Shiva XIV

Book One
of The Shiva XIV Series

by
Lyra Shanti

Copyright © 2014 Lyra Shanti
2nd Edition © 2016
Published by Timely Tales Press
Cover Art by Timothy Casey
All rights reserved
ISBN-10: 069235638X
ISBN-13: 978-0692356388

This is a work of fiction. Names, characters, businesses, places, events and incidents are either the products of the author's imagination or used in a fictitious manner. Any resemblance to actual persons, living or dead, or actual events is purely coincidental.

Dedicated to my beloved soul-mate, Timothy, and my amazing phoenix-sis, Juniper. Your giving hearts and unwavering support kept me going in the darkest of times. Without the two of you, I never would have completed this story or found my true voice. I love both of you beyond what words can say.

TABLE OF CONTENTS

Prologue: Birth of Shiva the Fourteenth

When the Queen first ordered her son be proclaimed "Shiva the Fourteenth," it was already known to the high priest of the planet Deius that the infant would be the one to bring balance to the stars.

He was judged, and bathed, and welcomed with holy water, as with any other child born into the royal line of The Shiva. However, from the first sight of the child's body, the high priest knew that Queen Amya's son was the next true Bodanya, the second coming of The Great Adin.

So they prayed. They prayed into the early morning onward to the Gods of old while the priests sang and chanted, waiting for a sign or guidance.

By the third evening, the high priest, known as Meddhi-Lan, declared he had been given understanding by the previous Shiva about the child's true identity.

Then, the priests brought the child to the altar where only his birth mother was allowed to be present among them. Meddhi-Lan held him up to the ancient statue, The Star of the Sun, so that the child's eyes could look upon the spirits with awareness. After gently placing the newborn back onto the blanketed altar, the high priest walked to the center of The Holy Room while facing The Council, The Holy Order of the Dei. All the priests of The Dei then gathered in a circle around the altar, praying silently for guidance from their revered Gods of old.

Speaking with a resounding, clear voice, Meddhi-Lan declared, "No knife, nor stone, nor instrument of incision shall wound this child, for he will be now and forever known to us as The Neya Bodanya!"

Silence fell upon The Council as they could not believe what they heard. No one had been named the next Bodanya for hundreds of years.

Meddhi-Lan wet the boy's forehead with colored sand and water mixed with scented oils. He then chanted in a droning hum, which had been performed by The Holy Dei for thousands of years. With this ritual came the collective resonance of the entire priesthood. One by one, their song grew greater with each voice contributing to the epic drone.

Joining their collective song, the priestesses of the temple fell to the floor in the ecstasy of their tradition. Then, the royal infant was raised by the hands of the high priest. Meddhi-Lan waited a few moments, and with his eyes alone, he asked those present for silence.

"This boy has been named Ayn by his birth mother, Queen Amya. It is her right to call him this, but no commoner in the kingdom shall know him as Ayn. He will be known henceforth only as Shiva the Fourteenth."

Then, Pei, the adolescent student priest of Meddhi-Lan,

raised his hand, holding a replica of the great sun-star, Siri, and proclaimed, "All praise the Neya Bodanya, Shiva the Fourteenth! Rejoice! Adin! Adin!"

Soon, they all repeated Pei's chant as the infant was anointed by Meddhi-Lan with the symbol of the Siri-Star, the revered sun of Deius, encircling it with the holy light of Adin. Even Queen Amya chanted, though she was not particularly religious. She was, however, extremely proud of her beloved child.

Gently, with his forefinger, the high priest drew the symbols upon the child's forehead, coloring it with gold and silver sand. Then he, and all the priests and priestesses, fiercely prayed.

"Please, great Siri, the holiest of our Gods" said Meddhi-Lan in a hushed voice, "protect this boy from the fate of The Adin, for he may be The Neya Bodanya, but he is also an innocent, and worthy of a long, happy life. I beg you to be merciful in your judgment, and in return, I will guide and protect this blessed child for as long as I live. Holy Holy, Un-Ahm."

After his quiet prayer, Meddhi-Lan looked into the baby's eyes; how blue they were, how full of deep understanding. Just then, Ayn smiled with a radiant glow and grabbed onto Meddhi-Lan's finger. The high priest smiled in return, for he knew it was an answer from the Gods... or so he chose to believe.

Chapter 1: The Great Paradox

Meddhi-Lan sat upon the floor of his room and opened his private scroll. He remembered the ordeal of The Bodanya's birth with fondness, yet also with sadness and concern. He dipped his pen, which only the high priests of The Dei could manipulate, into the plasma-ink and gave one touch to the scroll. The neon white soon became a visible, clear blue with the words written:

In the year of 12.120.47, our Lord, The Bodanya Shiva, The Second Coming of Adin, was given to us on this Day of Seed, the twelfth of Api.

He then meditated, focusing his thoughts deeper into his memory, trying his best to depict The Bodanya's birth as accurately as possible. As the pen twitched, ready to write the words from his mind, Meddhi-Lan mentally blocked the pen's movement as his thoughts could not help but turn inward with worry.

Holiest of Gods, is this your plan? he questioned in his mind. He did not wait for an answer, and was about to scribe more of his testimony into words upon paper, when Pei, his student priest, knocked gently on the door. "Enter," said the high priest while still in meditation.

Pei bowed halfway in reverence to his mentor. "My Lan," he said, "Amun-Lan and some of the other priests wish to speak with you. They have requested that you meet them in The Holy Room."

Meddhi-Lan opened his eyes, awakening to conscious thought as the plasma-powered pen gently fell onto the smooth carpet of midnight blue.

"Tell me, Pei, do you think as they do about the matter in which they are concerned?" the high priest asked as he carefully watched his student.

"I know not," replied Pei, trying not to offend his beloved teacher.

"You should speak your mind, young Ney," Meddhi-Lan said while getting up to redress himself in his proper blue Dei robes. He then turned to his student and spoke, dead calm and direct.

"You are frightened too. Are you not?"

Pei did not like to be referred to as "Ney," for he was near to reaching full priesthood, and soon would have the respect of his teacher, as well as the rest of The Dei. Nevertheless, he understood his place and took a moment to respond, unsure of what his answer should be.

Finally, Pei replied, "Yes, a little, my Lan."

"It frightens you... because of the unusual nature of his being?" questioned the high priest with his left eyebrow raised.

"Yes... and no," said Pei shaking his head and feeling naive in his thoughts, which he knew his teacher would undoubtedly sense.

"Yes and no? I assume you are in a state of unbalance - of paradox - and not of the oneness of The Un?"

It was Meddhi-Lan's way to gently tease his student. Pei was a highly intelligent young man, and near his attainment of awareness, but he still could not look upon his teacher with equal mind. His robes were of red with no blue along their trimming, and he did not yet shave his forehead or wear the belt of a Lan. Though he still had many doubts, he was loved like a son by his teacher and was Meddhi-Lan's favorite among the student priests.

"I... do not mean to speak in a paradox, my Lan. I simply have not yet come into the light. I admit, though, it is difficult to understand the meaning of The Un's ultimate design when a child has been born to us who is so... unusual."

"Yes, Pei," said Meddhi-Lan as he gently rested his hand on his student's shoulder, "and we must expect that there will be some opposition to my pronouncement that he is indeed the reincarnation of The Great Adin."

"Because of fear?" Pei asked nervously.

"Yes," replied Meddhi-Lan, "and also because of the length of time that has passed before his return to us. It has been hundreds of years since The Bodanya has chosen to live and walk upon our planet - so many years, in fact, that The Council was already in disbelief when Amya gave birth to him."

"But she *was* the woman to conceive amongst the white flowers in the time of The Great Adin's rebirth," argued Pei unnecessarily.

"Yes, she was," replied Meddhi-Lan with a slight smile.

"And so the prophecy has been fulfilled."

"Of course," sighed the high priest as he placed his unfinished scroll back into an oval chest that hung on the wall. "It has all been written and prophesied, my young student."

"Then..." said Pei as he forced himself to ask, "why was The Bodanya born with... both male and female flesh?"

Meddhi-Lan winced at the rawness of Pei's question. He stared at the ancient blue and silver chest on the wall, adorned with the holy markings of The Dei, as if looking for an answer within its design.

"This was not foreseen... was it, my Lan?"

The high priest slowly turned to face his student.

"No, Pei. It was not."

--

For nearly a thousand years, The Council of The Holy Dei had believed themselves on the brink of doom. The galaxy of Un-Ahm was slowly becoming desolate and barren. With each passing year of drained plasmic energy and decreasing power supply, the people of Deius looked to The Dei for wisdom and light.

This was now the time of The Great Paradox, also known by the few remaining scientists on Deius as Polarity Syndrome. It was first suspected by the priests of Deius when the sun of the planet Hun imploded, killing all of Hun's inhabitants instantaneously. Scientists disregarded the event as an isolated, natural incident within The Un, but the Deiusian holy men saw it differently. They believed the death of Hun was a sign from the Gods, and a warning of the doom to follow. The Dei priests believed Hun's demise was the first massively tragic event in a series of horrific disasters yet to come.

Soon after, fear led to panic and panic lead to war.

Planets rivaled each other for control of plasma, and for religious reasons as well. Adding to the calamity, the other known galaxy with intelligent life, Dru-Ahm, refused to offer any aid, for fear of bringing war and possible contamination upon themselves. The people of Dru-Ahm had always considered themselves to be higher life-forms than most and had made it clear to the planets of the Un-Ahm galaxy that they would be facing their plasma crisis alone.

The years then passed with much anxiety and paranoia while planets fought over who would have the last controlling share of plasma. Soon, the over use of plasma began destroying plant life and subsequently caused sickness in a wave of mass proportions, especially among the poor and destitute.

After the planet Sirin had become nearly barren of its vast oceans and jungles, the planet leaders of the Un-Ahm galaxy were asked by the queen of Deius, Queen Amya, to sign a treaty which promised to mine plasma carefully and on rare occasion. Hoping to end the spread of Plasma Sickness, the leaders anxiously signed the treaty. However, the illness still spread – even to the wealthy and privileged. No one seemed safe, and it made most either look to their Gods or to science for the answers.

The modern citizens of Deius, however, no longer recalled the days of science; they looked only to the priests of their kingdom for comfort and truth.

Not since the original Bodanya, The Great Adin, had the Holy Order of the Dei any insight into what may solve their crisis. Though they believed many incarnations of the Gods had secretly graced their sands throughout time, only the pure bloodline from the "Shiva" royal name was trusted by The Council to be the true heir to the Deiusian Kingdom.

The royal line of Shiva began with the first incarnation of Adin himself, in the year of 11.213.70. It was written that during Adin's rule as king, The Dei believed he would define existence in his own lifetime, as well as heal the power supply of the galaxy.

However, according to legend, in his twenty sixth year - only three years after his crowning - Adin, Shiva the First, was violently murdered by the hands of his own half-brother, Siri, whom the planet Sirin had been named after. It was also written that, even though Adin had appointed his younger brother as king of Sirin, Siri was jealous of his older brother's power, for he wished to become the new Bodanya, the universe's holiest of spirit-guardians, as well as high ruler of all the planets of the Un-Ahm galaxy.

According to The Dei's legend, Adin forgave Siri just before he died, making it possible for all men to forgive those who succumb to their jealousy and hatred.

After three days of resting within his sarcophagus, Adin's spirit rose from his body and spoke with his brother, giving him a full pardon, as well as counseling him on how to rule Sirin with light and love.

Unfortunately, after years of war and excessive mining of plasma, Sirin's lush lands eventually fell into ruin and despair, causing most Sirini to question their once great king, as well as their own beloved Gods of old.

Thus, the use of prophecy was even more depended upon. Priests focused all their minds and souls into the gift of prediction and meditation, in order to foretell the next coming of The Bodanya Shiva.

Through the hundreds of years that followed, twelve of The Shiva royal line had lived and died. Unlike The Great Adin, however, they were kings, not Gods. Many had spoken with truth and wisdom, but none had cured the galaxy of its ever-draining energy.

Some blamed the chaotic nature of the stars. Some

blamed the ones from the past who did not care for their planets. Some even blamed scientists for discovering the uses of plasma in the first place. Most, however, simply became desperate in their hope for a man to come and save them from their doom, as it had been prophesied for so many years.

On his deathbed, Shiva the Thirteenth promised his priests that he would return in spirit-form to light the way for the return of the first Bodanya Shiva, The Great Adin. He had told his high priest, Amun-Lan, that Adin would be reincarnated in the season of The Seed, which was now upon them.

And so it was, and so it shall be, Meddhi-Lan heard the famous Deiusian chant spoken in his mind. He had been given the title of High Priest from his predecessor and teacher, Amun-Lan, many years ago, and now, after receiving the vision of Adin's return, he embraced his role as the Neya Bodanya's Lan. In fact, he felt nothing but pride. No matter who might contest his decision to teach the God-child, he vowed he would do so until his death, for he loved the boy with all of his soul, and in a way no other priest could understand. Despite what the other priests believed, Meddhi-Lan was certain that this particular Shiva was indeed a boy, no matter what his body seemed. Meddhi-Lan knew it in his heart to be the truth.

Meddhi-Lan closed his eyes and made a silent soul-promise to forever protect the new king of Deius. Though, for Meddhi-Lan, The Bodanya would always be known, first and foremost, as his most beloved boy named Ayn.

Chapter 2: The Influence of Meddhi-Lan

*O*ver the past forty years, Meddhi-Lan had watched his planet become the enemy, like a serpent swallowing its own tail. Split in two halves, the rejected followers of science, now in exile, fought against the believers of the Gods of Un-Ahm, or The Un, as it was more commonly called. Meddhi-Lan believed that Deius had gone from being a planet that was once the most powerful in the galaxy to a weak and dying planet with inhabitants who do nothing but chant and pray. As much as he believed in the power of prayer, he did not think it replaced scientific advancement. He had hoped the queen of his planet, Amya, might somehow reconcile and heal their people, but that seemed an impossible feat.

Unlike his fellow priests, he did not watch his planet's demise without emotion and was unable to remain detached when he heard of the rampant poverty and sickness that plagued his planet. Dedicated to making a difference, Meddhi-Lan spent most of his life learning the ancient ways of The Dei. He hoped that doing so would help him become truly aware and prepare him for when Adin would inevitably be reincarnated.

As a child, Meddhi-Lan had seen the unrest of his people

first-hand during The Great Civil War. He had witnessed his father killed at the hands of science followers, or as they were more commonly known, The Tah. It was his violent childhood that prepared Meddhi-Lan to become the strongest and noblest man within the council of The Dei. It was also his dedication and pride that made him such a respected leader among his fellow priests.

Meddhi-Lan's greatest asset, though, was his inner will, which helped him to become the youngest high priest in the history of The Dei, and it was the underlying reason The Council did not often question his words.

However, shortly after the birth of Shiva the Fourteenth, The Council had broken their usual loyalty and banded together in effort to confront the high priest to cast doubt on his proclamation.

Meddhi-Lan, with proud face and hardened will, entered The Holy Room, followed by Pei, seconds behind him. He found The Holy Order standing in a semicircle around the great floor-painting of the Gods.

Pei couldn't help but notice the irony of the scene with his fellow priests gathered to question the very Gods that were painted below them. Looking at the floor's painting, he was captivated by the brilliance of the gold and blue colors of oil that reflected upon their stern, skeptical faces.

They bowed to Meddhi-Lan, who bowed in return. Then, as customary, the student-priests broke the silence with an ancient chant about the Gods and their wisdom. When they finished, Meddhi-Lan spoke without reservation.

"My fellow priests, I have made my decision, and I shall not make a second judgment, for the child *is* The Bodanya. Of this, I am certain."

The room fell silent. Only the eldest priest, Amun-Lan,

who had once taught Meddhi-Lan, had the courage to publicly speak against him.

"How can you be certain?" asked Amun-Lan. "With all due respect, High Priest, and greatest student of mine, have you not seen the child's form?"

Meddhi-Lan turned his head and calmly replied, "I have seen his form, yes."

Then Jin, Amun-Lan's newest and youngest student, came forth to speak. "Yet, you do not question its purpose?" he asked, though he did not officially have the right to speak out of turn.

Meddhi-Lan was slightly offended, but kept his control, for he saw a bit of his younger self within Jin. He also saw himself in Pei, who was only a couple of years older than Jin, yet possessed maturity beyond his years. Meddhi-Lan understood him far better than Jin, and it was partly why he decided to personally mentor Pei instead.

"*His* purpose is to be The Bodanya Shiva," Meddhi-Lan rebuked, "and *that,* he will be, no matter what his physical form."

One of the elder priests, who did not know how to easily accept Meddhi-Lan's proposal, continued with another doubting question. "How can the child even be considered one thing or another?" he asked. "How do you know what it is? How do you know it is the true Adin?"

"How can you even call it a he?" blurted Jin who seemed unable to keep his rebellious tongue quiet.

Meddhi-Lan, clenched a fist and closed his eyes in effort to calm his soul. If Jin had not been a student of Amun-Lan, Meddhi-Lan would have lost his temper and asked for the boy's dismissal. Instead, he quietly gathered his wits, planning how he would clearly explain the situation.

"He is The Adin," Meddhi-Lan stated firmly. "There is no question. The Gods have granted us his soul in the form that he himself has chosen. It does not matter if it is different than before, or if it is different than any other being in The Un. He is The Great Adin, and I will call him by whatever he would have me call him."

Meddhi-Lan then walked in front of the young student who had angered him. He smiled and softly said, "Jin, perhaps you do not yet understand that the body and the soul are not of the same material. However, The Great Adin knows this, and he has come to this understanding with his Godly, subtle grace – all so that he may teach us with his infinite wisdom."

Jin's face lost its color as he had been clearly defeated by the high priest's noble words. All Jin could do was nod, turning his glance away from Medhhi-Lan's penetrating gaze. The high priest then turned to face the elders, as well as the rest of The Holy Order.

"In this life as Shiva, the Fourteenth, Adin will guide us with his plans when he has come to a proper age, and when he is officially crowned king. Until then, we shall not question the ways of the Gods, or the royal line of the Shiva!"

The council rested their heads and softly chanted, "So it was, and so it shall be."

Pei couldn't help but smile, for his Lan had won over the council of priests just as he had done many, many times before.

--

By the time Ayn had reached his seventh year, he had already proven himself to believers and doubters alike. His mental abilities were beyond those of his predecessors, and it filled Meddhi-Lan with hope, yet apprehension.

Ayn had been raised by the high priest like a son, with visits to his mother only once or twice a month. He had never known his birth-father, though Meddhi-Lan had said he was Amya's favorite slave. Unfortunately, he had died from illness when Ayn was only an infant, and Ayn had no recollection of his father's visage. Nonetheless, he imagined his father as a tan, strong-backed man with a slave's strength of will to match. Having never seen a picture or painting, however, Ayn couldn't be certain of his father's actual image.

Ayn's mother, Queen Amya, he had seen many times. She was a strikingly beautiful woman with long black hair that reached to the length of her ankles, though she usually wore it wrapped tightly on top of her crown in a braided bun, disguising its extraordinary abundance. Her olive skin was smooth as silk, and her eyes were round and deep with a hazel richness. Her full lips and robust, yet feminine figure made her the ideal of womanly beauty for many Deiusian men, and Ayn could sense the power she had over them.

He felt a deep, instinctual love for his mother, though he was not allowed to see her often. The elder priests told him that it was tradition for a holy man to be removed from matters of the flesh; all attachments were denied, even more so for The Bodanya. Their traditions and rules saddened Ayn, but he also wanted to become a great holy man who would make them proud, especially his beloved teacher, Meddhi-Lan. Knowing that he could not fight his destiny, he instead tried to meditate on happier feelings.

It was Meddhi-Lan who taught him the methods of meditation, as well as many of the ancient ways known to the Holy Dei. When Ayn felt sad or angry, he instead concentrated on the beauty that surrounded him. He often remembered the first time he saw the white ona flowers bloom in the months of The

Seed. He also remembered when he was given his pet, Duna, and how he repeatedly licked Ayn's face every time they greeted. So many things Ayn could remember to counter the sadness when it came into his mind.

However, on his seventh birthday, he woke with a deeper, darker sadness, as well as confusion, and his usual meditation wasn't working. He had many questions to ask his teacher, about his planet, his people, and most importantly, about plasma, which he had read was "the blood of the universe." Ayn wanted to understand everything and wondered if he would ever receive the answers he sought. Meddhi-Lan was never one to avoid a question, if asked in earnest, but Ayn knew there were things his teacher kept away from him ever since he was a small boy.

He could feel it — sensing the burden that Meddhi-Lan held upon his shoulders. Ayn wondered if it was because of the psychic abilities born within him. He hoped he had not made Meddhi-Lan keep an anger inside because of jealousy or fear. Ayn also hoped with all his soul that his teacher would forgive him for the many times Ayn woke him in the middle of the night.

He could not help the scary dreams that caused him to make the sensing candles fly and the room to shake. It was not truly Ayn's fault if his mind was so strong it made the plasma-lights blow out, causing everyone in the temple to think the Gods were angry with them. All Ayn knew was to trust his teacher. He decided to ask Meddhi-Lan his questions, trusting his Lan enough to divulge his fears.

"That is what The Neya Bodanya would do," he told himself with a nod of his head.

--

Ayn found Meddhi-Lan reading in The Holy Room of Thought, but before he was close enough to speak, Meddhi-Lan smiled and said, "Blessed morning and blessed birthday, my young Bodanya."

Pei was there as well, sitting beside Meddhi-Lan with his hands folded in prayer and a widening smile on his lips.

"Blessed morning, my Lan," Ayn said, quickly bowing in haste.

Meddhi-Lan sensed the child's anxious energy and turned to him with his eyebrow elevated.

"You have questions?"

"I do, my Lan," Ayn replied nervously. "Is it too early in the morning for them?"

Meddhi-Lan turned to Pei and both men grinned, amused.

"It is never too early for questions from The Bodanya, is it my Lan?" Pei asked his teacher with a knowing glance.

Meddhi-Lan laughed with a mixture of pride and love coming though the sound of his deep voice. "Of course not, my Ney."

Pei smiled, knowing that his teacher was thinking fondly of him. These were the times that Pei almost felt as if they were a small family unto their own. Being an orphan, Pei was pleased by the idea. Ayn was like a younger brother and Meddhi-Lan, a father whom he loved dearly.

Pei then got up and walked over to Ayn, leaning over to match Ayn's height.

"But first," Pei said with a cheerful tone, "we must give you your birthday reward, my Neya Bodanya."

Ayn felt the sadness slightly lift from his heart. He could see that Pei was hiding some sort of object behind his back, and he was filled with curiosity.

"My reward? Am I not getting too old for rewards?"

"You're only as old as you wish to be," replied Pei with a warm grin. "Come now, can you guess what it is?"

Ayn smiled at his brother-in-spirit and said, "Yes, I think I can."

Meddhi-Lan closed his book, then watched his two students with affection.

"Do your best then, Bodanya Shiva," teased Pei.

Ayn closed his eyes and opened his mind to the sounds of The Un. He saw Pei's surrounding colors inside of his aura. It was a golden hue with purple and orange, denoting a sense of well-being and hope. Ayn had noticed many people in the Kingdom with this type of color surrounding their souls, but Pei's was the brightest he had ever seen.

Pei could tell that Ayn was sensing his soul, and it made him smile. "Are you meditating clearly, Your Holiness?" Pei asked.

Ayn broke his concentration and opened his eyes with make-believe anger.

"Of course I am!" he defended himself while hiding his laughter.

Meddhi-Lan stood up and put his hand on Ayn's shoulder.

"If you can guess what your reward is," Meddhi-Lan whispered into Ayn's ear, "then I shall answer any questions that you have, provided I know the answers."

Ayn nodded and closed his eyes once more.

He felt The Un open, and in an instant, it was revealed to his mind. "It's a toy boat!" Ayn exclaimed. "A boat that flies with the sun-star engraved on the front!"

Pei laughed and opened his hands to show him his toy. "You are correct once again," he said with a nod to Meddhi-Lan.

"I'm always right," Ayn replied with nonchalant confidence.

"Especially when you want something," Pei teased as he mussed the top of Ayn's long black hair.

"And he did want a flying boat. You were right," the high priest said to Pei.

"That is because he has told me of his dreams to fly," Pei replied.

Meddhi-Lan smiled and knelt to the young Neya Bodanya.

"And someday you will, Ayn," he whispered. "Someday you will."

Chapter 3: Visions of the Bodanya

The truth of Ayn's birth was never completely known by the people of Deius. Even the members of the royal family were unaware of the secret the priests dare not tell. Meddhi-Lan himself did not trust the superstitious tendencies of the people, for fear they would assume The Bodanya's physical form was a dark sign from the Gods. For that reason, he kept Ayn's duality hidden, even from the scrolls of The Holy Room.

All that was written on the day of Ayn's birth was that he was the true coming of The Great Adin and that he was born with the knowledge of The Un.

Meddhi-Lan knew that Ayn's defect was the one thing the priests feared might bring them shame and possible doom. There was simply no way for them to understand why or how Ayn had been born with both male and female form. Only Meddhi-Lan seemed to understand, and it was he who officially declared that Ayn was of the more masculine sex, having mostly male features.

Not since the days of ancient times had Deiusians suffered from so-called defects such as Ayn's. It had been thousands upon thousands of years since the last known specimen of the rare "intersex" condition, and the priests did not understand why it had happened, especially to their own Bodanya.

They attempted, at first, to meditate upon the meaning behind the defect. Each of them believed there was a deeper reason behind the veil of his dual gender, but none could guess the minds of the Gods, so they left the impossible task to Meddhi-Lan. It was also the high priest's duty to not only raise the child, but guide him along his path to enlightenment.

For Meddhi-Lan, Ayn's destiny seemed clear since the day of his birth. He believed Ayn to be at one with The Un, and his unique body merely reflected the truth of the essence of the universe.

Through the years, Ayn grew well and was loved by most, especially by the high priest. In fact, Meddhi-Lan had uncontrollably allowed himself to act as the boy's father.

However, even as loved as he was, Ayn couldn't help but feel he was the only one of his kind. It seemed to Ayn that evolution and science had defeated his condition years ago, yet there he was, like an old relic from the past. It made him wonder why the Gods would be so cruel, and he often felt sad and alone.

Meddhi-Lan was painfully aware of Ayn's sadness, though he did not know what he could say to cheer his young student.

Nonetheless, Ayn depended on his teacher for guidance, and on his seventh birthday, he came to Meddhi-Lan's private room, asking to speak with him.

After Ayn explained his feelings, he asked his teacher why the Gods had cursed him so.

Meddhi-Lan tenderly replied, "My boy, I understand your confusion, but you are not cursed, you are blessed. And I am afraid you are asking me questions that only you may answer in time."

"But... y*ou* are the Lan, not I!" said Ayn, close to tears.

"Yes, I am your Lan, but it is *you* who are The Neya Bodanya and-"

"No, I am not!" said Ayn, defiantly. "I am not The Bodanya, and I am NOT The Great Adin!" He then covered his face and wept.

His teacher felt his pain, but did not reach for him. "There is no use in denying your true self," Meddhi-Lan said, gentle, yet stern.

Ayn continued to weep into his hands, then fell on the lap of his teacher.

Meddhi-Lan broke his cold reserve and softly petted the back of Ayn's head.

Ayn then looked up at his teacher with tear-streaked cheeks and asked, "Am I truly The Neya Bodanya? The true rebirth of Adin?"

"What does your soul tell you?" asked Meddhi-Lan.

Ayn thought for a moment, trying to hear his inner sound, but all he could hear was his pain. "I do not know, my Lan," he replied, "but how can I be The Great Adin when I am so..."

The high priest gently raised Ayn's chin and said, "You're so what?"

"Incomplete!" blurted Ayn.

"My Shiva... Ayn, you will listen to me now," said Meddhi-Lan as he wrapped his strong arms around his beloved student. "You are not incomplete. You are the most illuminated soul I have ever known. Of this, I am certain."

"I am?" asked Ayn, blinking his teary, blue eyes.

"Yes, Ayn, you are. You have the rarest of all souls. It is both wise and innocent all at once, and I am honored to have been chosen to guide you," Meddhi-Lan said as he wiped the tears from his beloved boy's face.

"But it is not my soul that I speak of, my Lan. It is my body that is incomplete... and so very different."

"Yes, it is different," replied his teacher, "but it is not necessarily incomplete, my child."

"But why would the Gods want me to be like this?" asked Ayn as he looked upwards to his heart's father.

"They have their reasons," Meddhi-Lan assured him, "and one day, when you are ready to hear them, they will tell you."

Ayn did not believe his teacher's words, though he hoped they were true. Breaking away from Meddhi-Lan's arms, he stood up and paced.

"Why can it not just be corrected?" asked Ayn. "I know there are scientists that understand the body. Perhaps they could perform a surgery to eliminate the unwanted parts. Did they not once do such things in the past? Can you not find someone for me? Please, my Lan! Please!"

Meddhi-Lan feared Ayn may become hysterical. He gently touched Ayn's hand, guiding him to sit down.

"It is not fair!" cried Ayn. "Why won't you help me be whole?"

"Because it is not for us to make such decisions, Ayn."

"Whose decision is it then?" Ayn asked with a sniff.

"Only the Gods may decide, though it is your choice as

well... when you have come of age and your mind is ready."

"But!" blurted Ayn.

"Remember, my Ney," said Meddhi-Lan with a calm voice, "our laws tell us that no child on Deius may be harmed or even altered. They are born pure and exactly how the Gods have intended them to be. This law applies to The Bodanya even more."

Ayn looked away, holding back his impatience and rebellious anger.

"Of course, you are also The Second Adin," added Meddhi-Lan, "and it is well within your rights to claim your form any way that you see fit."

"Then I-"

Before Ayn could finish, Meddhi-Lan said, "But you must come to that decision when you have come of age, and no sooner."

Ayn pouted and sighed. "That will take forever!" he replied.

"Do not worry, my Ney, you will come of age soon enough," said Meddhi-Lan with a comforting smile.

"Not soon enough for me!" said Ayn as he lay his head on his teacher's lap.

"You must honor the traditions of The Dei," said the high priest as he petted Ayn's long black hair, "they are holy and without flaw."

Ayn looked up at Meddhi-Lan's pointed, manly chin.

"Without flaw?" asked Ayn with a doubtful sneer. "But that is impossible, my Lan, for all of The Un is flawed."

Meddhi-Lan smiled and said, "My blessed Bodanya, you once again did not step into the trap."

Ayn proudly nodded, realizing that Meddhi-Lan had been testing him. Feeling a little better, Ayn yawned and soon fell asleep on the lap of his beloved teacher.

--

Shining like the great Siri God in the sky, Adin was armored in smoothest gold to reflect his strength and will. Even his princely crown was a jewel-encrusted laurel made entirely of gold.

He was well aware, to most in his kingdom, he seemed a God. Yet, Adin did not understand why. In his mind, he merely looked the part with waves of shoulder-length blond hair, sky-blue eyes, and statuesque, masculine form. Even still, Adin felt he had never truly proven himself, and it was for that very reason he allowed his father to convince him to become a warrior in the first place.

As a child, Adin would have rather learned about science, metaphysics, and the stars, but his need to prove himself to his father was so strong that he had focused all of his energy to become the greatest swordsman Deius had ever seen. He was only eighteen years of age, and yet he led his father's Deiusian army into battle.

Sitting on top his black steed with his blue eyes blazing in the bright sun, Adin looked at his troops, then held up his hand to speak. "These Ohrians will pay for their arrogance! Let us show these lost science worshipers that they cannot invade our planet without penance! Let us fight with the strength of our ancestors at our side, and in their presence, we will triumph! For honor! For justice! For the glory of Deius!"

His troops of thousands erupted into thunderous cheers as they raised their swords high into the air.

This was the moment Adin was waiting for as he turned his horse around to face their sworn enemy, the Ohrians. With their nearly impenetrable silver-colored armor, crafted from the rare Linthil diamonds, their incredible speed, and advanced weaponry, an Ohrian soldier was a formidable foe. Adin's father had been in battles with them before, so he had told Adin what to expect. However, nothing could prepare Adin for the violence and bloodshed of war.

In the thick of fighting, and after witnessing several of his childhood friends and cousins instantaneously die as their limbs were torn from their bodies, or worse, their heads cut clean off with Ohrian lasers, Adin found himself unable to control his own anger.

In retaliation, he jumped off his horse and swung his sword without restraint. He felt the rage inside of his heart meld with the metal of his sword as he sliced through hundreds of Ohrians. By the time the battle was over, Adin could barely feel anything. His heart had grown as cold as the lonely, frozen mountains in the northern hemisphere of his planet.

Seeing all the death before him, much of which he himself had dealt, Adin cried and dropped his sword to the bloodshed ground.

"Why, Gods?!" he screamed to the heavens as he fell to his knees. "Is this what you want us mortals to do to each other? Is this my path? Is this... it?!"

Suddenly, the earth shook and Adin felt the ground beneath him split open. He looked down and saw that there was nothing but lava and stars. It was the blood of Deius, and it was going to swallow him whole!

Adin began to laugh and cry all at once. He knew that the Gods were answering him, but he didn't want to know the truth. He wasn't ready.

"I'm not ready!" yelled Ayn in a panic. "Please, Gods, no! I'm not ready yet!"

Meddhi-Lan came to his side immediately and said, "Hush, my boy. It was only a dream."

Looking around at Meddhi-Lan's room, which was decorated in colors of blue and tan, Ayn realized where he was and that he had, once again, fallen asleep in his Lan's room.

"I'm sorry, my Lan," said Ayn as he groggily rubbed his eyes.

"Did you have a disturbing dream?" asked Meddhi-Lan as he poured Ayn a glass of cold water.

"Yes," replied Ayn who hastily grabbed the glass, and then quickly drank its contents.

"What was it about?" asked Meddhi-Lan.

"Well..." said Ayn, "it was a battlefield. There were Ohrians with laser weapons, and they were in these shiny, silver suits of armor. I was there too. I was... well... I think I was The Great Adin."

Ayn gave his Lan embarrassed eyes as he bit his bottom lip.

"I see," replied Meddhi-Lan. "It makes sense that you would dream of having been him. It was your past life... perhaps your most important one. "

"But," said Ayn, confused, "how do you know for certain I

was him?"

"Because I had a vision too once."

"You did? About me?"

"Yes, Ayn," said Meddhi-Lan with a smile, "it was on the day of your birth, actually. I did not dream of battle, but while meditating, I saw your face. Then I saw Adin's face... and it was one and the same. I was certain from that moment forward that you were The Bodanya and that you would bring balance to Deius, and to the entire galaxy.

Sighing, doubtfully, Ayn leaned on his beloved Lan's shoulder. "I don't see how I will be able to do that," he said with a pout.

Meddhi-Lan smiled and stroked Ayn's hair. "You will do it by being you. I have the utmost faith in you, Ayn."

"Thank you, my Lan, but... what if I can't? Will I end up falling into the blood of the stars?"

"What? Where did you get that idea?" asked Meddhi-Lan as he looked down at Ayn, picking up his chin.

"It's what I saw in my dream," replied Ayn with a sigh. "You see, Adin doubted his path, and then the ground opened up and he saw, well, I guess I saw... the blood of the universe! I guess it was plasma. My Lan, what exactly *is* plasma?"

Meddhi-Lan sighed, not knowing how to explain such complicated notions to a boy of seven years. Despite Ayn's keen, inquisitive mind, he was still a child, and Meddhi-Lan didn't want to push Ayn too hard, too fast.

"Plasma, my dear boy," said Meddhi-Lan as he got up and reached for one of the scrolls on his shelf, "is indeed the blood of the universe. It is the essence of life which runs through all of creation, and even through death. It is the unseen power within the fabric of time and space, and without it, we would all cease to exist."

Ayn nodded as he looked at Meddhi-Lan's scroll. He then looked at the priests' illustrations of plasma and asked, "So, is it similar to a giant river, but it runs through time and space?"

"Somewhat, yes," replied Meddhi-Lan, "though it is more accurate to say that plasma is even more powerful than a river, yet less visible to the eye."

"Then... how do we know it's really there?" asked Ayn.

Meddhi-Lan smiled and said, "Because Adin meditated extensively and found plasma to be truth. He also became friends with a scientist named Sri Unda, and with her help, he was able to spread the truth throughout the galaxy. You see, through spiritual instinct and scientific process, Adin was able to bring enlightenment to our people. This, among other reasons, is why he was such a great man."

Ayn's brow knotted in thought. "Why did I dream about him being a warrior who killed so many people if he was such an enlightened man?"

"Well," replied Meddhi-Lan, "sometimes the Gods test us, and in doing so, they force many painful and difficult tasks upon us. They do this, you see, in order for us to learn so that we may become wise."

"And The Great Adin became wise after he fought in war?" asked Ayn.

"Yes, he did," said Meddhi-Lan with a gentle, loving smile. He then put back the scroll and said, "and so will you, my Bodanya. First, however, you need proper sleep."

Picking the boy up, Meddhi-Lan carried him back to Ayn's

bedroom.

"No more bad dreams, little Bodanya. Is that understood?"

"Yes, my Lan," Ayn sleepily replied, "but... can you stay with me?"

Meddhi-Lan smiled and said, "Alright... but just for a little while. I have much writing to do."

"Will you write about my dreams?" asked Ayn with a playful grin.

"I very well might," replied Meddhi-Lan.

Ayn then cuddled up in Meddhi-Lan's strong, safe arms, and found himself fast asleep, dreaming only of images that were happy and warm.

--

It was written that the second Adin would return with a mighty power to restore balance to The Un. Most of the religious commoners on Deius believed those words to mean he would destroy their planet's enemies, as well as heal The Un of The Great Paradox.

All of Ayn's abilities were further proof to the religious. It was a light emerging from the darkness, and they were filled with a renewed hope and pride.

However, to Ayn, his abilities were not a source of strength. He hated them. He wished he would wake up one day and not see or hear anything but his own wishes and thoughts.

His mental powers kept him awake at night, for fear he would once again dream of a stranger's death or his mother's tears. He could always sense it. He could always see when she was in pain, and his insight made him hurt deep inside his soul. He never once felt the hope he gave the people of Deius. He only felt two things when pondering his existence: confusion and shame.

Having been trained in the ways of The Dei, however, he could remember many things when meditating, and it would help his state of mind. He would often bring along Duna, his furry, four-legged animal friend, when meditating or wandering the halls of the temple or reading the ancient scrolls under the Saras "Enlightenment Tree" in The Holy Garden.

Sometimes Ayn would feel happy and forget his body altogether. He would run with Duna through the ona flowers, forgetting time and space, only to feel the oneness of The Un. Other times, he was filled with sorrow. He dared not let himself look down at his strange flesh. He would look away if being bathed or if he had to relieve himself. He would not allow himself to think of his physical form, and he lived through his childhood as if in a prolonged dream.

One night, he awoke from a nightmare about his mother; she was dying.

He entered Meddhi-Lan's private chamber and touched his shoulder. Meddhi-Lan was fast asleep.

"Please, my Lan. Please wake up. My mother is ill," begged Ayn quietly. Meddhi-Lan's eyes opened, and he saw Ayn in his white sleeping robes. "She is dying," added Ayn in tears. "Please help me see her before she leaves her body."

Meddhi-Lan rose and quickly got dressed for the small journey to Queen Amya's palace. Traveling by The Dei's traditional, and somewhat primitive, transportation of horse drawn carriage, Ayn was extremely glad The Royal Palace wasn't too far from The Holy Temple. He figured they could have just walked there, but the priests would have never allowed it.

When they arrived at the palace, they were greeted by two of Queen Amya's slaves. One was male, the other female, and they were both dressed in long, tan robes. Ayn did not understand the royal family's use of slaves, since The Dei did not have many themselves. However, his mother was queen of the Shiva royal line, and though she was the leader of the movement to treat slaves with respect, she was not a proponent of true change. To her, slaves were as much a part of their culture as their ancient scrolls or paintings of the Gods. However, she always treated her slaves with extreme kindness. It made Ayn wonder why she didn't just set them free.

Ayn never truly understood his mother, though he loved her nonetheless. She was like the white ona flower: graceful and beautiful, yet mysterious and rare. Unfortunately, when he saw her lying in her bed of blue silken sheets, she did not look like an ona flower. She looked sickly and stained with sweat, and he felt afraid as she reached for his hand.

"Come here, my sweet son... my prince," she pleaded softly.

Ayn slowly went to her side and sat down. He held her cold hand as she brought his to her cheek. He could feel her sickness and how weak her body had become. He also sensed that she had been struggling with the illness for a long time. It seemed to him she was already accepting her death, even if he was not.

He imagined the old paintings from the scrolls of The Dei where the Gods had supreme power over life and death. He wanted to become like a true Bodanya of legend and reach into her body to find the source of the illness so that he could give her his light in place of her pain, but he knew he was not powerful enough, and his teachings told him that if it was her time to die, he must let her go.

"Mother," Ayn said in a whisper, "I am here. Do not be afraid."

He heard himself speak, but could not feel what he was saying. It was, once again, much like a dream.

Her face was still beautiful, even if it was wet with cold sweat, and she smiled at Ayn with an exhausted, but relieved expression.

"Good boy," she said.

A few moments later, her body went limp. She was gone.

Ayn did not cry, for he told himself that his mother was with the Gods in The Un, but from that moment on, he put his feelings into a scroll-jar in his mind, refusing to feel them. It was his mother's death that gave him the resolve to face his path. He knew he had no other choice but to become The Great Adin.

Chapter 4: Pei's Expectation

*P*ei was ordained as a Lan, a teacher of The Holy Order of the Dei, and soon afterward, was given the arduous task of tutoring Ayn when the young Bodanya had reached his thirteenth year of age.

Despite the difficulty, Pei felt it was a great honor to teach alongside his former Lan with the guiding of The Bodanya Shiva. He hoped that he, like his teacher, would one day earn the title of High Priest, becoming well-known to the Dei as "The Great Pei-Lan."

"Do you see the light of The Un?" asked Pei.

He and Ayn sat under the pale lavender of the Saras tree, surrounded by the brightly lit stars of the night sky. There was nothing to be heard in the solace of the garden except for the humming of the plasma-candles that were placed in a circle around where they sat.

"Yes," whispered Ayn.

"Do you hear the singular chord of The Un?" Pei questioned as he probed further into his student's mind.

"I hear the oneness, yes," replied Ayn.

"Good," said Pei. "Now, do you feel the vibration of that oneness?"

Ayn opened his mind's eye and saw the darkness of space and time. He saw the swirling colors of plasma-light and the shimmering energies of the souls who had come to rest. The beauty and the immensity of the sight filled Ayn's spirit with peace. He thought about how wonderful it was that The Un was so open to him.

Ayn had always been able to see the spirits within the living dark of The Un, but the vibration Pei referred to was another matter. He knew the energy his young teacher was asking him to sense was more than a mere feeling or movement. The Great Vibration of The Un was known to The Dei as "The Elusive Voice of the Unity of the Gods." For Ayn, the vibration was the most difficult to sense.

It was not difficult because he feared it, but because it was hidden within the clattering sounds of The Un's chaos. Sensing The Great Vibration was not easy for even the most skilled priests. Ayn knew that Pei could only feel moments of the elusive sound, then it would disappear into The Un's collective void once again. Ayn was not sure if even Meddhi-Lan could probe deeper into the feeling of The Un, but he was certain Pei was not as mature as his elder Lan, and he found it amusing that Pei was his meditation guide.

There was also another difficulty in sensing the vibration. It was known to the Holy Order that the prophecy would only be fulfilled when the reincarnation of Adin linked himself with the oneness of The Un. This was interpreted by most of the priests to mean that he would fully understand the power of The Un, thereby destroying the chaos that was infecting the galaxy. To them, it was Ayn's destiny to reach past their own abilities, finally ending the threat of The Paradox.

As of yet, however, Ayn felt he had no such power. He indeed could sense the vibration in The Un, as well as hear the collective song, but no more than the young teacher who sat in front of him. He felt the enormous expectation on his shoulders, and to Ayn, the pressure was like a thick fog blinding his inner eye.

"What do you sense?" Pei again asked him.

Ayn pushed his mind to see through the fluid of light. He looked past the colors, past the textures - deeper into the void.

"I sense… the energy," he replied.

"Do you see and feel the plasma within The Un?"

"I see it, yes, and I think I can feel it, but…"

"You must seek to understand it, Ayn"

Despite his somewhat vague words, Ayn knew what Pei truly meant. It was supposedly The Bodanya's destiny to see past the riddles of space and to stop the inevitable doom that lurked over his people, but how? Ayn wondered how his two teachers would react if they knew he had not the answers they hoped for.

"I only see the particles of light," said Ayn, "but I cannot understand its meaning, my Lan."

Pei reached for Ayn's shoulder and gently held it. "Do not simply see, my Bodanya," he whispered to his student, "you must feel the light and seek to know it."

Ayn felt lost within a cloud of expectation, trying his best not to become annoyed at Pei.

Meddhi-Lan found his two students sitting under The Enlightenment Tree. He smiled and sat down nearby, waiting silently for their lesson to reach its goal. *How beautiful,* he thought as he joined them in the oneness of The Un. Meditating on his love for his students and the life force surrounding them, he soon felt Ayn's presence slowly approaching from behind.

"Do you think you can surprise me, Bodanya Shiva?" Meddhi-Lan asked with his eyes still closed in meditation. Ayn burst into an uncontrollable laugh, then wrapped his arms firmly around his elder teacher.

"Nothing surprises him," Pei said with a hint of a smile as he walked toward them.

"Well," Ayn replied, smiling, "it is my life's goal then - to one day surprise him when he is caught unaware!" Ayn giggled and continued embracing his mentor with overflowing affection.

Sometimes Pei felt a twinge of jealousy, but only moments before he would silence the feeling. It was not Ayn who molded their destiny, and Pei was well aware of that fact, nor could he blame Meddhi-Lan for adoring Ayn any more than he could blame the Siri-Star for rising or the snow for the falling on the Quay-Karah Mountains. Meddhi-Lan showed Pei affection as well, but at times, he felt like a shadow in the light of the burning sun.

"Come, my Bodanya, it is time for your next lesson," Meddhi-Lan said as he rose to his feet with a graceful, upright position.

"But I am not ready!" Ayn whined in protest. This made Pei smile and slowly shake his head.

"Not ready?" questioned Meddhi-Lan.

"No," Ayn replied defiantly. It only took a few seconds for Meddhi-Lan's raised eyebrow and slight smile to make Ayn burst out laughing yet again.

Ayn loved his teacher's face. He loved his serious, dark eyes, strong jaw and determined brow. He often stared at his beloved Lan and idolized his masculinity, as well as his grace.

"Come Shiva, you must begin your next lesson," Pei said without jest. Ayn could tell that Pei was slightly annoyed with him.

"But I'm hungry," Ayn said, testing his boundaries, "and that makes me not ready yet."

Pei looked at Meddhi-Lan for guidance.

"Ayn, go now to the Meditation Room. I will be there shortly," Meddhi-Lan said in a serious tone.

Defeated, Ayn bowed. "Yes, my Lan."

As the boy left, the two Lans looked at each other.

"Will he never act his age, my Lan?" Pei asked, calmly.

"He is still a boy, Pei. You must give him more time to find his age."

"We do not have more time to give, Meddhi."

Pei suddenly felt out of bounds and lowered his head to his teacher. "Excuse me, my Lan, for speaking so plainly. I am merely concerned for his future... and for our future as well"

Meddhi-Lan let a moment of silence fall before responding to Pei's words. He brushed his fingers against the softness of the ona flowers and breathed their scent into his body. He briefly meditated on the serenity of the garden.

"Pei," he finally replied, "you are not expected to keep your feelings to yourself, nor is it a crime to speak plainly with me, or to anyone of The Council. I do not take your words as disrespect."

Pei looked up at his Lan with a hint of sadness, sensing the underlying sharpness within his Lan's words.

"However," continued Meddhi-Lan, "it is my purpose to

guide The Bodanya Shiva into adulthood so he may fulfill his path's journey. I have asked you to help me in this purpose so that you too may find adulthood, and honor, within your own path."

Pei lowered his head once again. "I am sorry if I am not reaching those goals fast enough, my Lan."

"No Pei," Meddhi-Lan said as he lifted Pei's chin, "you are reaching them faster than you realize."

Chapter 5: Time to Wake Up

*A*yn loved to meditate. He would sit alone in the darkness remembering his name, remembering his previous incarnations. It brought him comfort to face the pitch black of his mind. It was as if he could face death itself and find peace within the quiet nothing. Yet, Ayn was well aware that the darkness was not merely peaceful. Often his teachers would remind him to meditate on the sounds of The Un, and in doing so, he knew that the darkness was only a veil for the truth; the truth of chaos. Sometimes, though, Ayn very much liked to forget the truth.

He sat on the floor of the dark room with his legs in a triangle waiting for Meddhi-Lan to begin his lesson. Ayn was always happy to spend time with his beloved teacher, but today, he feared what his Lan might tell him. He sensed that something was not quite right, and he wondered if he had done something wrong.

Meddhi-Lan opened the door and quietly sat down in front of Ayn who had his eyes shut. His Lan would usually smile and play along with him, but this time he seemed more serious and distant than other meditations. It was as if Meddhi-Lan wanted him to become fully aware of The Un's power in one sitting. That idea made Ayn nervous, causing him to scratch the top of his right foot.

Ayn could sense it was not a meditation class that Meddhi-Lan had in mind. In fact, as of late, his Lan had been concentrating on teaching Ayn about science, which was not a subject to which many in the kingdom paid much attention. Ayn himself dreaded these classes, except for being able to spend time with his favorite Lan. At every chance, Ayn would try to distract Meddhi-Lan from the lesson with either a joke or a smile. Meddhi-Lan was not easy to distract, however, and always found his way back to the lesson.

Ayn could see Meddhi-Lan even with his eyes closed. His presence was immense and made Ayn worry. He did not want to open his eyes, for the idea of seeing his Lan angry with him made his stomach ache.

"Ayn," Meddhi-Lan said sternly. "Ayn... Wake up. It is time for your science lesson."

Ayn did not move, nor open his eyes.

Meddhi-Lan leaned over, putting his hands on Ayn's shoulders.

"Ayn... No more games. You must learn now. It is time to wake up. "

Ayn slowly opened his eyes and pouted.

"Why are you angry, my Lan?"

"I am not angry, my Ney."

"Yes, you are."

"I am not."

Meddhi-Lan was lying, Ayn could tell, and he seemed more stern than usual. His teacher turned away from him, opened a scroll, and then sat in front of Ayn with his knees apart. He was still not looking at Ayn, as if it doing so would cause him grief.

"If... I have done something wrong, I truly am sorry! And I will not do it again. I promise. I vow!" Ayn's voice cracked as he spoke with hints of his impending adolescence coming through his words.

Meddhi-Lan couldn't help but gently smile. "No Ayn," he replied, "you have not done something wrong. It is The Council, and even Pei, I am a little angry with, but it is nothing to worry about."

Meddhi-Lan stood up and walked towards a large scroll case. He pulled out a small magna-screen from a drawer and placed it on the floor in front of where Ayn was sitting.

"You are not happy with Pei?" Ayn asked his teacher.

"I am not... unhappy with him." Meddhi-Lan replied mysteriously.

Ayn could tell that his Lan did not wish to talk more about it. He decided to let it go for the time being.

"This day, we will study the components of space, and of plasma itself," Meddhi-Lan said as he touched the oval screen with the tip of his finger, energizing its power with a blue light. In three dimensions, Ayn could see the magnetic pulse flowing through the strange device. It was not the first time Meddhi-Lan taught him with the use of the magna-screen, but it was not something he often used. It was a device once used by the scientists of Deius, though none in the science field remained on their planet. It was a mystery to him as to how his Lan had acquired it. Ayn was planning to ask him, but only after the lesson had ended.

"In the beginning, we did not know what the plasma was. We tried to analyze the physical properties, but to no avail. We did not understand until Sri Unda, the renowned scientist, came to the truth of plasma when she wrote the groundbreaking, but controversial book, The Magnetic Connection in the year 11.120.16."

Ayn wished he could keep his attention on his Lan's teachings, but it was nearly impossible. His mind kept drifting into other places: the fountain pools in the royal garden, the Sirin-fish that swam nearby, the birthday celebration his Lan was planning for Ayn's coming fourteenth year, and the crowning coronation that came with it, which Ayn dreaded most of all.

"Ayn..."

Meddhi-Lan's face looked displeased and serious.

"Sorry, my Lan! I am truly sorry. I, um... I will concentrate now, I promise."

Meddhi-Lan got up and stood with his arms folded.

"You must understand why it is so important for you to learn about the workings of The Un, my Ney."

"It is because The Dei wish me to defeat it," Ayn interrupted with a numb sadness in his voice. He could not help but dislike most of The Holy Order, for they all seemed distant and bland. Every time he walked by their lonely souls, he somehow sensed a hidden anger... or perhaps a confusion. Ayn was never sure, but he felt as if they feared him and he also knew how much pressure they placed onto the shoulders of his Lan. He knew how their prophecies dictated what shall be, or at least, what they expected for Ayn's future. He often wished they would just leave him and his Lans alone.

"No, that is not why, my Ney," Meddhi-Lan replied. "You see, despite The Council's order that you must not learn about The Un from a scientific approach, I have decided it is only through a full understanding that you will become one with The

Un."

"And this makes you angry with Pei? Why? Is he on The Council's side?"

Meddhi-Lan released a small sigh and unfolded his arms. "No," he said while rubbing his neck, "Pei is merely questioning me, which is his right." He then reached for Ayn's hand so that he could pull him to his feet. "Listen to me, Ayn," he said, looking into his student's eyes. "You are not here to be anything for anyone but for yourself. And The Dei will come to their own understanding in their own way, in their own time."

"But!"

"No, Ayn. When I say listen, you must do so," said Meddhi-Lan, firmly.

"Yes, my Lan," Ayn softly replied, lowering his head.

"I know that you are fearing many things and that you are tired of being of such great importance, but-"

"Am I?" Ayn interrupted once again, tears forming in his eyes.

Meddhi-Lan became quiet and looked at Ayn with intense concern.

Ayn turned away from his Lan and nervously pulled at the long braid that hung from the bun on his head. "Am I... of such great importance?" he added as he walked to the scroll case, folding his arms. Then he turned to face Meddhi-Lan who seemed deeply troubled.

"Please, my Lan, tell me what would happen if I should fail... or if I stare and stare into the void and find no answer to be given, or not one that the priests in The Order would want to know? Then, will I be of such importance or will I be useless, and judged as not the true Adin? What shall happen if I fail? Please, can you tell me?" begged Ayn, his voice beginning to crack and quiver.

Meddhi-Lan could see the pain in his beloved boy's eyes. They were welling up with water and fear, making them appear even bluer than usual. Meddhi-Lan's own eyes felt as if daggers were cutting into them by the sides. He had not slept in days. He could not sleep due to the planning of Ayn's fourteenth birthday; a day with endless opportunities for both their allies and their enemies.

However, Ayn was not worried about his enemies. He was more aware of the ones who called themselves his followers. In the past years of his childhood, Meddhi-Lan had managed to convince The Dei that Ayn's complex gender was the will of The Great Adin and was all part of the prophecy that had long been awaited.

Unfortunately, Ayn could feel their confusion and doubt over the matter, which only fed his own fears having to do with his body. He could not understand why The Un would make his mind undoubtedly male, and yet, create his body with both male and female genitalia. Why include both? Was it truly planned like The Dei chose to believe? Ayn could not think of it in such a way. He knew the chaos of The Un too well, and for him, it felt more like a sick joke - a joke being played on him and his entire planet, just to amuse the Gods. If so, he was definitely not laughing.

Ayn began to cry into his hands and fell down upon his knees onto the floor. Meddhi-Lan gently knelt beside him.

"Ayn... my Ney," he softly spoke as he lifted Ayn's chin. "You will not fail. You cannot fail. It is impossible for you to do so."

"Why?" Ayn replied in a whimper. "Because I am... The Adin?" He lowered his face into his hands once again, feeling defeated.

"No," Meddhi-Lan replied as he re-lifted Ayn's chin, "you cannot fail because no matter what path you choose or whichever answer you shall receive, you are you... and that is enough."

"Not for them," said Ayn with a sniff. "They want me to simply fix it, as if The Un were a broken wheel that must be remade or replaced. But it is not, My Lan!"

"Shh, Ayn, I know," Meddhi-Lan hushed as he put his arms around Ayn to comfort him. He wanted to tell his beloved boy that it would be alright and that The Dei will accept whatever fate had in store for them, but he knew his words would have run past Ayn like wind through clouds. Instead, he simply cradled Ayn and rocked him in his arms.

In a matter of moments, Ayn fell asleep. Soon after, Meddhi-Lan gently picked him up and carried him to Ayn's room. He then lay the exhausted boy onto the bed. He removed Ayn's sandals and covered him with a silken, light-blue sheet. He then sat in a chair, watching over his favorite student, worried for his very soul.

In the darkness of Ayn's bedroom, Meddhi-Lan silently prayed. He did not pray to the Gods, but to The Un itself. *Please, mighty Un,* he pleaded in his mind, *Please give Ayn the strength to face his own soul. I beg of you to keep him safe in your care. Let him grow to become a man so he may fulfill his purpose.*

Meddhi-Lan looked again at Ayn who was quietly breathing as he slept. Meddhi-Lan noticed how peaceful he seemed, even if for just the moment. Soon, the high priest felt tears flowing down his face. Ayn was his to teach and protect, yet he was helpless against the pain that tore at his beloved boy's heart. Meddhi-Lan loved him beyond measure, and wanted to take him away from such pain. Yet, he knew it would only cause Ayn more harm if he ran from his destiny. However, it was always at the back of his mind to take Ayn away - far away to perhaps Kri or somewhere else beyond their planet. Ultimately, he never acted on his fantasies, for he knew Ayn's destiny would only find him once again until there was nowhere else to run.

Meddhi-Lan sighed, then wiped away the tears from his face. If only he could protect Ayn with his love alone. If only there was a way to keep him in this moment forever; a gentle boy asleep in the peacefulness of the night.

Chapter 6: The Dream

*I*t always began like this: the silver stream and the ona petals falling slowly to the ground. At first, it was serene and beautiful, but then the rain fell, and Ayn could sense the doom in the air.

He saw their eyes glowing white in the darkness - all twelve of them, with their black, hooded robes hung low. They seemed to look at him with an intense anger. Then, all at once, they pointed in the same direction, and when Ayn looked, he saw the shape of his fate.

It was the legendary tangled tree, the sweat encrusted blood, and the once Great Adin hanging by the branches of hatred.

Ayn's heart raced in fear as he tried to turn away from the spectacle before him, but the men in robes blocked him from returning to the ona gardens. They surrounded him in a semi-circle and began singing traditional chants in their guttural, low voices. He was trapped and forced to move forward into the past.

Adin was bleeding. His wounds seemed too numerous to even comprehend. It was as if someone had cut him with a sharp, many sided sword in his ribs, his arms, his legs, and his stomach. He hung there, naked, rotting in the sun.

Ayn cried in horrible pain. He could not look at the spectacle of blood and sweat any longer. Just as he felt he could take no more, he noticed something odd coming from Adin's wounds. It was not blood. It was clear, yet glowing. It was plasma itself.

He felt the need to look closer, but did not want to go near the dying Adin. Instead, he used his mind's eye to look harder at the substance.

Suddenly, he was inside a white room with only walls. He heard a voice telling him to be diligent in his thoughts. He assumed it was his beloved teacher and tried to find where he was, but to no avail. The room was empty and cold.

Then the sound began. At first, it was a whisper of noises amidst orchestral music, but soon, it grew into a thousand sounds melding into a dangerously loud cacophony that deafened Ayn's mind. It became too loud for anyone to withstand, and Ayn fell to the floor in shock and terror.

Then, he saw the middle of the floor crack and split until it expanded into a gaping hole in the center of the room. Ayn looked at the hole and saw nothing but pitch black darkness. He felt a complete and utter fear take hold over his soul.

It was a vortex, creating a vacuum of power that was sucking the room inside of its mouth. Everything, including Ayn, was being pulled by extreme force into the hole. At his last reach for the security of the room, he was sucked into the darkness... into the black abyss.

There, in his mind, Ayn saw it like never before. The particles of static mixed with the plasma of life's energy, and its residue was before him as visible as the stars. It was silent and still, but Ayn could feel an enormous depth within the image. It was the connecting gravity within darkness and the true source behind the static and creation. It was immense!

However, Ayn could not hold the image to him. It fled the moment he thought of The Dei and their expectations. He then found himself surrounded again with the twelve hooded men and their glowing eyes. They pointed and sang.

He would not look this time.

He had his eyes fiercely closed in a stubborn act of will. Just then, he heard a familiar voice beckoning him and looked to see where it came from. It was Meddhi-Lan standing in front of him with an extended arm. He looked gentle and kind and seemed to know the way back to the gardens. Ayn was filled with sudden warmth and hope, and he ran to join his beloved teacher.

Just as Ayn took Meddhi-Lan's hand, he looked up to see his teacher's face. It seemed wrong, pale, and confused. Ayn looked closer and noticed blood. It was slowly pouring from his Lan's mouth.

Ayn felt his entire being split in two.

"NOT MY LAN!" he screamed. "NO! NOT MY LAN!"

--

"Wake up, Ayn. Wake up, please!" Pei begged as he gave his student a gentle shake to the shoulders. Ayn awoke to see the worried, pale face of his second teacher, sitting beside him on the bed. It calmed his heart to look at Pei, his brother-in-soul.

Ayn sat up and wiped his face. He could feel the wetness of tears and wondered why.

"Was I crying in my sleep?" Ayn asked, confused.

"Yes, my Ney, you were," answered Pei as he got up to pour Ayn a glass of water.

"Strange," Ayn quietly replied.

"Yes, very," Pei remarked before giving Ayn the glass. He then looked at his student carefully. He could tell Ayn was already deep in the act of forgetting, a device his brother-in-soul seemed to use more and more as of late. It worried Pei greatly, though he kept his thoughts to himself.

Ayn looked at Pei and smiled at him, as if nothing had been wrong. *Perhaps he is excited about his birthday today*, Pei wondered.

Just as his thought ended, Ayn's smile turned to a frown. Reading Pei's mind, Ayn pouted and said, "I had forgotten about that."

Pei did not know why Ayn dreaded the celebration so vehemently, but remembering how easy it was for The Bodanya to hear the thoughts of others, he scolded himself for thinking too loudly.

"It will be a glorious day, Ayn. You will see," Pei said with a comforting smile. Ayn wished he could believe his secondary teacher, but a strong sense of dread lay deep in his mind.

Pei got up and walked over toward a large closet. He opened the purple veils that hung as drapes, and then turned to look at Ayn with a hint of a smile. "Which robe shall it be today, my Bodanya Shiva?"

"None," said Ayn, covering his head with a sheet.

Pei looked at Ayn and gave a sigh. "Come now, my Bodanya. Today you will be crowned, and all of Deius will rejoice in your name. It is not something to be sad about."

"I'm not sad," Ayn mumbled under the sheet.

"What are you then?" asked Pei as he uncovered the sheet from Ayn's head.

Ayn looked at Pei with a frown.

"I'm worried."

"Worried about what?"

"About everything."

Pei laughed and said, "Ayn, you cannot worry about everything. There is far too much in this world to think upon the entirety of it. Why don't you tell me what in particular is worrying you today?"

Pei looked at Ayn who was pouting and looking away. Taking Ayn's silence as a test of will, Pei further prodded, "Are you nervous about the ceremony being complicated? You must remember, it will mainly be the priests who will be doing the chanting and reciting. You do not have to do much, except to stand and be crowned." Pei's attempt at cheering his little brother-in-soul did not seem to work. Ayn just sat in silence.

Pei was about to focus once more on choosing a robe for Ayn to wear when Meddhi-Lan swiftly opened the door.

"He's awake?" asked Meddhi-Lan.

"Barely," Pei quietly replied.

Meddhi-Lan looked at Ayn, who still seemed to be in some far off land. "Come, Ayn, you need to be ready soon," said the high priest. "You must bathe and have something to eat — something small, just to get you through until the coronation feast."

Ayn heard every word his Lan said, but he was terrified of looking at him. He did not want his dream to be like the others - the prophetic kind. He was afraid if he made eye contact with Meddhi-Lan, he would be inviting an unnecessary evil into their lives, forcing fate's hand.

"Ayn," said Meddhi-Lan as he walked over and sat in a nearby chair, "what is wrong?" Ayn could not help but succumb to his desire to tell his Lan about the dream. He began describing the rain and the petals, and the twelve men with white eyes. However, as soon as he came to the hanging of The Adin, he could no longer bring himself to speak.

Pei sat upon his knees on the floor near to his teacher. He looked at Meddhi-Lan, as if asking him for help to decipher what Ayn was describing. Meddhi-Lan put his hand on Pei's shoulder, then sat by Ayn on the bed.

"Go on, Ayn. You must not be afraid to open the door to your hidden feelings," said Meddhi-Lan in a sympathetic tone.

"Is that all they are? Feelings?" asked Ayn with a panicked vulnerability.

Meddhi-Lan knew Ayn was afraid of his prophetic dreams, but he did not want him to be frightened of his own mind. "Ayn," he softly said, "not all dreams that you have will come to be. There will be some dreams that are only reflections of emotions and desires. It is best that you learn to tell the difference between the two, though only time and courage will help you do so."

Ayn understood his teacher's words, but did not feel comforted by them; they seemed rushed and determined. "But... my Lan-"

"Listen to me Ayn," Meddhi-Lan said with a firm, yet gentle voice, "we have only an hour or two before the guests will be arriving. You must try to concentrate on the positive that is around you." He looked at Pei and nodded to him. "Do you see how you are surrounded with only our eyes?" Meddhi-Lan looked deeply into Ayn's eyes. His teacher's dark-blue eyes were the kindest Ayn had ever known.

Ayn could not hold back his tears and flew into Meddhi-Lan's arms. "There, there, my boy," said the high priest. "It is alright. No need for tears today."

Ayn looked up at the only father he'd ever known and silently swore to The Un that if anything ever took his beloved Lan away, he would refuse to be The Bodanya Shiva, Second Adin.

Pei smiled, yet felt a strange sensation, as if he were looking at them through a darkened window. He immediately distanced the feeling and got up, returning to the closet, hoping his teacher would soon make Ayn feel safe enough to face his destiny.

"Ayn..." said Meddhi-Lan with a hint of a smile, "I was going to give you your present after the Coronation, when we had a moment of calm, but I think maybe now would be best."

"Oh, yes, please!" Ayn said as he wiped his tears.

Meddhi-Lan gave a wink, then pulled something from behind his robe. It was a round, red-colored medallion tied to a gold chain.

"What is that?" asked Ayn, forgetting all about his fear.

"It is an ancient artifact that has been in your family for generations. Your mother wanted me to keep it safe until you were of age and ready to protect it with your full strength."

"Is it magic?" asked Ayn.

"Yes, I believe it may be," Meddhi-Lan replied, grinning. "I would like you to wear it for your coronation so you may remember that you carry your mother's spirit with you."

Meddhi-Lan hung the medallion around Ayn's neck, then wiped the remaining tears from Ayn's cheeks. "There is nothing to fear, Ayn," he said in a calming voice. "You will be surrounded by joy and admiration, this day and from here on, and I will be with you, always."

Ayn smiled, fighting back his fears, then hugged his Lan tightly. He knew nothing could harm them if their bond remained impenetrable.

Trying his best to hide his overwhelming emotions, Pei turned around and held up two robes for Ayn's approval. "Do you like the white or the gold?" he asked with a cheeky grin. "Neither," said Ayn, who bounced out of bed with a renewed spirit. "I like..." Ayn paused as he stroked his fingers across the robes of the closet, "...the blue!"

Meddhi-Lan was pleased and proud. He reminded Pei that Ayn must be bathed and ready by the mid turning of the sun. Then, he nodded at Ayn and bowed. "See you soon, my Bodanya Shiva."

Ayn bowed and smiled, returning once again to his usual joyful innocence. He turned to Pei and motioned for him to close the veils so that he may change into his chosen holy robe. Pei understood and pulled the veils shut.

"Pei?" Ayn asked as he was dressing.

"Yes, Ayn."

"Will there be, um... many people today?"

"Oh, yes."

"How many?"

"Quite a lot, my Ney."

"Well, how many? More than fifty?"

"Yes, Ayn... I would say, hundreds will come."

"Hundreds?" Ayn poked his head out from the veils. "How can there be hundreds coming? Were they all invited?"

Pei laughed and looked into the gold-framed mirror that hung near Ayn's bed. With slight vanity, Pei checked to make sure that his hair was smooth and in its proper place.

"Well," said Pei as he finished fixing his long, braided hair, "there will be hundreds from the Kingdom who have desired for many years to witness your crowning. But if you mean only the guests who will be dining with us and those allowed to watch the ceremony-"

"Yes! That is what I meant," said Ayn as he came through the veils.

Pei smiled and said, "Well, then perhaps fifty or so people - only our allies and their close relatives."

Pei found Ayn to be full of questions, even during his bath, which usually made him quiet. From the time Ayn was a small child, Pei had been assigned the duty of washing him. It was usually a slave's place to do so, but the secrecy involved with Ayn's physical oddity made it necessary to break from tradition. However, Pei was never truly comfortable helping Ayn bathe - not so much because of his complex genitalia, but more due to Ayn's reserved anxiety about the matter. This day, however, Ayn was much less reserved.

"Will there be anyone from other planets arriving?" Ayn excitedly asked as Pei rinsed the soap from his hair.

"Yes, I expect a few," said Pei.

"And will there be anyone of my age?" Ayn asked, even

more excited.

"I think so, my Bodanya," Pei said with a smile. "Now rinse yourself, and I will see you downstairs in the great hallway."

Ayn suddenly felt frightened again. "Pei?" Ayn anxiously asked as his teacher was about to leave the bathing room.

"Yes?" Pei replied. Ayn gulped and looked at his teacher, hoping he would understand without words. "Do not fear, Ayn. It is what I had said before... today will be a glorious day."

With those words, Pei left the room, leaving Ayn with nothing else to hold onto, except the mere hope that at least some of his dreams would never come true.

Chapter 7: The Morning of the Coronation

*M*eddhi-Lan was not a political man by nature. He was extremely well spoken, and could handle himself with great confidence, but he was not comfortable with the role of diplomat.

Yet, here he was nonetheless, awaiting the arrival of two important political leaders. The first, and more welcome, was King Atlar, elected ruler of the neighboring, allied planet, Kri. Thousands of years ago, it was populated by the same scholars and scientists that formed the kingdom of Deius, but it had since become its own vastly rich and prosperous planet. Through the last hundred or so years, Kri had been governed by a family of dignified kings who had tolerated and respected the religious doctrine of The Dei. Meddhi-Lan was hopeful that the current king, who had once been his closest friend, would appreciate and respect the importance of their Bodanya's crowning.

The second dignitary whom Meddhi-Lan was scheduled to welcome had a more questionable nature. His name was Lod Enra and was of an alien race from the planet Ohr, which circled near the outer rims of the Un-Ahm galaxy. He was officially an ally, but Meddhi-Lan had heard the Ohrian king was not all that fluent in Uni, the native tongue of Deius and the language that most in The

Un galaxy accepted as their universal speech.

Having once been Deius' sworn enemy, the Ohrian government usually kept rather distant. With their unique language full of fluid sounds, as well as their advanced technology, beings from Ohr were a mystery to the priests of The Dei.

Meddhi-Lan, however, had reasons beyond unfamiliarity to be skeptical and nervous. Lod Enra and his family were, until recently, considered enemies of Deius, and their visit was cause for suspicion among many in The Dei. Meddhi-Lan, however, remained hopeful that The Bodanya's coronation would bring an end to past grievances and old conflicts.

Forgetting the past would not be easy for many Deiusians. It had been roughly ten years prior when Ohr had attacked Deius during the infamous Xen War. During that time, it was King Atlar who had been able to force peace upon their three great kingdoms.

Now, it was up to Meddhi-Lan to keep the peace and bring understanding between their different cultures. With the queen gone, and Ayn still too young to govern, Meddhi-Lan was completely in charge. The Dei had long been the true governing body of Deius, but Meddhi-Lan believed it was the high priest's job to work with The Shiva, and to bridge the gap between royalty and priest, like balancing the body and spirit.

As for Ohr, it was known to Meddhi-Lan that the Ohrians did not believe in a higher power, choosing to follow only science and mathematics. This made Meddhi-Lan a bit nervous, for he feared Ayn's life may be endangered. He assumed it may be an upsetting concept to any non-believer if The Dei's prophecy had indeed been fulfilled.

However, Meddhi-Lan felt sure that the Gods were watching over his beloved Ayn, and it was that very notion that drove him every day, every hour. He would even play the part of diplomat, just for the final moment when all people from every planet would see Ayn be crowned Bodanya and king.

The giant silver doors of the Holy Temple opened slowly to the sounds of beckoning horns being played by the royal musicians of the palace. Meddhi-Lan stood and readied himself. Only he and two other priests were there to welcome their allies. To his right, stood his elder and former teacher, Amun-Lan. To his left, Pei hurried to find his place.

Pei was nervous, yet confident Meddhi-Lan would handle the situation with grace and wisdom. He serenely smiled at his Lan who nodded in return. Meddhi-Lan could not show his Ney how deeply unsure he truthfully felt, especially with his previous teacher there beside him.

The open doors revealed a tall man with thick curls of golden hair. He was standing, arms folded, between two well-dressed soldiers who wore the flame-shaped insignia of Kri on their armored chests. "Meddhi! How long has it been, my dear friend?" Atlar loudly exclaimed as he entered the hall and embraced Meddhi-Lan as if they were long-lost brothers.

Meddhi-Lan did not quite expect such a bold entrance. He had once been close friends with the man who was firmly holding onto his arms, but he had not spoken with Atlar in many years. Meddhi-Lan felt glad, yet slightly uncomfortable.

"It has been a very long time, Your Majesty," Meddhi-Lan said with a slight smile. To that, Atlar heartily laughed, then patted Meddhi-Lan on his left shoulder.

"A very long time indeed!" replied the Krian king. "But, please, Meddhi, call me by my name. We are old friends, and I am honored to be with you again on this triumphant occasion!" Meddhi-Lan half-bowed and smiled. Atlar bowed halfway in return and folded his arms with a twinkle in his eye.

"Let me introduce to you my daughter, Ona," Atlar joyfully exclaimed. He turned around, and from behind, a beautiful young woman with dark auburn hair appeared. She bowed and gestured a circle with her hands, which was an ancient Dei symbol for peace and unity. Meddhi-Lan returned the gesture and politely nodded his head. The king then continued; "Her mother, Queen Pira - Gods rest her soul - named her after your planet's holy flower. Pira was, after all, originally the princess of this wondrous Kingdom of yours."

Meddhi-Lan smiled with a knowing nod.

Pei, who had never seen a woman of his own age with such beauty, was unable to control the rush of fluid that formed inside of his mouth. He gulped and turned his face from her sight. Meddhi-Lan sensed his student's urgency, but kept his mind on political matters, hoping Pei would try to do the same.

"I am honored to bear witness to the crowning of the new Bodanya," she said to all three priests. Her maturity and grace immediately struck them, as well as the depth of her voice: both strong and softly feminine. Pei could not help but stare at her. He had never seen such smooth waves of dark hair, pale skin, rose colored lips, and piercingly green eyes. He was suddenly lost inside the beauty of the princess who stood before him.

Meddhi-Lan cleared his throat and said with a smile, "Your Highness, we are the ones who are filled with honor and gratitude." He turned to Pei, then to his former teacher. "This is the order's elder, Amun-Lan... and this is my personal student and recent graduate, Pei-Lan."

"It is good to see you again, King Atlar. You are most welcome among us," Amun-Lan replied.

Pei finally snapped out of his trance as he nodded politely and bowed.

Meddhi-Lan looked at King Atlar with a smirk, which made the king quietly laugh. Atlar then extended his hand for his daughter to take. "Come, my dear," he said to her, still amused at Meddhi-Lan's student, "we have much unpacking to do before the coronation, and I am sure it will take you at least a full season to choose what you will wear." She took his hand and smiled.

Pei could feel his heart race as he watched her. Raising the side of her pale blue dress, which hung low to the floor, Ona gave Pei a slight smile, then walked on with her father. He wondered if he had ever truly seen anything as lovely in his entire life.

"Pei," Meddhi-Lan said with a direct, commanding tone, "please escort King Atlar and Princess Ona to their guest quarters. Then, I would like it if you could meet me in the Coronation Room for a brief discussion."

Pei looked at Meddhi-Lan as if he'd been caught doing something inappropriate. Meddhi-Lan simply nodded politely at him. Pei then bowed and quickly withdrew his feelings from being seen or felt. He motioned for the king and his lovely daughter to follow him. They obliged along with their entourage of guards and servants following close behind.

--

In the kitchen, Ayn was sneaking around looking for more to eat. He did not feel that the amount offered to him for breakfast was nearly enough, and he wondered why Meddhi-Lan thought a small breakfast, consisting of only a handful of fruits and a slice of sweet bread, would be enough for the next Shiva Bodanya. Perhaps he thought of him still as a child? Ayn began to get a strong feeling of defiance and walked past various servants, smiling at them nonchalantly.

He saw a plate of cured meats and cheeses and grabbed as much into his hands as he could manage. A servant girl looked at him curiously, then quickly bowed as to not catch his eye. Ayn simply smiled, then stuck a rolled slice of cheese into his mouth. He then half-bowed at the girl, whom he had easily charmed, then hurriedly exited before anyone had the notion to tell his teachers about what he was doing.

--

Meddhi-Lan was busy controlling his anxious energy, pacing the floor of the great hall. Amun-Lan stood calmly, watching him. "Meddhi..." said Amun-Lan, "the Ohrians shall come when it is time - no later, no sooner."

Meddhi-Lan turned to face Amun-Lan and gave him a slight sneer. "I wish it would be sooner," he mumbled, then continued to pace.

Meanwhile, Pei unlocked the ornate, gold and green framed door to the guest rooms for the king and princess of Kri. Many kings had stayed with them through the years, and Atlar felt right at home, having stayed there previously as a young man.

The princess, however, felt a little uncomfortable, though she did not show it. She could not help but miss her home immediately after having left it, and she wondered if she would be able to sleep in a strange bed in a kingdom that was not entirely familiar to her.

Pei vaguely sensed both of their emotional states, but attempted to keep his awareness to a minimal. He would not let himself unfairly probe Ona's mind simply because of his attraction for her. He wasn't the greatest at such mental gifts anyway.

He cleared his throat and watched as they entered the room and looked around. "Will this do?" he asked the king. "Oh yes," replied Atlar with a contented smile. The king turned to his daughter and opened his arms. "And what does the princess think?" he asked as he wrapped her in his arms.

She serenely smiled, then nodded. "It's beautiful," she replied.

Pei could not move. Yet again, he felt entranced by her beauty. He wanted to bow and turn to leave, but his feet stuck themselves to the floor.

"Father! Look!" The princess exclaimed, wild eyed, as she ran to the large windows at the end of the room. She then swung them open, and to her delight, the view displayed lush gardens with waterfall-pools that ran throughout the length of the green. "Can you see this, father?" she said beaming with joy. "Look! There are mother's favorite flowers! *My* flowers! Do you see?"

Atlar walked over to his daughter and put his hands on her shoulders, smiling. "Yes, Ona," he replied, "Didn't I tell you how much you'd feel at home here?" He kissed her forehead, then began helping his servants with the unpacking of their belongings.

Pei was amazed at how different the king of Kri was to that of their own planet's royalty. Never had there been a king or queen who helped a servant unpack; it was simply unheard of. He also had never seen such open warmth between parent and child. As Pei watched him further, there was something emanating from the Krian king: a genuine goodness. It made him feel love for a man he did not even know.

Pei's mind was suddenly caught off-guard as the princess turned around and smiled at him. She was radiant beyond his wildest imagination with her noble, high forehead and oval, angelic face. He watched her standing by the window, hypnotized by her waves of dark auburn hair blowing in the breeze as the sun gently kissed it, exposing subtle hints of red. He felt as though he was caught in the haze of a dream. *Is she smiling at me?* he asked himself, nervously. *Does she smile at me on purpose or simply because I am the only one to smile at in the room?*

Ona gave Pei no clue as she gracefully ran to her father with a girlish innocence. She then helped him with the unpacking of their belongings.

"I..." said Pei nervously, "I will take my leave then... if everything is to your liking." The king grunted in approval as he continued helping the servants.

Ona was more aware than her father of Pei's presence. She walked over to him and half-bowed her head. "Thank you, Ney-Lan," she said as she raised her head to look at him eye to eye. Pei gulped and could not think of words any longer. "If you don't mind me asking, what is your name?" she asked with her head slightly cocked to the side. The young man, in love for the first time in his sheltered life, struggled to remember how to speak.

After a few moments he shyly replied, "Pei, Your Highness."

Ona smiled at him, forcing his heart to fall even deeper in love. "Pei-Lan, we thank you," she sweetly replied, "and look forward to seeing you at the coronation."

Pei bowed and swiftly left the room. He felt he had to forcibly pull himself away or he might never leave. It was as if he were waking up from the deepest meditation he had ever experienced.

--

The king of Ohr, Lod Enra, was greeted at the silver entrance gates with a handful of Deiusian Royal Guards, as well as Meddhi-Lan who had gotten tired of waiting in the hall. He walked up to Lod Enra with a confident approach and shook both his hands in the style of Ohrian custom: fist inside fist with the guest always having the inner one. This seemed to make the Ohrian king feel more at ease as he followed Meddhi-Lan past the guards and into the great hall. His wife and their teenage son walked behind the king with their slanted eyes watchful and aware.

Once the Ohrian family was safely inside the hall of the palace, Meddhi-Lan apologized for the overabundance of guards. "But," he explained, "it is for your protection as well as ours." Lod Enra raised an eyebrow, which was thin and white. He and Meddhi-Lan looked at each other for a moment. Then, Lod Enra said in a heavily accented Uni, "I assume you are the leading high priest to your new Lord Shiva?"

Meddhi-Lan immediately sensed the truth behind the king's slightly sarcastic tone. The Ohrians were, for the most part, a non-religious race who looked down on those who still believed in Gods. They had once followed Gods of their own, but that was thousands of years ago, and it seemed to The Dei that Ohrian royalty believed themselves superior to other races in almost every facet of existence, especially when it came to Ohr's rejection of religion in favor of science. Despite their prejudice, Meddhi-Lan was well aware of how important Ohr's new allied relationship to Deius was, and he was not about to jeopardize it for the sake of his pride. He assumed Lod Enra felt the same, which was why the Ohrian royal family had come to the coronation in the first place.

"Yes, Your Majesty, my name is Meddhi-Lan, and I am the high priest of The Holy City. We are honored you could join us for this momentous celebration, which represents a new era for our people, as well as a new era for our entire galaxy."

Lod Enra paused for a moment, then nodded. "This is my

wife, Loda La," he said in a serious tone, "and this is my son, Zin Ra." Meddhi-Lan looked at the fragile woman with silver hair and her handsome, adolescent son, then bowed to them both as they did in return. "We are very tired. It has been a long journey," the king explained while opening his hand for his wife's fist to rest in.

"Please," Meddhi-Lan said, "follow me to your guest quarters so that you may rest before the ceremony." The Ohrians nodded their heads and walked with him through the halls to their rooms.

As Pei headed toward the Coronation Room, he noticed the Ohrian family walking behind his Lan. How strange they were to him. They resembled his own people enough to be somewhat the same with hands, legs, feet, etc, but they also had overly smooth skin; it was fine and nearly opaque. Their eyes were slanted upward with a shading of silvery green on their eyelids, which did not seem to be applied by a cream or powder.

Pei noticed how they walked too, almost gliding across the floor, and he silently marveled at them. There was also something about the Ohrians he found particularly intriguing: their gills. He had heard that Ohrians evolved long ago from a fish-like creature, but he had not imagined they still had the slits on the sides of their necks. In fact, Pei had noticed that the queen was wearing a pair of round, circular objects that hung from the slits, just below her ears. He assumed it was some kind of jewelry, but he wasn't quite sure.

It was both wondrous and frightening to the young Lan's mind to think of the differences between Ohrians, Krians, and the Deiusian people. He had never seen so many differences, especially among the females.

At the temple, the Dei priestesses often hung their heads down when they approached a priest of The Holy Order. He was also used to how the priestesses reacted to him in a polite, distant way, and how they usually dressed in fully covered clothing. The priestesses, however, resided on the eastern side of the temple, nearer to the palace of the royal family, and so he didn't spend too much time with them. As Pei thought further on the matter, he began to question if he had ever truly seen a woman outside of The Holy Order.

While lost in thought, Pei suddenly heard Meddhi-Lan's voice speaking inside his mind. "Pei," said the high priest, "what are you doing? I am waiting for you."

Pei shook from his thoughts, then quickly walked to the Coronation Room, feeling more like a Ney than a Lan.

"I'm sorry, my Lan," he said as he entered the room. Meddhi-Lan was standing near the door with his arms folded.

"It is not necessary to hide your thoughts from me, Pei. I simply wish your mind to be as clear and concentrated as possible during these next few days, for we have important matters at hand."

"Yes, my Lan."

"It is our highest concern to think of nothing but the Shiva's crowning and of his well being."

"Yes, my Lan."

"You must understand, Pei," Meddhi-Lan said with a sigh, "that I need you to focus your energy so that when I need your help on matters of politics, you will be able to do so readily."

"Yes, I understand. I am truly sorry, my Lan."

"And please *stop* calling me your Lan!"

Pei had never heard Meddhi-Lan's voice with such fierceness. A little shaken, he lowered his head in shame.

"Pei... please," said Meddhi-Lan, calming himself, "do not

misunderstand me. I am not your teacher any longer, and you may address me as your equal now."

"But you *are* my teacher... and always will be," said Pei with his head down.

"No, Pei," sighed Meddhi-Lan, "I need you to think of me as your equal and treat me as such so that I may depend on you when needs be. Ayn will need you today as well."

Meddhi-Lan then pointed in the direction of a large, golden throne, which stood in front of them like the God of the sun. It had a circular disc at the top with wing-shaped rays of metallic sunlight coming from its sides. "Today," Meddhi-Lan continued as he walked in front of the throne, "Ayn will be crowned king, as well as proclaimed the savior, The Bodanya, of all Deius. This, Ayn fears more than anything else in the world. We *must* get him through these fears. Do you understand, Pei? You can no longer afford to think of yourself as merely my student. Today, you are Ayn's teacher as much as I am, and together, we will help him become his destiny."

"Of course, Meddhi," Pei said as he raised his head to face his former teacher.

"Good," said Meddhi-Lan with a strong nod of his head. "We should not be distracted by other thoughts, whether they be desires or insecurities. Agreed?"

"Yes, I agree," Pei replied, trying his best to appear confident in front of his teacher.

Meddhi-Lan gave a sigh and turned to face the throne before them. He knew Ayn would soon be sitting there, looking for guidance. He also knew there would be nothing he could say or do to entirely prepare Ayn for leadership; it would have to be something he discovered for himself. Meddhi-Lan and Pei looked at each other and nodded, fully aware of the arduous path ahead of them.

--

Ayn did not understand what was taking so long. He had been told to wait in the dining hall until Pei arrived to escort him to The Holy Chamber of the Adin: a large room that had not been occupied since the original Shiva.

He felt anxious and a little sick to his stomach. *Where is Meddhi?* he thought to himself. *Have they forgotten that I am here?*

Ayn could no longer take the waiting. He decided to explore into areas of The Holy Temple he had never seen before. Getting up, he walked through the oval doors that connected the dining room to the hallway.

Ever since he was a child, he had been carefully watched. He was told not to go to the servant's quarters or anywhere near the back entrance of the gardens where the merchants and scholars were sometimes allowed to pass.

At times, however, Ayn would sneak into the gardens when no one was looking. He would peek through a sliver in the stone wall, and for a moment, he could see the outside world.

He saw the merchants in their black and gray suits and thought they looked extremely serious, which he did not like, nor understood. He also saw people of different colors walking with baskets of fruit and vegetables in their arms. He assumed they worked for the merchants, and he wondered if they enjoyed being in the sunshine or if they disliked every minute of it. Ayn questioned many things, but most of all, he wondered about the peasants.

He had often heard mention of them from his mother and occasionally from the mouth of a priest, but he did not know one firsthand. He had never seen a peasant and didn't understand what it meant to be one. He only knew it meant they were not wealthy and that they did not live for long, suffering from illnesses or accidents, which often caused death. Of course, he had seen a deadly illness - Plasma Sickness - come to his own mother, The Queen, so he was quite aware that it was not just a peasant's curse. However, he wondered if they felt The Great Paradox in a way that was perhaps more spiritually inclined than a rich man or royal member might.

Today, though, Ayn was more interested in the hidden places of his own home. In the past, he had often tried sneaking into the closed off area which used to be the private living quarters of Adin. He'd get close enough to peek through the roped off barrier, but before he could reach it, he was usually caught by a priest and told it was off limits, even to a Shiva. However, he figured no one would object after he was crowned and proclaimed as the next Adin.

Silently, Ayn walked through the hallway. He then came to a burgundy curtain and quickly ducked behind it. It was a secret passage to Adin's library, and a place Ayn was not allowed to enter.

He had followed Meddhi-Lan once before and got as far as Adin's reading room, but he was found and told to go back to bed. He never understood why he was not allowed into such places if they were originally *his* quarters from his past life. The Dei were full of such inconsistencies, however, and Ayn learned to accept their strange rules and secrets. Accepting it was one thing, but he never stopped being curious. In fact, he was more curious than ever before.

Ayn opened the door to the secret staircase that led down to a circular path. It was dark, but dimly lit by the tiny plasma-candles which hung on the walls. He then opened another door and came to an elevated pedestal. He stepped on it and said, "Un." In a rush, the pedestal zoomed upward as Ayn braced himself as best he could.

He then found himself behind dark-blue curtain. He lifted it to the side, and as soon as he could see that the room was empty, he slipped out from behind the curtain. Ayn smiled to himself, feeling rather clever and mischievous. *They must all be too preoccupied with the coronation to even notice where I am!* he thought.

He then entered a room with a long table and many chairs. There was a large map of Deius on the wall, as well as an ornate plasma-chandelier, which hung from the ceiling. He assumed it was some kind of planning room, perhaps where Adin and his council would meet for discussions of great importance. He had seen it before, however, and quickly ran past to get through to his destination: Adin's library.

--

"Why did you not act more friendly when we arrived? Do you not realize how crucial this visit is for us, politically? Zin? Zin, answer me!"

Silent and staring into the distance, his son did not give an answer.

Lod Enra was not pleased with his son's defiance. It seemed to the Ohrian king that the prince did not share in his own logical approach to living, nor did his son seem to care about a future political career. Because of this and more, Zin Ra was not at all what the king had wanted in a son and an heir.

"Why do you sneer at me when I am talking to you?" he

demanded from his son. "Zin, do you hear me?"

"Zin Ra, your father is addressing you," Loda La reminded her son as she brushed her long, fine, silver hair with a bluish jade comb.

The prince sat on a chair with his arms folded. His fair, but stony face turned away from his mother and father. A few moments of silence passed until the king threw up his arms and walked out of the sitting room, heading into the master bedroom. He then slammed the door shut.

The queen twitched from the noise, but quickly shrugged it off. She opened a bottle of perfume and began applying the scented oil behind her ears. She looked into the mirror and could see her petulant son staring at her through the glass. It made her uncomfortable to be so intently watched by his anger-filled eyes. Fed up, she turned around to face him.

"Listen to me, Zin," she said, strict and cold. "I want you to behave for your father's sake, and for mine as well. This is not a situation that you can tamper with simply because you are bored or feeling rebellious against your father."

"I am *not* bored," said Zin Ra in a monotone voice.

"Then why must you start with your usual attitude?"

"I have no attitude, Mother."

Even though he was almost the spitting image of her, Loda La felt no patience for her only child. She shook her head and got up, walking out of the room. She then went into her bedroom, closing the door behind her.

Zin smiled to himself, grateful to be alone. He silently walked to the front door. Finally, it was his chance to escape, and he was going to take it.

--

Meddhi-Lan could feel many disturbing vibrations in the air. Most of all, he was intensely aware of Ayn's nerves and could sense Ayn was not where he was supposed to be. As the hour grew closer, Meddhi-Lan feared Ayn might be late for his own coronation.

"Pei, I want you to find Ayn and bring him to The Holy Chamber."

"Where is he?" Pei replied.

"He is probably in the gardens somewhere, though I'm not sure. Find him and meet me in the chamber in half an hour. I have to gather The Council and run through the details of the coronation ceremony."

Pei nodded, then headed toward the gardens, though he was unsure where Ayn was hiding. It was always difficult for Pei to sense Ayn's presence, especially as he got older. Ayn loved to play games, and he seemed to be getting better and better at them.

--

The library was bigger than Ayn had imagined. It was an immense room, seemingly endless in its winding glass stairs and plasma-powered escalators. Ayn had to rub his eyes when he saw the grand design on the wall. It was a vibrantly colorful painting depicting the birth of Adin as he emerged from The Un's womb, reaching for the knowledge of the stars. Ayn felt like a trespasser. He wondered if he should go back to the dining room and wait for

Pei.

"So..." he heard a voice say," you must be the new Shiva?"

Ayn whirled around to see a young man standing in front of him. He was someone Ayn had never seen before – a young man near to his age, and yet, with his opaque skin and silver hair, he was quite different in appearance.

"Who are you?" Ayn asked nervously.

"I am known as Zin Ra, and I am Ohr's one and only Heir Apparent," he replied in a sing-song, sarcastic tone, "but you can just call me Zin, if you'd like."

Ayn had never seen anyone from Ohr and was slightly overwhelmed. He looked at Zin's features: sparkling aqua-colored eyes and fine, shoulder length hair of pure silver. It was awe-striking. Yet, Ayn was still cautious. He didn't know if Zin was there to hurt him or to be friendly. He wondered how Zin had even found the secret passageway.

"What are you doing here?" Ayn asked as he slowly backed away from the strange prince.

"I was curious," said Zin, "and I wanted to meet you." The prince then leaned on a desk, crossing his arms.

"What? Why?" Ayn replied, even more anxious.

"Because, supposedly, you are a God," said Zin, smirking. "Are you not?

"Me?" Ayn replied, confused and not sure how to answer. "A God?"

"Well, not a God exactly," Zin said as he picked up a book lying on the desk entitled The Past and Future of Deius, "but more of a so-called Messiah, the one who will lead Deius into purity... or some such nonsense."

Ayn was in a shock. He did not know what to do and had no idea how the Ohrian prince found his way into Adin's chambers. He was petrified of what Meddhi-Lan would say, and began thinking of ways to explain himself if his teacher found them out.

"I... don't know what you mean," said Ayn, pushing the words out of his mouth.

"Oh come on," said the prince, coyly, "you are the one they say will rectify the so-called paradox of The Un, aren't you?"

"I am... not..." muttered Ayn, barely able to think straight.

"You are not... what?" Zin teased with a smirk.

Ayn felt vulnerable, and in a split second, decided to call for his Lans within his mind. He closed his eyes and concentrated.

The prince could tell that Ayn went somewhere else in his thoughts. Zin smiled, then gracefully walked to Ayn and whispered, "Don't worry, I won't tell anyone that you're just a man... like the rest of them, no better and no worse."

Ayn opened his eyes and saw Zin's aqua eyes staring right through him. It penetrated Ayn's soul, as if he had known this Ohrian prince before... in some other time and place. The familiarity was instant, yet it frightened Ayn, making him turn away.

"I am... not..." said Ayn, trying his best to speak.

"You are not what exactly?"

For the life of him, Ayn just couldn't find the words.

Zin laughed under his breath and sat down in a chair. He opened a book and pretended to read the pages within.

Ayn took a breath and found himself studying the cocky

Ohrian prince in front of him. Questions popped up in his mind. *Is he my age? Why can he speak Uni so well? What does he want with me?*

Zin looked up at Ayn and grinned at him. The two boys then looked at each other for a moment, curious and somewhat confused.

"So," Zin said, breaking the awkward silence as he rose to his feet, "since I don't want to call you Bodanya, should I call you Shiva? That isn't your real name, is it?"

"No, my name is... Ayn."

Zin smiled again and approached Ayn with such a closeness that their faces almost touched. Ayn nervously swallowed. He couldn't believe he had told a stranger his real name, and now the odd behaving Ohrian prince was invading his personal space. Ayn wanted to run away, but felt transfixed.

Zin stared at Ayn and attempted to reach into his mind. Much to Ayn's surprise, the two of them became lost in another world, a child's world of depth and imagination. They somehow understood each other's souls in a way that most never do.

Ayn could sense the Ohrian prince's urge for freedom, his romantic and poetic nature, his need to praise and adore fine works of art, and most of all, his deep love for music. In return, Zin felt the depth of Ayn's pain, the longing for his mother, and the constant awareness of his great responsibility. The boys drew to each other unconsciously until their foreheads gently touched. Ayn felt scared of this intimacy, but could not stop his longing to be understood by another person of the same age.

Zin opened his eyes and looked at Ayn's pale face. Tears began forming at the edges of their eyes. It was as if they had performed an old blood-bonding ritual, but in their minds alone. Their closeness was instant, and Zin lifted his hands to wipe the tears from Ayn's cheeks. He softly brushed his fingers against his own cheek, mixing the tears together.

"See?" whispered Zin as he held up his fingers of tears, "I am you, and you are me."

Ayn swallowed, overwhelmed by feeling too much.

Zin, however, was not afraid of his feelings. In fact, he was an anomaly of his people in that regard. He moved even closer to Ayn, wrapping his arms around him in a full embrace. He held him tightly, then kissed his cheek. Stunned, Ayn felt extremely uncomfortable. He'd never experienced such intimacy with anyone other than his Lans, and even then, it often felt as if they were breaking The Dei's unspoken rules. Physical closeness, especially among males in the temple, was simply not done. Ayn's thoughts raced as he struggled against his fears.

Why is he holding me like this? Ayn thought as he nervously smiled at Zin. *Is he confused? Does he think I'm female or is this normal behavior for an Ohrian? Does he just want to be my friend? Can I trust him? I want to, but...*

Pei suddenly flung the door open and looked at Ayn with a heavy brow. "Ayn? What are you doing here? Are you alright?"

The two young men immediately broke from each other's arms and wiped their faces. Ayn was filled with embarrassment and confusion.

"Ayn?" asked Pei yet again. "Are you alright?"

"I'm fine," Ayn snapped. "Where were you? I waited forever!" Folding his arms, he sat in a chair across from Zin and looked away.

"I had matters to attend. I'm sorry, Shiva Bodanya," Pei said, taking a formal tongue as he carefully watched both Zin and Ayn, trying to understand the odd situation through their expressions and auras.

"Well, while you were busy with whatever it is you were doing," said Ayn, defiant and defensive, "I got bored and decided to see what was, and still is, mine."

Zin let a smile escape from the corner of his mouth, then said, "I'm sorry if I should not be here, but I too became bored and wanted to see more of your great temple."

Pei looked at the Ohrian prince, tilting his head to the side, trying his best to listen past the boy's words and deeper into his heart.

"I am sorry, Your Highness," said Pei with a half bow, "but no one is allowed inside the private chambers of The Great Adin, and I must ask you to leave." Zin stood up and nodded. He looked at Ayn with a smile and then bowed to leave.

Ayn could not tell if he liked or disliked the intrusively arrogant Ohrian prince. Either way, he was glad Pei had come.

Once Zin exited the room, Pei closed the door and looked at Ayn with scolding eyes.

"Do you have any idea how much time you've wasted down here, Ayn?"

"I'm sorry, I just--"

"No, Ayn, you... *we* have to be in The Holy Chamber Room in merely ten minutes."

"I'm sorry..."

"You cannot do this again, Ayn. Do you understand me?"

"YES!" shouted Ayn, stressed and scared.

Pei did not expect Ayn to raise his voice at him. Ayn had

raised his voice before, here and there, but never quite as forcefully. For a moment, Pei was unable to respond. However, within a matter of seconds, Ayn's face went from anger to utter turmoil. He then burst into tears, making Pei feel awful and cruel.

Realizing how insensitive he had been, Pei wished he had not put such pressure on him. "I'm sorry, Ayn," he softly said, "I didn't mean to be so harsh." Pei tried to comfort Ayn with his arms, but his brother-in-soul recoiled from his touch.

"Where *were* you?" Ayn cried. Using his empathy, Pei felt the twisting in Ayn's stomach. He wanted to tell Ayn that it would be alright, but he did not know if it would be a truthful thing to tell him.

"Ayn..." he gently said, "calm down and relax."

"I can't calm down! I don't want this!"

"You don't want what?"

"THIS!" shouted Ayn at the top of his lungs.

Pei was completely taken aback.

"Ayn..." said Meddhi-Lan as he swiftly entered the library, "Ayn, look at me."

Ayn was breathing hard and feeling faint. He turned to see his elder Lan standing in front of him. "My Lan!" said Ayn as he ran to his beloved teacher, collapsing in Meddhi-Lan's arms.

Meddhi-Lan picked up Ayn and cradled him. Hugging Ayn tightly, he felt a deep sense of guilt take hold over his heart, as if he were leading his child to a slaughter. He then sat Ayn down on a chair and said, "Just relax, my boy, everything will be alright." He held Ayn's hand and led him into a familiar chant, making Ayn practice his meditation.

Gods, please help us, the worried high priest asked in a

silent prayer.

At the request of Meddhi-Lan, Pei went to gather the guests for the beginning of the ceremony. Pei was glad to carry out the task since he was unsure how to handle Ayn when he got that way. Only Meddhi-Lan seemed able to calm the boy, and that made Pei feel helplessly inept. Nonetheless, Pei forced himself to put aside his concern, telling himself that Meddhi-Lan would make everything alright in time for the coronation.

--

Zin had always been different. Since the time of early childhood, he did not think like an average Ohrian. He had a highly creative imagination, which caused him to be scolded often by his tutors and parents for excessive "day dreaming." They believed it weakened his mind, at least his conscious mind, which Ohrians valued far more than the subconscious. Scientific fact was the way of their people, and science was what his father wished Zin to study, as he did and his father before him.

However, the prince had something his father did not understand or approve of: a great sense of instinct that sometimes bordered on the psychic, often unnerving Lod Enra, as well as the queen. At times, Zin could sense when and where people or things were simply because he felt them. Unfortunately, the ability to use the subconscious mind had been draining from the Ohrian people for many years, almost to the point of nonexistence. Therefore, Lod Enra did not approve of his son's strange talent.

In fact, in effort to change his son, the king took away many of Zin's favorite objects as a child: his "magic" plasma-wand, his giant stuffed Eeir fish, and most prized of all, his elenon. He had been given the beautifully hand crafted elenon by his music teacher, Varvin, when he was three years old. Zin's natural talent on the eight stringed instrument had far surpassed many on Ohr, and it was something that made him truly happy. His father, however, eventually saw it as yet another distraction, blaming Zin's music for his disinterest in logic and science. On Zin's twelfth birthday, the elenon was taken away and was replaced with a large telescope. Though he had loved looking at the stars, Zin loved music more, and he never forgave his parents from that day forward.

Through the years, Zin became wilder and more difficult to teach. When Zin turned fourteen, Lod Enra sent him away to a special school on the third moon of the planet. It was an isolated sort of school for "difficult children," and to Zin, not at all a proper place for a prince. While in exile at school, Zin became even more rebellious, even pulling pranks, as well as talking back to his teachers.

Finally, at sixteen years of age, Zin was allowed to return to his father's palace, though Lod Enra had nearly given up, usually ignoring his son's presence altogether, which suited Zin more than being constantly scolded.

A year later, the king discovered that his own health was in jeopardy due to plasma poisoning; he was not able to breathe regularly and was easily winded. He could feel his kingdom slipping away, forcing him to train Zin as the next leader of Ohr. Because of this new burden, Zin understood how Ayn may have felt - like a caged animal in a zoo.

However, the prince was older than Ayn by roughly three years, and he had not been raised by loving priests, but by cold and scientific teachers. This factor had nearly turned Zin cold himself, though he swore he would never lose his heart, the way his father had. He vowed to be the absolute opposite, and so the cunning prince concocted a plan of escape while staying on Deius; it was only a matter of how.

Unbeknownst to Zin, Lod Enra had discovered his son's absence and sent his guards to find his ever-disobedient heir. They found Zin walking carefree in the hallway, then seized him by the arms, leading him back to his father. Zin knew he would receive a swift beating from his father, but the thought only made him smile in twisted satisfaction. He knew he'd be leaving soon anyway; it was fate.

Chapter 8: The End of Their Days

*I*n the Holy Chamber of Adin, the priests sat on their feet, meditating upon The Un. Pei briefly came into the room to inform Amun-Lan about Ayn's emotional state. He then swiftly exited, informing the guests who were lined up at the door that the ceremony would be starting soon. Amun-Lan got up and began chanting. He lit the candles surrounding the statue of Adin and meditated on The Bodanya, praying for his inner strength.

As Ayn awakened from his own meditation, he heard the sound of Meddhi-Lan's calming words: "You will be alright, my beloved boy. I will protect you."

Ayn believed him. As he often did throughout his childhood, Ayn chose to believe the words of his beloved Lan, and he hung onto the idea that all would be fine. He then opened his eyes and saw Meddhi-Lan hovering over him like an angel from ancient scrolls. Ayn smiled at Meddhi-Lan and lovingly touched his face.

"I am your beloved boy, yes?" Ayn quietly asked.

"Yes," said Meddhi-Lan with a gentle smile, holding back

his tears.

Ayn looked around him and saw that they were in Meddhi-Lan's room. He felt somewhat relieved, yet a bit ashamed for prolonging the ceremony.

"I am sorry," he said as he rubbed his eyes. "I passed out, didn't I? I do that too often when I go deep into meditation. I will learn to be better, my Lan, I promise."

Meddhi-Lan hushed him and said, "Today is possibly the biggest moment of your life, Ayn, and so it is understandable, but you must try to listen to the calmness of the ona flowers brushing against the wind. There, you will find peace... and answers."

Ayn listened and held Meddhi-Lan's hand for comfort.

"Will I be a good king?" asked Ayn.

"You will be the greatest leader our world has ever known," replied his teacher without hesitation.

Ayn felt a great sense of honor come over him. He got up and looked in the mirror. "I am ready," he said as he pulled his robe into place. Meddhi-Lan got up and nodded, beaming with pride for his beloved boy. He extended his arm to Ayn, and together, they slowly walked toward the Holy Chamber.

--

The priests heard the doors open and sighed in relief, knowing Meddhi-Lan had succeeded in reviving the spirit of their new Bodanya. Moments after, Ayn walked in with his head held high, tightly holding a holy object: the sacred symbol of three turning circles. It was a luminescent sphere, powered by plasma and rotating in place, as if by magic. Meddhi-Lan followed right behind Ayn while singing an old Dei holy song in his low, majestic voice. He sang the story of The Great Adin, about his death and rebirth, and the coming Age of Light. When they reached the altar, Meddhi-Lan bowed to Ayn, then bowed to the priests who did the same in return.

Ayn looked across the large, gold-adorned room and saw many faces. He saw Pei looking at him with pride, he saw Amun-Lan with his stern, yet wise face, and toward the back of the room, he saw Zin looking at him with a defeated, sad expression. He also saw a dozen or more people he did not know, many of whom were royals, sitting on the plush benches of the room with wonder and hope reflected in their eyes.

Meddhi-Lan crossed the room, and while singing, took the cup of holy oils from the altar. He dipped his forefinger into the cup and loudly proclaimed, "The anointing of the Adin." He then bent down to Ayn's bare feet and slowly poured the warm oil, making Ayn slightly squint in discomfort. The priests then sang in unison a song depicting how Adin survived the pain of the hanging tree. Pei stood up in the middle of the song and sang solo:

"He reached The Un and found the light,

Within the dark of a star-filled night,

Into the hidden layer of death and pain,

The Great Adin found life again!"

The priests sang and chanted, and Ayn closed his eyes. He did not feel or think - he merely stood still.

Meddhi-Lan closed the song with a single clap of his hand. He then helped Ayn to sit in a large, golden chair which was draped with purple silks and white ona flowers. Ayn was feeling as if he had drunk a thousand cups of wine and dared not open his eyes, for fear of becoming too conscious of what was being said and done.

Meddhi-Lan went to the altar and lifted a golden chest that was carved with the ancient symbols of The Holy Order. Also carved on the chest was a likeness of Ayn's mother, Amya, the late Queen of Deius. She held her child aloft to the heavens while a crown of the sun hovered above his head. Meddhi-Lan brought the chest to Ayn's feet, then turned to speak to the chamber of quietly awed spectators.

"This is the day of rebirth for our people and for all The Un's children," he said with a clear, proud voice. "Today," he continued, "we will bear witness to the fulfillment of the promise given to us by The Great Adin as we also honor the rites of the royal line of our planet." He then opened the chest and loudly said, "Let all who are present on this glorious day bear witness to the crowning of The Neya Bodanya, Shiva the Fourteenth!"

The priests chanted "Un" as the guests, filled with awe, caught sight of the beautifully crafted, golden crown. Accented with sapphire and amaranth, it shone like a star in the temple. Meddhi-Lan lifted the jeweled treasure and turned to face Ayn. He then raised the crown high in the air and proudly spoke the ancient Deiusian words, written years ago in their holy scroll's prophecy. "Bodanya, dri Un, lin Ara sine Jah!" said Meddhi-Lan. After those ancient words, the priests all quietly repeated their high priest, confirming the words as sacred truth.

Meddhi-Lan slowly circled behind the throne and lifted the sparkling crown above Ayn's head. The priests continued to chant as the guests listened to their voices mingling with the sound of drums pounding and crashing, which was the traditional music played by The Holy Dei in ceremonies of great importance.

The resonating sound of deep drums and crashing metal

objects continued to grow louder and louder until all who were present became enchanted and somewhat intoxicated by the sound of existence itself. Such primal, yet spiritually inspired music was the closest The Dei could come to the true sound of The Un.

Suddenly, there was a sound unlike any other in the room. It penetrated unexpectedly into the ears and hearts of everyone in the chamber. Even Ayn, who was deep under a meditative state, heard the explosive crashes and felt as if lightning had struck right beside him. It was a sound he'd never heard before, and never wanted to hear again.

Despite already being in shock, Ayn was even more surprised by the following sound of a woman's scream. Ayn opened his eyes and saw that the princess of Kri was shrieking, high pitched and filled with terror. He then turned to see what she was looking at, and the horror before him instantly broke his focus, as well as his heart.

Ayn saw his beloved teacher prostrate on the floor, his chest completely drenched in red liquid. Barely able to process the horror before him, Ayn heard more screaming, which brought him fully back into consciousness.

"No... please, Gods," Ayn whispered rigidly, as if frozen in time. The Gods did not reply, however, and all Ayn could do was accept what had happened, though it was almost too much for him to take. It was like his dream, but even worse!

In a matter of seconds, Amun-Lan flew to Meddhi-Lan's side, then ripped a piece from his own holy robes, wrapping it tightly around Meddhi-Lan's bleeding chest. He looked up and saw a dark-hooded man standing in the aisle while holding a plasma-gun. The man was about to re-load when Amun-Lan yelled, "Guards! Arrest him!" This was yet another sound Ayn had never heard.

Before the hooded man could reload his gun, The Royal Guard came bursting through the main doors to the chamber. They were too slow, however, and the hooded man ran toward the giant doors, knocking them down with the blunt end of his imposing plasma-gun. He had been stopped by the auto-locking doors, however, and he whirled around, aiming his gun at Ayn.

Pei was torn with emotion, but he acted on impulse, quickly seizing Ayn by the waist. He thought, *I would rather die than allow Ayn, my beloved brother, to be harmed in any way!* Protectively, he stood in front of Ayn, acting as a living shield.

By this point, everyone had scrambled or ducked under the benches. Only the guards remained standing, along with Ayn, and Pei in front of him. The hooded man stood by the door with his gun re-loaded, now aiming it at the guards who were running toward him.

"Drop your weapon!" shouted Amun-Lan, who was now holding Meddhi-Lan in his lap.

The hooded man maniacally laughed, which confused the priests greatly. "It is too late!" he shouted with a wild grin. "We will ALL be dead soon, and I will go to The Un, rewarded for my sacrifice!"

"Put down your weapon!" Amun-Lan repeated, unflinching. The hooded man, realizing he was out-manned, slowly lowered his weapon, but again started laughing.

Amun-Lan nodded his head, giving the guards the approval to move forward. As they rushed to arrest the hooded man, he surprised them by swiftly reaching into his pocket. He then quickly pulled out a small, blue vial, which he brought to his lips and drank down. In a matter of seconds, he fell to the floor.

The guards immediately inspected his body and found him dead. They also found a small, circular object in his hand, and brought it to Amun-Lan.

Pei felt utter panic and could no longer hold back. "What has happened?!" he sharply cried to Amun-Lan.

At that point, Ayn could not speak. All he could do was stare helplessly at his beloved Lan's blood-stained body on the floor. He was not moving, and Ayn could only assume that he was dangerously close to passing into The Un.

"I do not know," the elder Lan replied while looking at the strange, circular object in his hand. "All that I can say for certain is that we have been attacked - by whom, however, I am unaware. Clearly, this man did not work alone, which causes me great concern."

Amun-Lan then nodded to his fellow priests, ordering them to bring both Meddhi-Lan's body and Ayn into the secret chamber of Adin. He told the guards to follow Ayn and to protect him at all costs.

Pei tried to hold Ayn's hand as they walked, but Ayn refused it. Ayn was too hurt to be comforted; all he knew was that he would follow wherever the priests were taking his beloved Lan. Even if he had passed to the other realm, Ayn wanted to stay with him in any way possible for as long as he could.

Atlar helped his still shocked daughter to rise to her feet. "Are you alright, Ona?!" he asked, worried. "Yes, I think so," she replied, shaken, yet recovering. He then went to the body of the hooded man so that he could get a closer look. "This man is Ohrian," he said angrily as he removed the hood of the dead assassin. With this announcement, all eyes were suddenly on the king and queen of Ohr.

Feeling the heat of the room, Lod Enra felt compelled to react. "I do not appreciate your accusation, king of Kri!"

"Who else would have so much to gain?" snapped Atlar

with a suspicious glare toward Lod Enra.

"Enough!" Amun-Lan interrupted while still wiping Meddhi-Lan's blood from his hands. "We will soon see who is really to blame in the coming days. As of right now, we must all act as allies who shall unite in protecting Deius, and our new king."

King Atlar and Lod Enra stared at each other, distrustful and defensive.

The elder priest continued, ignoring their anger, "Your children must be kept safe, so I suggest you send them to their rooms. However, I would appreciate both of your counsel... if you will please follow me." The two kings nodded as they followed Amun-Lan out of the chamber and into the Holy Order's meeting room.

--

Ayn felt entirely lost. He thought for a moment that he had simply been dreaming, for it could not seem real to his mind. He sat on a chair in Adin's "Planning Room" – the same room he had secretly entered before the doom of the coronation. *Why did this happen? Why did this have to happen to MY Lan?!* he cried to himself.

Pei wasn't doing much better with his emotions. He helplessly watched as the few priests who were trained in the nearly lost art of medicine feverishly attempted to seal Meddhi-Lan's wound. It was nearly impossible, however, and his blood seemed to pour from all directions. Pei began to break. "Please, please, PLEASE!" he begged The Un over and over again in his mind.

Ayn knew it was hopeless, for he could feel how close Meddhi-Lan was to passing over. He had tried to reach his beloved Lan's mind, to say a final farewell, but he could not contact his Lan's conscious thought. It seemed Meddhi-Lan had become one with his dreaming, and soon, he would fall into the deep sleep of death. In despair, Ayn looked at his own blue robes, now stained with the spattering of his beloved Lan's blood. It made him want to throw up his insides as he began uncontrollably weeping. He shivered and shook, then fell to his knees.

Pei, noticing Ayn's collapse, had no choice but to remain strong for his little brother-in-soul who seemed even more torn apart than he. Unfortunately, just as before, when Pei reached for Ayn, he was refused. Pei could do nothing but watch Ayn's pain from a distance, and it broke his already torn heart.

Just then, Meddhi-Lan gasped as his body gave final jerks of movement. After one final breath, he was no longer physically living. The priests then covered him in a long, white cloth, hanging their heads low while silently chanting in honor of their deceased holy leader.

Ayn wailed and Pei cried tears of shock. Desperate for warmth, Ayn finally allowed Pei to embrace him, and they held onto each other as if it were the end of their days.

Chapter 9: The Darkness of the Tomb

Amun-Lan closed the door as soon as King Atlar and Lod Enra entered The Holy Room. Most of the priests were present, except for Pei and those who were attending to Meddhi-Lan's wounds. The room was silent and still.

"We must manage to see past our sadness so that we may be able to determine the nature of what has just occurred," Amun-Lan sternly said, breaking the silence. He looked at the faces of his fellow priests who appeared as if all life had been drained from their bodies. "Our prayers are with the spirit of our high priest," he continued as he walked to the center of the room, near the altar, "but at this very moment, we must evaluate what has just happened and discover who is behind this attack, for I am sure it was not that suicidal gunman alone who is to blame."

Atlar shook his head, then rubbed his eyes, as if he suddenly broke from a trance. "All I know is Meddhi just saved the Shiva's life!" Atlar nearly shouted. "He saw that assassin quicker than lightning and flew in front of the boy without a thought for himself! It was remarkable! He was as fit and fast as he was when he and I were young. He is a great, great man, and if he leaves this world having saved The Bodanya's life, then we must protect your new king as steadfast as he did! If we are to honor your noblest high priest, and my greatest friend, we owe him no less." Atlar tried to keep composure, but was unable to hold back the tears escaping from his eyes.

"Yes," said Amun-Lan, "Meddhi-Lan was my greatest student, and he would want us to protect The Bodanya Shiva at all cost, which we will." Amun-Lan reached into his robe and pulled out the object that the guards had retrieved from the gunman's body. "But this," said Amun-Lan holding up the object, "is what I am most concerned with at the moment. We do not know what sort of device this is, for it is a kind of technology foreign to us. We fear it may be a weapon, but we do not know."

"I have seen those before," said Lod Enra. "It is used for communicating and other forms of data transfer."

Atlar looked at the Ohrian king as if he had committed a crime by merely speaking. Amun-Lan, however, was curious and took a closer look at the object, noticing how smooth it was with its blue and silvery shine. "You have used one of these?" Amun-Lan asked Lod Enra.

"No, I have not," Lod Enra sharply replied, "but I know that many of my top scientists use them frequently to communicate."

"Interesting..." Amun-Lan responded as he further examined the object. It was a complete mystery to him and to the rest of the priests. Their lack of knowledge in science and technology had never quite bothered the priests before, but now, they were baffled and completely entranced, as if caught in the spell of the device in Amun-Lan's hands.

--

Ayn felt cold and numb as he sat in the corner of the Tomb. His heavy, tear-stained eyes were transfixed on Meddhi-Lan's motionless body as it lay on a stone slab, ready for the priests to perform their embalming ritual. Despite it being their tradition to do so, Ayn did not want his Lan to be embalmed as the other high priests had been in the past. He especially did not want it to be done so quickly after Meddhi-Lan had gone from this world. Unfortunately, there was nothing he could do – his Lan's spirit had passed, and Ayn could not remember what the feeling of happiness felt like; he only recalled the emptiness of despair.

Pei, still gathering himself, had not realized Ayn had followed the priests into the ancient burial chamber, even against Pei's wishes.

"Ayn?" he called. "Ayn?!"

There was no answer.

Pei finally grew the courage to enter the tomb and saw Ayn sitting on a stone bench, watching the priests anoint Meddhi-Lan's naked and pale corpse. Pei could not look at the sight and pulled at Ayn's shoulder. "You should not bear witness to this, Ayn. Let's go."

"No," Ayn calmly spoke, as if hypnotized.

"Stop being impossible!" Pei nearly shouted.

Ayn did not flinch.

Pei gathered himself and tried again. "I am sorry, my Shiva," he gently apologized, "but we must not watch while they perform the sacred rite of preservation."

"I am going to watch, Pei," said Ayn, transfixed on Meddhi-Lan, "but you may go if you wish."

Pei could not bear seeing his beloved teacher lying dead in

front of him, yet he did not want Ayn torturing himself with the sight either. "Ayn... you must know, they will remove his-"

"Yes, I know, Pei," Ayn replied, steadfast, "and I will be here to make sure that it is done correctly." Ayn seemed to Pei impenetrable, and it made Pei's anguish feel all the more heavy. "Fine!" Pei sputtered. "Then I will go, even if you do not. I'm sorry, Ayn, but I must. I cannot watch this, and I wish you would not either." With a twinge of guilt, Pei left the room.

How can he watch them dissect our Lan's body? Pei asked himself as he walked through the halls. He did not understand Ayn's behavior at all. It seemed as if the boy who was wailing in pain just a few minutes ago had somehow disappeared and a new, mysterious being had taken his place. He wondered if Ayn truly understood what he was about to witness, and for a moment, Pei thought of turning back around to forcibly retrieve him.

Remembering the feeling of the cold tomb, he couldn't force his feet to travel in that direction. Instead, Pei told himself that Ayn was now The Bodanya and that he must know his path well enough to make his own decisions. Even though Pei still thought of Ayn as a boy, he also realized Ayn had been forced to grow up immensely, especially in the last hour. Pei nodded his head, telling himself that the guards were standing at the doors, just in case something happened. Ayn was as safe as he could be, at least that is what he told himself as he left the catacombs.

Ayn, however, was not safe, most of all in his mind. He was viewing death as an end, an absolute, and he could no longer remember Meddhi-Lan's teachings. He could not believe that death was merely the beginning of a new life yet to come. No longer could he see the spiritual nature of the world. All he could remember was blood, pain, and darkness.

The priests did not want to extract Meddhi-Lan's vital organs in front of Ayn and refused to do so, even when he commanded them to do so with the voice of an angry young king.

"I said do it!"

"I am sorry, my Bodanya, but you will have to leave or we will not continue," said the eldest priest in a firm, yet sympathetic manner. Despite his politeness, Ayn became angered and stormed out of the tomb.

His anger was fleeting, however, and soon transformed to tears once again. This time, though, there was no Pei to hold him, no one to comfort Ayn in the darkness, and it jolted his heart into a place that goes beyond feeling numb. He now felt a shiver of insanity slip across his spine, and without knowing he was doing so, Ayn headed down winding stairs, toward a deeper, darker part of the tomb.

He walked until he found himself at the bottom of a spiral staircase. No light penetrated the room, so Ayn lit a torch, which he instinctively knew hung upon the left side of the wall. It was an old kind of torch that required oil, and Ayn had somehow known where to find it, as if guided by a secret memory or by the spirit of a long, forgotten past.

Slowly, the fire grew from the torch and poured its light onto the walls of the room. Ayn then saw that there were other torches he could set aflame. He lit them with the torch from the wall, then set it back into its holder.

When Ayn turned around, he saw something that made him want to fall to his knees: a large golden coffin, flickering in the haze of the room. It was extremely smooth and carved in the shape of a man, and on the surface, there was a life-sized painting of a young, fair haired king. He held a scepter and wore a blue and gold crown, and Ayn knew without a doubt whom it was depicting. He was absolutely certain that what he was looking at was the death coffin of The Great Adin.

--

Pei could hear loud voices coming from The Holy Room, which caused him to quicken his pace. As he approached the door, he nodded to the guard, who recognized him, and immediately let him through.

"No, that is NOT what I said!" Atlar shouted.

"You are obviously implying that I am responsible for this crime," Lod Enra contested, "and I do not appreciate such false accusations, especially when you have no proof!"

"Please, both of you," said Amun-Lan, doing is best to calm their tempers, "your argument is completely unnecessary."

Pei almost wished he had not entered the room, yet he felt more needed by Amun-Lan than by Ayn at the moment. Pei desperately needed to feel helpful so that his mind could be taken away from the loss of his Lan.

"The assassin was clearly from Ohr," Atlar insisted, "and for the last few years, you, Lod Enra, have done nothing but speak against Deius and their religious beliefs! Do you dare deny your previous actions?"

"I deny nothing," said Lod Enra in a stoic reply.

"Then I believe that is enough to at least put you under arrest until a trial may be set in motion!" Atlar said as he quickly turned to face Amun-Lan. "Please, my Lan, I implore you to arrest this man immediately."

Lod Enra scoffed and folded his arms, enraged by Atlar's request.

"I will do no such thing," Amun-Lan calmly answered. The king of Kri was completely thrown by his statement, and for the moment, seemed speechless.

"Please, if I may," said Pei, careful not to offend, "I suggest we do not arrest anyone as of right now, though I firmly believe an investigation is necessary. There is going to be a service for our fallen high priest within a few days, and I think it best if no one is allowed to leave the kingdom for at least a few weeks more - not until the investigation is over."

Everyone looked at Pei with sad eyes. "He is dead?" Atlar asked with his brow knotted in pain.

"Yes," Pei somberly replied. The king of Kri shook his head in disbelief, then threw himself in a chair, covering his face with his hands. Pei walked closer to Amun-Lan, then nodded to him, confirming his statement. "The healer-priests tried to seal his wounds, but he had lost too much blood," Pei further explained in a soft, sympathetic voice.

There was a moment of silence as the priests bowed their heads, quietly chanting their prayer for Meddhi-Lan's safe return to The Un. The two kings did the same in a show of respect, but soon after, they looked again at each other scornfully.

"Amun-Lan, I will stay for a little while longer," said Lod Enra, "for the service only, out of respect for your loss. As for an investigation, I will not stand for such a thing when my family and I are guests of your planet. We have done nothing wrong, and being that all three of us were present during the attack, I would consider it a breach of trust if you were to hold us any longer for an investigation. If you attempt such a thing, I shall promptly leave and tell my Minister of Foreign Affairs, as well as his constituents, that The Dei are indeed the nonsensical, backward thinking fools our planet has always believed them to be." He then swiftly exited the room.

"Coward!" shouted Atlar, pointing toward the door. Turning to Amun-Lan, he added, "Such rudeness is obviously a weak defense for his guilt!"

Almost relieved by the Ohrian king's departure, Amun-Lan shook his head, then gathered his wits. "King Atlar," said Amun-Lan, "forget Lod Enra for now. I have more important things to discuss with you. I want to speak with you as well, Pei" he added while directing their attentions toward the small, silver-blue object in his hand. "I want you both to take a look at this."

"What is it?" asked Pei.

"I do not know," replied Amun-Lan, "but I want you to keep an eye on it, and then find a way to understand how this strange device works."

"That self-righteous Ohrian wouldn't tell us how to open it," said Atlar as he walked closer to Amun-Lan, "but I will do my best to find out its secrets. You have my word."

Pei nodded and said, "I too will do my best." Pei didn't know what he could do to help the Krian king in unraveling such a mystery, but he was dedicated in doing whatever it took to honor his beloved, fallen teacher.

--

Lod Enra marched through the halls of the palace, repressing his anger. He could not believe that all the work he had done to make peace between the three planets was now being so quickly dismantled.

Kurin Vax, his prime minister and closest friend, had assured him before they had left Ohr that everyone on their planet was behind the new alliance with Deius. If that was indeed the case, then Lod Enra was sure Ohr was being framed by an unknown enemy who desired revenge against The Dei. He didn't know who that might be, but he almost didn't care. It was all too confusing and dangerous for his liking!

"Get your things packed, my wife!" he said as he pushed the door to his room wide open.

"Why? Are they sending us away?" Loda La calmly questioned.

"No, it is quite the opposite," he replied. "They are demanding that I stay and perhaps be brought to trial, which I will not allow to happen. I will stay for a few days, out of respect, but something feels wrong about it all, Loda. I promise, I will leave as soon as I am able." His wife looked at him blankly, unable to think of what to say. "Now, I may have to stay," he continued, "but they did not demand you must remain with me. Therefore, I wish for you to go with Zin back to our home and wait for me there until all this is finished."

Loda La stared at Lod Enra in disbelief as her rather stressed husband sat on an ona-patterned chair located near two large windows, which overlooked the gardens. Trying his best to release his anxiety, Lod Enra shook his head and sighed.

Loda La called to her servants and began packing for the trip home. She hesitated for a moment, then slowly approached her husband, resting her hand on his shoulder. "This is not your fault, my king," she whispered, "and they will come to see the truth soon."

Lod Enra looked at his wife with saddened eyes, and for a moment, was calmed by her warmth. His rest was brief, however, as he suddenly realized something wasn't quite right. He stood up, erect and rigid, as though his body had been transformed into wood.

"Where is Zin?" he asked.

His wife stood up and sighed. "I do not know," she replied, "but I have already sent a guard to find him." Lod Enra's brow turned downward. "Why did you let him leave the room in the first place?" he nearly shouted.

His wife looked at him with disdain. "Perhaps I did not have any choice!" she defensively snapped. "You know very well that he is a willful child and barely controllable these days!" she added with a sneer.

She turned away as Lod Enra threw his hands in the air, heading toward the front door of the room. "Keep packing, and I will see you off at the loading area," he commanded as he opened the door, "and do not worry, Loda," he added before exiting the room, "I will find our son!"

--

Ayn nervously licked his bottom lip, then slowly approached the ornately crafted, yet somewhat faded, gold and blue coffin. He had an unrelenting urge to unhinge the sides, pull the lid, and take a good look at the decayed flesh that once was The Great Adin. Instead, out of fear, he stared at the coffin with wide eyes and breathed at a quickening pace.

The painting on the top of the sarcophagus was painted in fine detail, and Ayn was astonished at how much it resembled Adin's likeness, described in books and paintings throughout the kingdom. Specifically, Adin's eyes were painted deep blue, and his mouth was depicted as full, yet masculine. As Ayn focused on the image, he felt that Adin had the look of a young king who died before his time.

Could this man who lay inside really have been me in a previous life? Ayn asked himself. He felt his heart beat faster as his lips became dry and chapped. Curiosity overpowered his mind while his hand slowly reached toward the lid of the coffin.

"What do you think you'll find in there?" came an unexpected voice behind him. Ayn whirled around and saw a figure in the dim light holding a small plasma-light in his hand.

"Zin?!" shouted Ayn, surprised, yet somewhat relieved. "What are you doing here?"

"I am here because you are here," the Ohrian prince replied. He then walked over and stood next to Ayn while raising a brow.

"So... this was The Great Adin?"

"Yes, I... suppose," said Ayn, unsure.

Zin nodded, then shrugged. "Do you want to know what I think?" he asked.

"Not really..." Ayn sarcastically replied, distrustful and wary.

Smiling and unfazed, the Ohrian prince put his arm around Ayn's shoulder, leading him toward the stairs. "I think, my friend," said Zin, "that you spend too much of your time dwelling in the realm of death. Instead, you need to walk in the land of the living."

Ayn was annoyed, yet slightly grateful that he was being taken away from the coffin of Adin. Because of his conflicted feelings, he allowed the prince to lead him by the hand as they head up the winding stairs and away from the hidden tomb.

"Yes, perhaps you are right," Ayn said as he took one last look at the beautifully painted blue eyes on the coffin.

"Of course I am," said Zin as he led him back to the upper levels of the tomb, "and now, I want you to leave all of it behind."

Ayn stopped in his tracks and said, "What?"

"You heard me well enough, Great Bodanya," said Zin with a hint of mockery.

"What do you mean by leave all of it behind?"

"Exactly as I said. Leave this rotting palace, this overbearing prophecy! Get out now, my friend, and come with me - to freedom!"

"Come with you... where?" asked Ayn, backing away from the Ohrian prince. Zin shook his head and looked at Ayn with sympathetic eyes.

"Don't distrust me," he said as he gently reached again for Ayn's hand. "I know you are scared and hurting, but I am the one person in this world who truly cares for your soul. You know it to be true!"

Ayn was a little offended by the idea that this strange boy would dare assume to know who cared for his soul. After just losing Meddhi-Lan, Ayn was tempted to slap the Ohrian prince's pale face! However, as Ayn looked deeper into Zin's eyes, he felt the familiarity from their first encounter, and it forced him to listen to Zin's proposition.

Smiling, Zin put both of his hands on Ayn's shoulders. "Listen, my friend," he explained, "I have a ship that is ready to fly. It's one of my father's cargo ships. All we need to do is board it, and we will both be free! You, from this trap of prophecy and selflessness... and me, from the cage of my father's limited scope of reality." Zin released an emotional exhale, then looked at Ayn with pleading eyes. "So... what do you say?"

Ayn looked to the side where the walls of the catacombs

seemed almost prison-like, and he began thinking over the idea of running away. *What would happen if I left?* he asked himself. *Would Pei hate me? Would Amun-Lan and the rest of the priests be lost without their Bodanya?* Ayn rubbed his forehead, worried and confused, and unable to make a decision.

"No," said Ayn after a few moments. "I cannot leave."

"But!"

"No, Zin, I will not leave my kingdom."

"But it's not safe here, Ayn. I can't let you stay!"

"I will not go! They are my people! I am their Bodanya!"

"You are just a boy, Ayn! And someone is obviously out to kill you! That plasma-shot was meant for you, not your teacher! Don't you realize that?! I have only just found you, Ayn! No... I will not let anyone harm you, and that is final!"

Then, without warning, Zin swiftly grabbed Ayn, throwing his new friend over his left shoulder. He looked around to make sure that no one had seen them, then hastily made his way down the other side of the stairs to where it led back out to the loading docks of the palace. Ayn struggled, but not hard enough to stop Zin's determined mind.

Unbeknownst to Ayn, Zin had planned his escape for a long time, and with or without his new soul-friend, he was going to be free.

Chapter 10: The Coming of Yol Notama

*T*he healer-priests were extremely careful with the holy jars that held the vital organs of Meddhi-Lan. They slowly walked to The Holy Room with their heads held low and did not even acknowledge him when Atlar passed them by. Unaware of the objects they carried, he still sensed an ominous aura about them as they went by.

Atlar walked briskly through the halls until he found his daughter by the loading area near the outer gate of the palace. He greeted her with a short embrace.

"Now," he said to her, "you know what to do?"

"Yes, Father - I will go home to organize the army while you act as diplomat here on Deius."

"Yes, exactly," he said, nodding nervously. "Now, remember that you are my only heir, and when I am gone, the people will look to you for guidance and leadership."

"Yes, Father, I know," she replied with a hint of worry on her face. She was not worried for herself, but her father who seemed thoroughly shaken by his friend's sudden death.

"And right now," the Krian king added, "I need you to be firm with the men of The Council – don't let them bully you. Tell them your words are my direct orders and that we cannot wait while they have their endless conferences!"

"Yes, Father," she softly replied, "I'll try my best to convince them to take action." Ona then smiled at him and brushed back the stray lock of golden hair that fell over his brow. "Do not worry, I will be strong."

The king sighed and looked at his proud, loving daughter. "I am the one who isn't feeling very strong at the moment," he admitted. "To be honest, I am more upset than I am able to put into words."

"Oh, Father..." said Ona. She put her arms around Atlar and held him tight. "You and the high priest were close friends as young men, weren't you?"

Atlar silently nodded, holding back his tears. "We once were, yes," he replied, clearly affected. Breaking out of it, he wiped his tearful eyes, then pulled back from his daughter's arms. "But we will discuss that at a later time. Right now, I am going to make sure whoever did this is properly punished." Ona nodded in agreement.

"Now, wait a few moments before taking off. I will confirm that your departure is legally authorized by Amun-Lan, and I will contact you soon, my sweet, brave daughter." He kissed her cheek, then watched as his only child walked onto their large, envoy-class ship. He briefly closed his eyes and prayed to the Gods, hoping they would protect his only daughter.

--

Pei could not find the opening anywhere. No matter which side he viewed the blue sphere from, there didn't seem to be any creases or latches - nothing obviously visible that a person could pull or twist. "The object appears to be completely impenetrable, my Lan," said Pei with a perplexed frown.

Amun-Lan came closer and inspected the sphere that Pei held in his palm. After he looked at it for a moment, he stroked his chin and said, "Perhaps it is a new device that only an Ohrian scientist may operate correctly?"

Amun-Lan sighed and sat on a pillow on the floor of The Holy Room. With his head held low, he meditated and hummed in a deep drone. It seemed to Pei, for the first time since Meddhi-Lan had been struck down, Amun-Lan was finally displaying his grief. Pei was about to go to him and share in his pain when Atlar hastily entered the room.

"Amun-Lan!" the Krian king exclaimed, "I am sending my daughter back to Kri to gather military aid. We shall have justice!"

The old priest got up from the floor with Pei's help, then went over to Atlar, resting a hand on his shoulder. "My dear boy," he quietly replied, "you do not need to gather an army so soon. We have not even found who our enemy is, and yet you wish to attack someone?"

Atlar looked at Amun-Lan, confused and slightly angered. "But, my Lan," Atlar protested, "we must be prepared!"

The old priest and the Krian king looked at each other with their eyes locked in a mental game of will. After a few moments of gridlock, Atlar released a grunt and threw his hands upward. "Talk some sense into him!" he demanded as he looked at Pei and sat on a chair, folding his arms tightly.

Pei had never met Atlar previously and was a little taken

aback by his commanding, blunt style of speech. He looked at Amun-Lan, who was looking away, as if lost in a dream. Pei realized he was now on his own to communicate with the highly emotional Krian. "I believe Amun-Lan is right to say that it is perhaps too soon to think of war," said Pei, cautiously, "for the path of war is destructive, and it cannot be good for any of our planets."

A strange, grimacing smile crept across Atlar's face – it was an expression Pei had never seen before. The Krian king got up and laughed. "Oh, I see," he said as he approached Pei. "You are perfectly fine with what they did to Meddhi?" Pei felt his stomach turn as Atlar continued. "Wasn't he your Lan? Aren't you the slightest bit angry that he was shot down like a dog today, and all we have left to show for it is THIS GODSFORSAKEN... THING?!" Atlar then grabbed the sphere from Pei and threw it across the room.

Pei stood frozen as Atlar took a deep breath, holding himself back from yelling at Pei any further. "Fine," the king concluded, "ignore what has happened, if you wish, but don't expect me to sit idly by and-"

Atlar was suddenly interrupted by a bright blue light that had burst across the room. The light was coming from the center of the floor where the sphere had landed. It quickly caught the attention of all three men.

"What is that?" asked Pei.

Amun-Lan went over to the object and tried to touch the light. "It is not real. It is a holographic image," said Amun-Lan as he waved his hands through the light.

"What did I do?" Atlar asked, confused.

The old priest nodded his head while thinking. "I believe you must have somehow opened the device," Amun-Lan replied.

Once again, they were distracted by a new surprise: a loud clicking noise, followed by a muddled kind of interference. Then, just as they thought the disturbance had ended, a clear image began transmitting from the sphere on the floor.

To their shock, they saw the virtual image of a man with straight, white, shoulder-length hair standing in front of them. He was wearing a white and blue wreath of serpentine ornaments on his head while his face bore a scar that was shaped like a new moon on his right cheek. All who were present noticed his strange attire as well: a white tunic with a blue belt and a silver symbol on it, which looked like a snake, slithering around his waist. His outfit was neither particularly Deiusian in style, nor any other culture known to the men who were witnessing the image.

"Good afternoon, priests of Deius," the man said with his arms crossed in front of his chest. "I am Yol Notama, the leader of The Tah: a great army that you, in your ignorance, unknowingly created. Though you have chosen to ignore us through the years, we are here, and now, at your very doorstep. I am giving you this message to warn you that we will no longer stand for the tyranny of your prophetical rule and false superstition. Prepare yourself, you hypocrites of religion, for you will be held accountable for your crimes, and not by your supposed Gods, but by the people of Deius!"

Pei noticed how the man in the hologram did not blink, nor show signs of emotion, yet he was most definitely not of Ohrian decent. The man looked Deiusian with lightly tan skin and slightly slanted eyes. Pei's mind wondered of what origin this man's supposed army descended from and if they were all Deiusians. *Who are The Tah? Why do they hate us?* Pei silently questioned, slightly panicked.

"So take heed," the white-haired man continued, "for your high priest's death was only the beginning. I assume that he has died valiantly to save his prodigy, which I respect. At least he had some small amount of honor. However, all of you will be on trial soon enough. Consider his death a warning for what lies ahead of you. In approximately sixty seconds from the end of this message, your so-called Bodanya will be swiftly executed with a plasma-bomb, which has already been planted by one of my most courageous and cunning spies. After eliminating your supposed savior, you will all be next. You can expect a swift attack. Prepare yourselves and be ready for the beginning of your end. I sincerely hope your make-believe Gods hear your prayers."

As Notama's sinister grin faded with the end of the transmission, a shudder ran through Pei's spine while his mind tried to process the truth behind the man's threats, and if it was even possible. "There is no way!" shouted Pei. Just then, the strange sphere rose up into the air and spun with bizarre clicking noises. "I don't understand this!" Pei yelled to Amun-Lan, who seemed just as confused, if not mortified. "Amun-Lan! Did you hear me?!" Pei again shouted as he waved his hand in front of Amun-Lan's eyes.

"It is no use, Pei, he isn't listening," said Atlar. "Pei, listen to me. You need to go find The Bodanya, and quickly, and I'll meet you at my ship. Do you understand, Pei? We need to get your king out of here!"

Atlar shook Pei's shoulder, forcing him to forget about Amun-Lan's trance-like state. Pei nodded and darted for the door.

Then, out of nowhere, there was a loud, thunderous noise followed by an unbearable wave of intense heat that threw Pei backward. He fell to the ground and was unable to think. The room seemed to be shaking, but he couldn't quite tell.

Ayn! Pei cried in his mind. *Ayn, I am coming!*

Within seconds, however, his mind went dark, and he could no longer keep conscious.

Chapter 11: The Aftermath

*T*here was a distinct, vile smell in the air that violently woke the young priest up with a choking cough. Pei's throat was burning, and his eyes were as dry as the Deiusian desert to the East. Nonetheless, he forced himself to open them so he could take in his surroundings.

At first, he could only see smoke in a haze of scattered debris, but as his eyes focused, he realized the devastation at hand. The entire room seemed shaken to its core with large blocks of stone that had toppled over to form a thin layer of white ash, covering everything like snow.

Pei coughed and attempted to stand. He felt his right arm pinch with pain as he stood, and his face felt flush from light burns. Everything else seemed fine; he was more mentally hurt than physically. He then immediately searched to find Amun-Lan.

He saw the other priests lying on the floor, some in twisted positions and others seemingly unconscious, but alive. Looking around, he panicked when he couldn't easily find where Amun-Lan had fallen.

"Amun-Lan?" he called out with a voice that was rough and hoarse. Coughing, he repeated, "Amun-Lan?!"

Just then, he heard a man coughing. Pei followed the sound to find someone lying on the floor, half covered by ash and pieces of stone. Pei ran to him and immediately threw off the debris from his body. As he did so, Pei saw the familiar blond locks of the Krian king and worked faster to alleviate his body from the rubble.

Atlar coughed, then uncontrollably let out an angry cry. Pei looked and noticed that his leg was twisted in a strange manner.

"Can you move?" Pei asked him.

"Barely," replied the king, with a strained face, "but I've no choice. I'm not going to die here!"

Atlar reached for Pei's shoulder and slowly forced himself up, ignoring the shock waves of pain that were shooting through his body.

"We have to go find the boy... the Shiva," he said to Pei with a look of determined will.

"I know... but I can't find Amun-Lan," Pei replied in short breaths.

"It's more important to find your Shiva, is it not?" Atlar snapped. Pei nodded nervously. He was in a state of shock and had no idea how to think straight. He only knew to follow Atlar's commands.

"Now, help me walk," Atlar ordered as he leaned against Pei's arm. They slowly walked toward the door, carefully avoiding the bodies on the ash-covered floor.

Just as they were leaving, Pei noticed the white and blue robes of Amun-Lan camouflaged under the debris. He told Atlar to wait as he rushed to uncover the old man's body. It was too late; Amun-Lan laid motionless with dried blood on his lips, his eyes wide open. It was a sight Pei never before imagined, and it broke his spirit. He screamed in soul-agony, throwing random pieces of stone across the room.

Atlar, not willing to watch Pei lose his mind, grabbed the flailing young priest by the shoulders, forcing him to get up. "Stop this, Pei!" he shouted at him. "We have got to get out of here – NOW!" He grabbed Pei by the chin and looked directly into his eyes. "Do you understand me? We must find out if The Bodanya is alive, and then get the hell out of here!"

Pei released a few final tears, then nodded in agreement. The shock wore off quickly when he thought about Ayn as he hoped against hope that his brother-in-soul had survived the blast. "Yes," he said decisively, "Ayn is all that matters now."

Then, the two men pushed open the door with all their combined strength and saw the same type of view as inside The Holy Room: guards and servants strewn about on the floor indiscriminately, some with broken limbs, others moaning in helpless lament.

Steadily, they made their way through the halls as Pei tried to locate the secret passages to the rooms of Adin. It was all in shambles.

When they approached near to the door of the once great library, they felt a strong heat coming from inside the room.

"It's a plasma build up in there," Atlar said as he put his hand up to the door. "We'll get a face full of poisonous flames if we open it."

"But Ayn was in there!" Pei yelled. "I left him in the tombs below!"

Atlar looked down, and it seemed to Pei as if he were

saying a silent farewell.

"NO!" shouted Pei with more emotion than he had ever displayed in his entire life. "He CANNOT be dead! I refuse to believe it!"

It was too much for the young Lan to process, and he began violently screaming, his hands clenched in tight fists.

"It's too late," said Atlar, sympathetic, yet stoic. "We must get out of here, and fast! Do you hear me, Pei? We've got to make it to my ship!"

Atlar reached into his pocket and pulled out a black, oval-shaped transmitter. "Ona?!" he loudly spoke into the device. "Ona, can you hear me?"

After a few seconds of silence, there was a small amount of feedback, followed by his daughter's voice. "Father? Father, what has happened?"

"No time to explain. You've got to fly the ship around to the rear of the palace and wait for me there. We have been attacked. The entire temple is in ruins! Do you understand? Fly the ship to the back area of the palace!"

"Yes, Father, I understand," his daughter replied.

"Thank the Gods she's alive," Atlar said as he put the transmitter back into his pocket. "We have to go, Pei. We have to get out of here before-"

Just then, there was a crash followed by the sound of men shouting. Atlar and Pei heard screaming, followed by the sound of plasma-guns being fired rapidly.

"Come on!" commanded Atlar as he grabbed Pei by the collar of his torn, ash-covered robes.

Hurriedly, they ran through the halls, passing the survivors of the temple and nearby palace. The noises of gunfire and screaming made Pei want to be sick, but he knew he had to keep moving. He had to reach Atlar's ship no matter what!

When they came to the doors of the back exit of the palace, the sun seemed to vanish, and dark, gray clouds covered the sky. To Pei, it seemed an omen of great doom, and he felt his soul twist in grief.

"There she is!" said Atlar as he pointed toward the giant, gold-trimmed, Krian ship. He then pulled Pei's arm and ran with him toward the opening.

Ona greeted her father with a slightly frightened embrace. Seeing Pei was also present, she bowed to him, then hurried them both inside the ship's huge hatchway.

"We must leave quickly," Atlar said as he took his seat, pulling down the safety buckle. "Pei, you've never traveled into space before, have you?" In reply, Pei anxiously shook his head. "Well," Atlar added, "then I suggest you buckle up, and hold on to your stomach!"

Ona showed Pei to his seat, then placed the buckle over him. She gave him a reassuring smile, and for a moment, the darkness in his heart lifted ever so slightly.

The sleek, gold-colored ship lifted from the dock, making its way over the landing, then into the air. In the span of a few moments, they were thrust into the hovering atmosphere of Deius. Pei felt as though he had been caught inside of a dream. He looked out through the window near him and saw Deius becoming smaller and smaller. He then fell into a deep, desperate sleep.

Chapter 12: A New Destination

*A*yn could see his home planet from the oval window he was staring through. The sight of it made him feel cold and empty, as if he'd never see Deius or anyone he knew ever again.

Ayn turned to the young, Ohrian prince who was sitting next to him, hoping to find answers in his eyes. No answers came, however, as Zin gave Ayn a mere hint of a reassuring smile, which seemed to fade quickly.

"Where are we going?" asked Ayn.

"We're headed for the planet X-314," Zin responded with a far off gaze in his eyes.

"I've never heard of that planet," said Ayn, his curiosity sparked. "Is it outside of our galaxy?"

"No," Zin replied, awakened from his far-off thoughts, "it's a small planet, just outside my planet's borders. Maybe you would recognize it by the name of Xen?"

"Oh yes!" Ayn said with a glimmer of his former self. "I remember Meddhi-Lan once told me that-" Ayn suddenly stopped, overwhelmed by the painful loss of his Lan. All at once, he was filled with memories: his beloved Lan smiling, teaching, scolding, dying...

Zin noticed the tears forming at the corners of Ayn's eyes. He took Ayn's hand and held it.

Ayn was holding back everything – fighting his own soul's sweet and loving nature. *No more tears,* he thought. *It is over and gone. My home is no more.*

"Do not worry, my friend," said Zin as he held Ayn's hand, "we'll be safe where we're going. No one will even know who we are."

"How is that possible?" asked Ayn as he swallowed his tears.

"Well, Xen is mostly barren with only modern style cities, except a few, newly restored country-side areas here and there. I've heard that the only people left are the exiles."

"The what?" Ayn asked.

"The exiles," Zin repeated, "the ones who were either banished from Deius as traitors or the people from my own planet who were considered rebels or criminals. Of course, the Ohrian mafia rules the government, but I hear they usually turn a blind eye to most who exist there. I don't think they'll care about us. We should go unnoticed."

Ayn had absolutely no idea what Zin was talking about. He hadn't ever heard of Deius sending traitors to a barren planet. In fact, he could barely even process the notion of an exile or someone who was banished from their own planet.

Zin saw the lost look in Ayn's face and tried to explain it further. "When X-314, or Xen, was less inhabited - before the Plasma Sickness - it was a beautiful planet full of lush trees and ocean. After the natives left, most of them relocating to Deius, all that was left was an outpost called X-314. It was a city that our leaders could control without anyone suspecting their actions. After the civil war on Deius a few hundred years ago, your kingdom's leaders sent many of their unwanted people to the now relatively desolate planet."

Unwanted people? thought Ayn. *And when was this supposed civil war? Why didn't my Lans teach me about any of this?!*

"Basically," Zin added, "my planet's leaders have long been using Xen as a place to send their rebels or discontents, which is funny considering how much criminal activity goes on behind closed doors - on both Ohr and Xen. My father doesn't even seem to care. It's ridiculous."

"Zin! Why would we go to a planet full of rebels and criminals?" Ayn fearfully asked.

"Calm down, Ayn. It isn't as bad as you may think."

Ayn looked at him blankly.

Zin continued to explain as he got up to check on the ship's coordinates. "Xen may be home to criminals and such, but it also has a great reputation for being the best place to go if you're an artist." Zin stopped as he touched oval shaped buttons on a screen. Ayn wondered what it was that he was doing. He knew it had something to do with the mechanics of the ship, but had no idea how Zin was able to understand it. "In fact," Zin continued, "despite the mafia practically running the place, I'd say this is the ideal planet for the likes of us." Seemingly content, Zin smiled as he sat back down with Ayn, crossing his legs.

Ayn could not understand the Ohrian prince sitting with him. For all the immediate closeness they shared between their souls, they seemed completely opposite of each other in every way.

"Don't worry, Ayn. It will be alright."

"How can you say that?" Ayn asked with a piercing look.

"I just know it. How much worse could it be than where we've come from? You with those so-called holy men who want you to be their God figure – their puppet idol! And me with my father's denial of my true soul. I think we're far better off on a planet where only artists and rebels are to be found."

"You may have been unhappy, Zin, but I was not," Ayn said as he looked away, folding his arms tight.

"Yes you were, Ayn. You just haven't admitted it to yourself yet."

Ayn became angry, but kept it inside. Who was this Ohrian prince? Who did he think he was to tell Ayn what he felt? Holding back his rage, Ayn stared out the window.

"You should eat something," said Zin as he got up. "There are dried foods and drinks in the cold bin over there - to your left."

Ayn nodded, but didn't get up. He didn't feel hungry, just tired and emotionally drained. All he wanted to do was find a way to become numb. He closed his eyes and tried his best to meditate, the way Meddhi-Lan would have told him to do.

"Are you alright? What are you doing?" asked Zin, puzzled at Ayn's behavior.

"I'm listening," Ayn said with eyes closed.

"Listening to what?"

"To the hum of the ship."

Zin sighed, unable to comprehend his new friend. He then walked over to the control panel of the ship and sat down in the pilot's chair. He had set the coordinates for Xen, but was beginning to wonder if it had been the right decision. He'd wanted to see the infamous outpost planet his entire life, especially after reading about the many wild musicians and artists that lived there, but was it safe? Then again, he no longer believed any place was truly safe.

It didn't take long before both young men began to drift in their minds. After a few minutes, they soon fell fast asleep.

--

Pei awoke to her beautiful, loving face in the twilight of a new day. She smelled like flowers and scented oils. *Is this a dream?* he wondered, still half asleep.

"Good morning," Ona spoke softly near Pei's ear, her sympathetic voice coaxing him awake. "We have arrived at my home planet, and I am to take you to the palace."

Pei sat up and wiped his eyes. He immediately noticed the change in the air, which was somehow cleaner and crisper, and it made it easier for him to breathe. He wondered if the mountains of Kri were located near the palace and if he would be able to see them from where they were.

"Where is your father?" he asked the princess with a calm, yet concerned face.

"He is already preparing to speak to our kingdom's council... about everything that has happened."

"Will he ask them to help us?" Pei questioned as he stood

up.

"I am sure that he will, Pei-Lan."

"I am honored that you remembered my name," he said as he followed her through the ship's enormous hatchway.

"Of course I remembered. You are a very brave priest, and I hope you will find rest and comfort in my home."

Pei felt a mixture of happy and sad, pain and pleasure. He was deeply wounded, and yet, he felt a sense of relief when he looked at the graceful beauty before him. Princess Ona seemed to Pei as if she moved like a veil in the wind, like a dancer in a religious concert from days of old. He could not keep his eyes off her as she led him through the sky-high, golden gates of the Krian palace.

Kri was extremely different from Pei's home planet; it was warm and pleasant with hardly any signs of plasma poisoning. Even on Deius, if one traveled to certain areas of various cities, there was a thickness in the air that made it hard to breathe. Kri, however, seemed even more beautiful to Pei than his own kingdom.

He followed Ona blindly through the halls, looking away from her momentarily to view the white marble statues and other forms of Krian art that decorated the palace. He saw a marble statue of a woman in a lavish robe holding an apple in her right hand as well as a statue of a nude man with his arm hanging over his head. Pei had never seen such impressive and seductive artwork before. He was astounded.

The most beautiful display of art, however, was the giant fresco of Krian Gods that covered the ceiling and walls of the main hall of the palace. There were colors of red, blue, and gold, all carefully painted on proud, noble faces. As they walked, Ona informed him that her great-grandfather, an artist and inventor, was responsible for the beauty that decorated the palace. "He was a genius," she told him as they passed through the halls. Pei felt as though he had stepped into another galaxy altogether.

"Come," Ona said as she motioned with her hand, "follow me, and I will take you to a room where you may rest." Pei nodded and walked with her to a large room. It had a classic, Krian air about it, complete with a curved lounging chair and a painting of two young lovers in an embrace.

"Will this do?" Ona asked.

"Yes, thank you," Pei shyly replied.

He was overwhelmed and in culture shock. He didn't know how to feel or what to do. He could only manage to feel a mix of emptiness and transparent despair.

Ona watched Pei sit down on the lounging chair. He seemed to her like a lost boy who needed help. He sat with his eyes forward, motionless and seemingly void of emotion. She didn't know what to say to him. Everything she could think to say seemed vapid and hollow. She was about to take her leave when she saw his eyes tear up with his mouth turning downward. Pei covered his face and uncontrollably cried.

Ona rushed to his side, feeling a strong urge to help the sad priest in front of her who had recently seen the death of his own brethren. She could not fathom how lost he most likely felt; how alone and betrayed by his Gods. She found herself gently cradling Pei while hushing him until he slowly became quiet again.

She uncovered his hands from his face and gave him a sad, but tender smile. He looked at Ona with melancholic longing. Her face seemed to him like the face of a Goddess, and her soul was like the light of the stars, though brighter than any he'd ever seen in the night sky.

"I am sorry, Your Highness," Pei said with a sniffle.

"It is alright," she cooed. "You have just lost your home and your loved ones all in one day. I cannot imagine how much your heart must be aching. It will take time to overcome such grief."

Pei nodded. He wanted to ask Ona to stay with him, not just for the moment, but for all eternity, though he knew he could not. She was a princess, and he was a meager priest. Plus, the Krian palace was her home where he was only a guest. Pei assumed King Atlar could come for him and ask him to leave at any given moment. Perhaps Ona would become tired of him and her sympathy would easily turn to boredom? He did not know what to believe in his mind. All he could do was continue to stare into her deep, green eyes, hoping he would somehow find an answer to his grief.

Ona sat looking at the priest before her, wondering what sort of life he had up until now. She slowly raised her hand and touched his face, wiping the residue of tears from his cheek. She knew she was behaving unconventionally, but true to her proud nature, she didn't really care. She wished to know him and to understand his people. Her mother was born the second princess of the Deiusian royal line, and through Pei, Ona hoped to find a revelation about her mother's upbringing.

"Pei-Lan," Ona softly addressed him.

"Yes, my princess?" Pei tenderly replied.

"Have you ever heard the story of The Priest and the Water Spirit?"

Pei shook his head.

"It is an old Krian myth," she said with a comforting smile. "It is the story of a young priest and his journey to the center of the ocean. You see, he had fallen in love with a water spirit who had taken the form of a beautiful young maiden, and so he vowed to marry her. Unfortunately, her father, the king of the ocean, did not want her to marry any man, let alone a priest. So she was taken deep into the center of the ocean where the priest could not find her. The priest, however, was so in love that it made him unafraid to face the storms and dangerous whirlpools of the ocean. So he built a small boat and with the help of Delma, the Goddess of mercy and love, he was able to penetrate the ocean's core and retrieve the water spirit."

Pei was transfixed on Ona's eyes, completely absorbed by her.

"And then? Did he marry her?" Pei excitedly asked.

"Yes, but first, he cut his long, braided hair as a token of his devotion to her. He swore to only love her and no one else, not even the Gods."

"That is a beautiful story, Ona," said Pei quietly.

"It is a story about sacrifice and devotion... to whatever is your heart's desire. You see, the priest loved the water spirit more than he loved being a servant to the Gods."

"Yet, the Gods rewarded him anyway?" Pei asked.

"Of course," Ona answered. "Despite his betrayal to them, the Gods recognized his bravery and rewarded him for it."

"Krian Gods are very different from Deiusian ones," said Pei with a sigh. He then swallowed nervously as he felt Ona's hand reach for his shoulder. For a moment, they looked at each other in silence.

Ona felt uncomfortably close to Pei, so she carefully withdrew her hand, trying her best not to offend. Not knowing exactly why she had told such a story, she gulped and stood up. She was trying to cheer him, but she wondered if she had gone too far. "Pei-Lan," she said, regaining her equilibrium, "you are safe now, and my father wishes that you stay with us for the time being."

Pei sensed that Ona had pulled her feelings away from him, but he did not blame her for it. "How long does he wish for me to remain here?" he asked, trying to cover his nervous heart.

"For as long as you would like. You are his guest, and you are under Kri's protection."

Pei nodded, collecting his emotions. "Thank you" he said under his breath.

Ona gave him a brief smile, then walked toward the door. "If you need anything," she said, "please call for one of our servants. You will find the button by your bed."

"Thank you, Your Highness," said Pei as he forced a smile.

"Please... call me Ona."

"Thank you, Ona," Pei shyly replied.

"You're welcome. Now, please, get some rest. My father will most likely call on you tomorrow to give testimony to The Council about what has occurred today. You will need your strength."

Pei nodded once again. Ona then went to the door, turning back for a moment to smile at him before leaving the room. Pei felt his heart return to darkness the minute she was no longer in his sight.

He looked up and saw his reflection in a vanity mirror that faced him from the other side of the room. He stared at himself.

Am I plain? he wondered. Surrounded by mostly priests his entire life, he'd never really thought about his physical worth as a man before, especially not when it came to the attractions of women. Beauty itself baffled him, but he hoped he was indeed attractive, at least to the princess.

After a few moments of contemplative thought, he found himself walking toward the mirror, as if pulled by an unknown force. Somewhere within his subconscious, a voice told him what he must do.

Pei picked up a razor, normally used for shaving. He held the razor up, then closed his eyes. As if in a dream, he felt his actions a few seconds after they had occurred. He opened his eyes to see what he had done; his long braid of hair lay by his feet. Pei looked at the mirror once more, no longer a priest, but a man.

Chapter 13: Welcome to Xen

*T*he docking area was rather huge, bigger than Ayn had ever seen. It was busy with people, like ants scurrying around a fallen piece of fruit. Zin told him that the people were probably tourists, as well as ticket-takers of the loading dock. "They're the ones who take care of your ship while it is parked for any length of time," Zin informed him. Ayn thought it sounded dubious, but Zin seemed perfectly confident about it all.

After they had parked their Ohrian cruiser, Zin gathered up his belongings, which he had organized into a couple of black and silver suitcases. Ayn had no material objects to speak of, but it seemed that Zin had prepared for this moment for quite some time, having brought plenty of clothing and toiletries, enough for the both of them.

"Are you ready for a new life?" Zin excitedly asked.

Ayn wasn't sure how to respond. He wasn't even sure where he was or what his reality had become, so he merely nodded with a complacent stare.

Zin opened the hatch of the ship and took Ayn's hand. Together, they stepped onto the escalator beneath them.

Ayn was immediately awestruck by the buildings of the city. He had never seen such tall, angular shapes diving forward against the sky. He wondered if the architects who created them were angry with The Un, or perhaps they were infinitely proud men who needed to show the world what sort of creations they were capable of. Either way, Ayn was intimidated, yet intrigued. Xen was a city of massive and modern proportions, and compared to The Holy City on Deius, it seemed like a giant beast made of metallic skin.

When they touched their feet on the ground, Zin approached the ticket taker who greeted him with a wide smile.

"Welcome to the greatest planet in the galaxy!" exclaimed the ticket man who was holding a small rectangular machine in his right hand. He was odd looking to Ayn with his unshaven, scruffy face, and bluish-green hair.

Zin thanked the ticket-man and gave him some money, telling him to be extra careful with his ship. The ticket taker gave Zin a receipt, promising him that his ship would be looked after with the best of care.

Ayn nervously held onto his suitcase as Zin approached him while smiling. "Well, that's done," said Zin, stuffing the receipt into his pants pocket. "So what do you think? Amazing, isn't it?"

Ayn hesitated in his response, so Zin grabbed his hand and walked with him further into the city. The first thing they noticed was the sound of a mighty roar, which whizzed by them overhead. When they looked up, they quickly realized the whizzing had come from a fast moving train. As it rushed by, it looked to Ayn like a huge, crystal-white, smooth sort of snake.

"That's The Chord!" Zin shouted as it went by.

"The Chord?" Ayn yelled back. "What is it exactly?"

"It's the main way everyone here commutes. We should take it into the heart of the city!" Zin happily exclaimed.

Following close behind his new friend and guide, Ayn clumsily carried his suitcase, trying his best to keep the pace. They soon went upstairs, which spiraled and seemed to go on for miles. Finally, when they reached the top, they had to wait a few minutes for the next train to slide through the opened silver dome that covered them from the smog-filled sky.

When the oval doors to the train opened automatically, Zin smiled at Ayn with a wink. It was as if this was the happiest day of Zin's young life, and Ayn had absolutely no idea why. However, as they sat down upon the long horizontal benches, Ayn began feeling a sense of wonder and calm. It was the first time since the horror of his birthday that he didn't feel a deep emptiness and sorrow. He even felt a small amount of Zin's excitement as he peered through the window in order to watch the traffic of floating vehicles hovering below them.

"Look!" cried Zin. "It's the Hithra Temple!" Ayn followed Zin's pointed finger and looked to his right. Ayn could just make out a massive structure that had a marble surface with sharp triangular edges. He wondered what a temple was doing in a city that was known to be free of religion, but he didn't ask his excitable friend. Zin was in such a happy state, and Ayn didn't want to disturb him.

As the train raced through the city, it made several stops before Zin got up and motioned to Ayn that it was time to leave. The two halves of the oval door slid open and they exited the train quickly with luggage in tow.

"Where exactly are we going?" Ayn asked, already tuckered out.

"Well," said Zin as he paused for a moment, scratching above his right eyebrow, "I think we should just head into the artist's section of the city and see where fate takes us."

"Fate?" scoffed Ayn. After everything that had happened, he seriously wondered if fate existed. "Aren't your people scientists?" Ayn said with a hint of sarcasm. "Do you even believe in the concept of fate?"

"My people may not," Zin casually replied, "but I do."

Not knowing how to respond, Ayn walked on, silent and exhausted. By the time they reached the main transport area, Ayn felt as if he had been walking for a hundred miles. He didn't enjoy all the endless walking, and he could feel himself beginning to stray back into the pampered, princely brat he only recently left behind. He wished Meddhi-Lan was there to take him back home to his comfy bed in the temple. About to cry, Ayn stopped himself, for he didn't want Zin to see him break.

Zin could tell Ayn wasn't doing so well, so he stopped at a drinking machine and reached into his pocket, taking out a credit stick to pay for the drinks. Ayn immediately plopped onto the ground, crossed his legs and pouted. Zin smirked at him while waiting for the drink bottles to arrive at the bottom of the machine. However, the bottles refused to come. He tried again, and again, but nothing seemed to work.

"You're not gonna get anywhere usin' that kinda money, kid," said a man with a gravelly voice. "This machine only takes Xen coins," the man added. He had graying, long, thin hair and walked with a slight limp. He came over to show Zin the type of coins he was referring to. He then held up his own bottle of blue liquid, offering it to Zin. "Want a taste?" he asked. "No thank you," Zin replied, cringing. "I'd help ya out," the scraggly man said after taking a sip, "but I'm down to my last coin myself." With one more sip, he limped off and sat on a nearby bench.

Ayn was immediately frightened. Would they have nothing to eat or drink? Would they die in this strange place? He couldn't help but panic.

Zin put his credit stick back in his pocket and thought for a moment. "Come on, Ayn," he declared. "Let's go and find a place that takes credit."

Ayn lazily got up and followed behind Zin. They walked by various shops and cafés, though most of them only took Xen money.

Ayn was almost at his wit's end when Zin burst with an idea. "I know!" he exclaimed. "There's a trade shop over there!"

"So?" Ayn asked wearily.

"Well," Zin replied, his aqua-colored eyes wide open, "if we can trade something for some Xen money, then we'll be fine!"

"Trade something?" asked Ayn. "Like what?"

"I don't know," muttered Zin as he looked at his hands and legs, "but I'm sure between the both of us we must have something valuable we can trade for money."

Ayn was not pleased.

Chapter 14: The Council's Conclusion

Atlar knew it wouldn't be easy. He had been having it out with The Council as of late on matters of Deiusian religion, as well as Kri's new alliance with the Ohrian government, and things weren't going his way.

Through Atlar's twenty-year reign, he had often clashed with the majority of his elected councilmen, especially when it came to The Dei's insistence that their young Shiva was the reincarnation of their legendary God-King, Adin. Atlar himself didn't believe the boy was a God, but he did entertain reincarnation as a possibility. Besides, if Meddhi believed the boy would make a great king, that was enough for him.

Unfortunately, The Council didn't see things that way. They dismissed Atlar's visit to Deius as nothing more than a gesture of courtesy and good politics. None of them believed in The Dei's religious "nonsense." In fact, most of them believed Deius was haphazardly run by half-witted priests who knew more about chanting than affairs of state.

Atlar felt a bit differently, however. Having gone to school on Deius for the latter years of his adolescence, he had known

Meddhi for a long time, and he had seen his good friend grow from disillusioned orphan to wizened holy man with a devout sense of purpose. He trusted Meddhi to be quite capable of running Deius - blindfolded, if necessary - but how could he convey that to the twenty-four men who sat on The Council? It didn't help Atlar's position that his own wife, Pira, had been born the second princess in the Deiusian royal line. Her blood-ties to Deius were always a good excuse for certain members of The Council to accuse Atlar of partisan politics, and a few even callously called him a "Dei devotee" behind his back.

Despite his adversaries, Atlar was an extremely popular king, usually able to overrule The Council's objections, all the while convincing his people the validity of his plans. This time, however, he knew it would be quite difficult to hide his emotions while speaking on the floor. He could only hope that The Council would listen to him with, not just open minds, but open hearts as well.

The Council Room was designed as a giant circle of elevated, marble steps that surrounded a flat, square stage. As he approached the center of the room, Atlar felt as if the spirit of Meddhi-Lan was somehow with him. It was a feeling both reassuring and heavy.

"My dear friends," said the king, extending his arms to face his colleagues, "I am certain that you have all heard of the tragic events that recently took place upon my visit to Deius."

There was a small rumbling of voices among the room, all male, and most of them middle aged and older. Atlar could sense their uneasiness about the topic, but he continued nonetheless. "I am here to tell you that I have seen first-hand the terror and destruction that has befallen our good allies within the halls of the Deiusian palace. There is nothing left but rubble, blood and death - including the death of High Priest Meddhi-Lan, who was a dear friend of mine."

An elderly man then stood up and raised his hand to speak. It was Octian, Atlar's older half-brother, and one of the most respected men on The Council. Octian wore white robes of fine linen with a purple, bird-shaped crest upon his right shoulder, which fastened his robe together. His mere presence silenced the room.

"Yes, High Councilor Octian," said Atlar.

"Your Majesty, is it true," began Octian, "that the next Shiva of Deius has indeed been... killed?"

A hush fell upon the circle of councilmen.

Atlar's brow tightened as he swallowed hard. "I am afraid you are correct, Councilman Octian," he solemnly replied, "and I suspect that the man responsible for his death is none other than Yol Notama, the leader of The Tah rebellion."

The Council broke into gasps and shouting.

Atlar raised his hand, silencing the room. "Good councilmen, as you know from our past meetings, my Lirhan warriors have reported that The Tah is still at large on Deius, though it is perhaps worse than we feared. No one could have imagined they would have gone as far as to kill The Dei's God-King."

Next to stand was Raifar. He was a middle aged man with a red beard and a gentle face. He was also Atlar's younger brother and First General of the Krian Army. "But was his body ever recovered?" asked Raifar. "Did anyone actually witness the boy die?"

"I doubt there could be any other outcome," Atlar sternly answered. "Unfortunately, there was no time to search for his body. However, the room that The Shiva had secretly been hiding in was bombed by the terrorists. I cannot imagine how he could have survived the blast."

There was a slight grumble among The Council, followed by a solemn hush. Octian then raised his hand to speak. "My King, Brother, I mean no offense, but you say the word 'terrorist' without hesitation, even though most on The Council are quite aware that The Tah rebels of Deius have long been active, publicly stating that they merely fight for their freedom and equality under the extremism of The Holy Dei."

About half of The Council erupted in applause. The other half sat in silence, baffled or disgusted. The subject of The Tah was controversial on Kri, and Octian never shied from controversy, especially if it meant Atlar would be tested.

Octian raised his hand, capturing The Council with his venerable stature. "Please," he continued, "my King, if I may, these rebels who seem to have attacked the Deiusian Royal Palace are not necessarily terrorists. Instead, they are possibly just angry, fed up civilians who have had little choice but to become extremists against the threat of The Dei's tyrannical rule."

"Hear, hear!" said a few other council members.

Atlar felt the opposition inside the room growing within seconds. He knew he had to counter with a swift and strong rebuttal.

Just then, a red-haired woman entered from the side of the room. She was dressed in black and weaved between the men like an invisible serpent, unnoticed and unsuspected. Atlar saw her, however, from the corner of his eye. He had been expecting her, for Reese was his personal spy, as well as occasional lover. As soon as they made eye contact, she nodded, signaling with her fingers in a gesture that suggested she had vital information to give. The king nodded to Reese, but then he quickly turned his attention to The Council's chaotic rumbling.

"My good councilmen," said Atlar, "I assure you that the men who attacked Deius were not civilians, nor were they the unsophisticated Tah rebellion of the past. They were highly trained, and even used Ohrian weaponry, which means Ohr was possibly behind the entire operation!"

The Council roared in disbelief.

"Impossible!" Octian shouted above the other voices in the room.

Atlar, using only his magnanimous presence, hushed them by simply raising his firm, strong right hand. He waited until the room was silent, then said, "I speak the truth! I was there and saw it myself. Do you question your king's own testimony?"

He looked around at them like a fierce, proud lion. After a small pause, he returned to his gentler tone and said, "My friends... I have seen what sort of people we're dealing with and they are hardened terrorists. I have also seen the face of the man who waged this war against our allies, and believe me, he is not the leader of mere rebels. Notama made it quite clear of his intentions: to destroy The Dei and take over Deius for himself. Make no mistake. This was a terrorist action of epic proportion and nothing less."

The Council seemed confused as Atlar locked eyes with his elder brother.

After a moment of uncomfortable silence, Baran, a handsome man in his early thirties rose to his feet. He had dark, shoulder length, wavy hair and was wearing a black and burgundy robe as all eyes turned to hear him speak.

"May I suggest," said Baran with a deep, clear voice, "that we conduct a thorough investigation of the facts before we come to any firm conclusion about who was involved in the attack on Deius."

The Council agreed by politely clapping.

"And until then," Baran continued over the clapping, "I motion that the king, as well as The Council, refrain from making blank assumptions with only limited information at their disposal."

Atlar didn't normally allow men to speak over him or let them appear as if they were giving him orders, but Baran was different. He was the king's own beloved nephew, and the son of the much respected General Raifar. Such connections gave Baran the position of Second General, as well as a fair amount of respect within The Council. He was still relatively young when compared to the senior councilmen around him, but he had a debonair, manly quality that could often sway opinions.

Unfortunately, not all embraced him. In fact, Baran's charm greatly annoyed Octian and many of the elder councilmen. The king, however, was well aware that Baran's ability was something quite valuable.

"Yes, General Baran," Atlar replied, "I agree with your suggestion. In fact, I have already ordered our Intelligence Committee to conduct a widespread investigation. While we wait for their report, I ask The Council to vote in favor of my decision to send an elite unit of our Lirhan soldiers to the Deiusian borders."

There was another collective grumble in the room.

"Objection!" shouted Octian.

"Objection!" added another elderly councilman to his left.

Soon, a sea of objections came flooding like a wave of disdain.

Atlar looked around at the arguing men while fighting the urge to scream at the top of his lungs. *Why are they such fools? he thought. How can they hear of the horror on Deius, yet turn a blind eye? What is wrong with these aging councilmen?*

Just then, Baran stood up and swiftly moved to the center of the floor, directly in front of where the king stood. Everyone was silenced as Baran held up his right hand. "Fellow councilmen," Baran boldly addressed them, "I implore you! Listen to our king!"

The Councilmen stared at the general in awe. Never had anyone from The Council stood next to the king on the speaking floor, as if he were his equal. Baran's boldness had captivated the entire room.

"He is not asking for the full support of our entire army," Baran continued, "but merely for a portion to stand guard at the borders between Deius and Kri. Now, considering that we do not know how far these new Tah rebels will extend their hostility, or if they blame us as well for their grievances, I think it wise to send at least some of our soldiers to the border for the security and well-being of Kri."

Baran could tell he had reached The Council's need for self-preservation, so he continued with confidence. "I hereby vote that we send a limited military unit to the border to guard in effort to show our strength, for it would be foolish indeed if we were to give the impression we are just as easy to take down as our Deiusian allies."

The Council broke into patriotic cheers. Atlar nodded to Baran, who bowed to his king in return. With a subdued smile, Baran left the floor and went back to his seat.

"Thank you, Baran," said Atlar as he sternly eyed The Council before speaking once again. "My wise councilmen," Atlar addressed them while slowly turning around in a circle, facing the entire room, "I ask you now to vote on my decision. Those who vote to send a limited elite force to the border of Deius, say aye."

"Aye!" Baran shouted as he proudly stood up.

"Aye!" Raifar shouted, standing next to his rather persuasive son.

Soon, one by one, the rest of The Council, including Octian, found themselves bending to the king's will.

Chapter 15: Metamorphosis

Ona was about to knock on the door when she heard a loud thud, which nearly made her drop the tray of tea and honeyed biscuits she was bringing to calm Pei. Not able to shake the feeling of worry for the Lan, she had returned to his room hoping to soothe his nerves. However, after hearing such strange noises coming from his room, she feared she was too late.

When she opened the door to his room, the first thing she noticed was the long braid of black hair at Pei's feet. The second thing she saw was the razor, still in Pei's quivering hand. He was standing with his back to her, staring at the mirror, as if frozen in time.

Ona looked around the room for the cause of the loud thud she had heard, yet all that lay on the floor as evidence was a large bowl of water, usually used for washing one's hands or face. She assumed Pei had accidentally knocked it over, perhaps when shaving his face.

Oddly enough, Pei's face didn't seem in need of shaving, for it was dry and clean. She looked at him and became aware of how young his heart was, and how innocent and unworldly he seemed.

She looked further at his somber, stoic expression and was struck with intense pity. She instinctively came to him, took the razor from his hand and placed it on the table nearby. She then gently held his hand and rested her head against his shoulder, hoping it would bring him some measure of comfort.

The feel of her skin against his did more than bring Pei comfort; it completely woke him from the trance he was under, forcing up the tears that had been silently flooding inside his heart.

"Why, Ona?" he heard himself ask despite the lump in his throat. "Why did something so evil happen to us?"

The princess had no answer to give. Instead, she looked at Pei with her compassionate green eyes and held him with her loving, warm arms. Unaware of how deeply her actions affected him, Ona made Pei's heart skip a beat.

As Pei wept, taking sharp, shallow breaths, Ona touched his back with gentle strokes. In a few moments, he felt warmed by her loving nature, which pushed back his tears.

"There now," she softly whispered against his cheek, "it will be alright."

Ona then felt Pei's hands slowly reach for her sides as he pulled his head back, looking deep into her eyes, hungry for her in a way she had only read of in books. Surprised and curious, she found herself looking into his needy, gray-green eyes as he leaned in to kiss her soft, full lips.

The rush of blood that filled Pei's body was an intensity he had never known, and soon, he felt more than his blood rushing inside him, swelling his body. Embarrassed, he pulled away from her soft embrace.

"I'm so very sorry," he spoke with shame, turning away from her.

Ona stood, silent and thunderstruck.

Pei took a moment to evaluate what he had just done. His tear-filled eyes flickered back and forth in confusion. He gulped, then turned back around to face her.

"It's just..." he said as he took her hands in his, "you're so beautiful, my princess! And I can't help but love you!"

Ona felt a smile escape from her mouth. She didn't want to confuse him, nor lead him on, but she was genuinely moved by his sincere affection. Priest or not, he was the most handsome and romantic man she had met up to that point in her young life, and she couldn't help but feel affection for him in return.

Encouraged by her smile, Pei felt a new kind of courage well up inside his chest. "Ona," he said, holding her hands, "the story you told me earlier... about the water spirit and the priest - that was about us! Or it could be, if I am willing to sacrifice my dedication to The Un so that I may be worthy of you!"

Ona shook her head, somewhat shocked, yet touched. "Pei-Lan! My sweet priest... don't be silly. You're emotional and tired, and don't know what you're say-"

"No!" Pei interrupted, "I know exactly what I am saying, perhaps for the first time in my life! I know my destiny now, Ona, and it is not to be a priest for a dying religion that cannot fend for itself in times of danger. No, it is my destiny to become a man of strength and honor... like your father! I want to fight for my planet's freedom, and more than anything else, I want to be with you... to love you, cherish you, and give you all that I have, body and soul."

His eyes were penetrating and serious, which made Ona feel a little light-headed. What had she done to this man? He was willing to give up his entire life to be with her, yet she didn't really know how she felt about it all. Did she feel the same for him? She knew she liked him and felt a familiarity, but it was too soon! How could she know her feelings so quickly? How Pei knew his own was a mystery to her.

"Pei-Lan," she calmly replied, "I'm deeply moved, but..."

"Ona," he said, stopping her from speaking, "I am no longer a Lan, nor a priest, so please, call me Pei from now on. Don't you see, Ona? I am finally sober and awake - more than I have been in my entire life! Please, tell me you feel love for me in return. Your love is all that I need to survive and to become strong."

Ona stood paralyzed, unable to think, let alone speak. Unexpectedly, Pei took her face in his two hands, gently stroking her cheeks with his thumbs. "Your face..." he whispered, "is that of a Goddess from an old legend. I love you, my princess, with all my heart."

Touched, yet confused, Ona smiled at him and said, "Sweet Pei, you've gone through so much. Let us walk through the healing flowers of my mother's gardens. Tell me of your life, and I shall tell you of mine, and that will be more than enough."

Slightly embarrassed, Pei nodded as Ona led him through the gardens. The two held hands and let the magic of the gardens guide their fate.

Chapter 16: The Uncomfortable Exchange

Zin was becoming frustrated, especially with the scruffy looking, middle aged man behind the counter.

"How can you say that my ring is worthless?" he protested. "I'll have you know that this ring has been in my family for generations!"

Worried that Zin was about to give away their true identities, Ayn kicked Zin's ankle.

"Ow!" Zin blurted. Fed up, the annoyed Ohrian prince turned to Ayn and glared at him.

"What do you think you're doing?" Ayn asked under his breath.

Zin rolled his eyes. "I am trying to sell something in exchange for Xen money!" he replied in an angry hush. "What does it look like I'm doing?"

Ayn pulled him aside. "Well," Ayn whispered, "it looks to me as if you're behaving like a spoiled prince who demands to be served by his slaves." Zin opened his mouth, aghast, ready to rebut. "What I suggest," Ayn continued before Zin could talk, "is that we politely offer our valuables to this man, but in a way that makes us seem as if we are not as desperate as we actually are."

Zin took a moment to process what Ayn was saying. He then realized that his friend perhaps had a point. "Ayn," he said, "you are more savvy than you seem."

Ayn proudly smiled.

Zin turned around to face the pawn shop vendor once more, this time with a different approach. "My good sir," he addressed the vendor with a gleam in his eye, "I offer you the finest jewels of Ohr. In fact, these rings you see on my fingers have been worn by royal members for thousands of generations."

Zin waved his fingers, showing off his rings like a proud peacock. The man at the counter raised his eyebrows, seemingly unimpressed.

"It's no good," the pawn shop merchant said as he shrugged.

Zin could barely contain himself and said, "What do you mean it's no good?"

"Look," the merchant explained, "I see gems like that nearly every day."

"You do?" Zin asked, perplexed.

"Yeah, I do. Ohrian jewels flow into Xen like they're going out of style."

"But... I mean... how?" Zin stumbled, lost for words.

"Look, maybe I can give you a few coins, kid, but..." Suddenly, the pawn shop merchant stopped talking and began staring at Ayn. Immediately, Zin feared that the man had recognized The Bodanya of Deius. He didn't know how that would be possible, considering the priests had always kept Ayn secret, and would never allow any media coverage of their precious messiah. Even so, Zin was ready to grab Ayn's hand and run - just in case.

"Woah!" exclaimed the merchant. "Would you look at that?!"

Ayn turned to Zin with a fearful expression, silently asking for help.

"Is that a genuine relic from ancient Deiusian times?" asked the merchant as he marveled at something hanging from Ayn's chest. Zin and Ayn followed the merchant's gaze, which led them directly to Ayn's gold and red medallion. Zin remembered that Xen had been built by Deiusian kings and their artifacts would be greatly valued. He couldn't believe he hadn't thought of it before! "Ayn!" Zin nearly shouted. "Your medallion!"

Ayn frowned and walked a few steps backwards. "What about it?" he nervously replied. Zin then turned to the pawn shop merchant and asked, "How much for his medallion?"

The merchant squinted his eyes and thought it over. "Hmm... that depends on how old it is," he replied, "and I wouldn't be able to determine that unless I looked at it up close."

Zin rushed to Ayn's side and said, "Ayn, show him your medallion!"

"No!" Ayn said defiantly.

"This is no time to argue, my dear friend," Zin politely argued. "Just give him the medallion so we can get something to eat and find somewhere nice to sleep!"

Ayn pouted and shook his head.

Zin crossed his arms and looked at Ayn with stern,

demanding eyes.

"But Meddhi-Lan gave it to me!" Ayn cried out.

"Shh!" Zin interrupted, not wanting to attract attention.

"But," Ayn continued, now whispering into Zin's ear, "Meddhi-Lan gave this to me. It was his coronation gift... and it's all I have left from him." Ayn's face showed his loss, which Zin could not ignore. He felt terrible for Ayn, but he also wanted them to survive. Zin knew he had to make a hard choice - for both their sake.

"Listen to me, Ayn," he softly whispered. "I know it hurts to let your teacher go, but you must remember the truth of his teachings. Wouldn't Meddhi-Lan tell you his spirit is always with you? And that a medallion alone does not carry his teachings or his spirit? Would he not remind you that his spirit still resides within you and inside your memory of him?"

Ayn pouted while listening to his friend. He hesitantly nodded, then swallowed down his sadness. "I suppose you're right," he quietly agreed.

Zin nodded. "Besides," he continued, "we may yet get it back someday - you never know. But what I *do* know is that we need to get food and shelter. That is what's most important in the here and now. Wouldn't you agree?"

Ayn nodded halfheartedly. Zin motioned for Ayn to give the man behind the counter his medallion, and Ayn reluctantly did so.

"Oh, yes!" the merchant said as he eyed the ancient Deiusian relic. He then bit into the medallion, which made Ayn cringe. "Oh, yes indeed! This is a rare piece of jewelry! I wouldn't be surprised if it had been worn by a king!" the merchant exclaimed.

Ayn and Zin both silently squirmed.

"'Ey," added the wild-eyed merchant, "how'd you two come across a fine piece like this?"

Ayn and Zin again squirmed, this time more noticeably.

"Ah, don't you kids worry about it," said the merchant with a grin. "We don't ask questions on Xen. How you get your goods is your business!"

Zin exhaled and smiled while Ayn looked queasy from the whole ordeal.

"So, how much are you willing to give us for it?" Zin asked with a determined face.

"Oh, well... for this type of relic," the merchant stalled, "I might be able to give ya a lot more than what I got on hand. Why don't you both come back tomorrow, and I'll have the full sum of what this beauty's worth."

Ayn and Zin both felt immediately sickened by that idea. They could sense the innate attraction to wickedness and dishonesty within the man's nature. Waiting a day more would surely be the man's chance to cheat them somehow.

"No," said Zin adamantly, "I think we will just take whatever it is you can give us right now."

"Well, alright," the merchant replied, "but it ain't gonna be what it's really worth. It'll be your loss!"

"That's quite alright," Zin said as he held out his hand for payment.

The merchant frowned, looking disappointed. He then reached into his money-drawer and began counting out pieces of Xen money, which Zin informed Ayn was called "nex." It reminded Ayn of Deiusian money, which he hadn't seen himself, but had read about in stories.

The merchant handed Zin one thousand nex in bills and five hundred in coins. Ayn had a sinking feeling that the amount they had been given was not nearly equal to the value of his precious medallion, but he remained quiet. Zin quickly took the money, then pocketed it into his Ohrian style wallet, which was black and smooth.

"Nice doing business with you, my friend," Zin said to the merchant as he gave a slight bow.

"Likewise," said the amused merchant.

Zin led the way as he exited the pawn shop with Ayn trailing behind. When they were outside the shop, Zin joyfully shouted, "Yes!" He then attempted to playfully hit Ayn's hand in the air, to which Ayn stood still, confused at what Zin was doing.

"Oh come on, Ayn!" Zin nearly shouted. "We have money! We're going to live!"

Ayn immediately hushed him, worried someone unsavory might hear such a decree of wealth. "Zin! Don't you realize that we have just been robbed?" scolded Ayn.

"How so?" Zin asked, perplexed.

"That man gave us less than half of what my medallion was worth! By the Gods, it was once owned by The Great Adin himself!"

Zin looked at Ayn for a moment, dead-faced. "Ayn... I love you... I do... but you really are still caught up in that silly game, aren't you?"

Ayn pouted and folded his arms. "What game?" he replied, confused. "What do you mean?"

Zin sighed, then said, "I mean the game that those priests

played on you. Every day of your life, they told you stories about how The Great Adin did this and that... and how *you* were supposed to do it as well. Except, in this life, they expected you to do it even better than he did."

"So?!" Ayn shouted, defensively.

"So," Zin repeated, "you have been brain-washed into believing that Adin was some sort of great God-Man simply because they convinced you of its supposed truth ever since you were a baby. The truth is, Ayn, you don't even know if he lived as an actual person. It could all be a myth fed to the Deiusian people so they will obey blindly. Yet, you accept it as fact, merely because The Dei priests raised you to believe it, as if you're a simpleton like the rest of the people of Deius. I know you are not a fool, Ayn, so stop talking like one."

Ayn's eyes widened in anger and his very aura became inflamed with raw energy. Zin stood his ground, though he felt a little frightened.

"I am NOT a fool! And you are wrong! About all of it!" Ayn shouted.

Zin began feeling the eyes of the passersby on the street. "Look," he quietly spoke as he leaned in closer to Ayn, "it doesn't matter now. We can argue until we're blue in our faces about our religious differences and opposing beliefs, but let's do that later. Right now, all that matters is that we have enough money to get something to eat and drink, and hopefully sleep. Why don't we just focus on finding a nice restaurant or hotel for now?"

"Fine," Ayn defiantly replied. Zin sighed, trying his best to remember Ayn was younger than he was and had been raised even more cloistered than he had been. Zin knew that it would take time for Ayn to get used to how the real world worked, and in the meantime, Zin believed himself to be Ayn's protector.

Ayn, however, thought of things differently.

--

"Excuse me," said Reese, as she came upon Ona and Pei, who were walking among the gardens and exchanging stories of their youth. Reese looked at them for a moment, wondering if something more than friendship was sparking between the princess and the priest.

"Yes?" Ona said, hoping Reese bore no bad news.

"I'm sorry to disturb you, your highness," said Reese, "but your father wishes to talk with the priest... in private. He is to follow me to see the king."

Pei felt honored, yet unnerved. He wondered if Ona's father had somehow learned of their secret kiss, though he couldn't imagine how Atlar would have found out. Pei swallowed nervously, hoping for the best.

"Why does he wish to see Pei?" Ona asked Reese.

"I don't know, my princess."

"Well, then I'm coming too," declared Ona. Reese looked as if she were about to object, but instead, she smiled and nodded in acceptance. "As you wish, Your Highness. Follow me, please," Reese politely requested.

Pei had no idea what King Atlar wanted to see him about, if not the kiss. He hoped it had to do with Atlar's plans for bringing the murderer of Meddhi-Lan and Ayn to justice. He couldn't even think their names in his mind, for it brought too much pain.

Pei hoped Atlar was going to ask him for testimony about

the man who called himself Yol Notama. It would be difficult for Pei to remember what happened in detail, but he was determined to do whatever he could to help Atlar destroy The Tah. Despite his religious upbringing, Pei couldn't help but feel a deep sense of vengeance. He wanted Notama, and everyone responsible for the bombing, to feel the wrath of Kri's mighty army.

As he followed behind the strong-armed, red-haired woman whom he found to be astonishingly attractive despite her tough, warrior-like exterior, he looked over at Ona, who was walking beside him through the halls with a serious look on her face. He wondered if she had already forgotten the sweet kiss they had shared in his room. He wanted to say something to her, but felt it wasn't the right time. He decided to bring it up sometime later when they found themselves alone once more.

Reese led them through the vast hallways of The Royal Palace. Pei imagined he could easily get lost in such a grandiose, epic-sized structure; it made the palace on Deius seem small in comparison.

They soon took a turn down a smaller hallway, which lead to a private, hidden chamber. As Reese turned the golden doorknob of a green-colored marble door, they entered and saw that the king was sitting at a desk while wearing a regal, yet casual looking burgundy robe. Pei assumed that Atlar was wearing his night time attire because he was readying for bed. It made Pei wonder why the king would wish to speak with them at such a late hour.

"Good! Reese, thank you for bringing the Lan!" Atlar exclaimed as he stood up. "Ona, you've come too, I see," he added with a slightly displeased, albeit amused grin. Pei immediately bowed to the king, which Atlar responded to with a dismissive wave of his hand, as if to say there was no need for such formal behavior. Pei, a little confused, straightened up and nodded his head.

"Father," Ona quickly addressed him, "Why did you want to see him? He is tired and weary from his ordeal. Why bother him?"

The princess stood in front of the king's desk with her arms crossed, scolding her father with her eyes. Pei found her bold behavior surprising, but touching as well. He wondered if she was feeling protective for him. Did that mean she felt for Pei the same love he felt for her? His heart sped up at the idea.

"Calm down, my spirited daughter," Atlar said with a smile, "I have something very important to discuss with Pei-Lan - something I'd like to talk to him about in private, if you don't mind." Ona stood defiantly still with crossed arms. Realizing his daughter had no intention of leaving, Atlar walked to the front of his desk and directed his attention to the young priest.

"Now, Pei-Lan," said Atlar.

"Please, Your Majesty, just call me Pei."

"As you wish," the king replied. "Pei... I know you have been through a terrifying event, as we all have, though you perhaps even more." He walked across the room and motioned for Reese to shut the door. She complied, locking it as well with several plasma-locks. "But you must understand," Atlar continued, "right now, we have to focus our energies on more important matters,"

Atlar spoke with commanding majesty as he picked up a golden carafe and poured a glass of wine for himself. He offered a glass to Pei, but Pei politely declined the offer.

"More important matters, Your Majesty?" asked Pei.

"Yes!" Atlar confirmed. "We must not let our hearts have the time to grieve. We must turn our pain into strength!"

Pei had no idea what Atlar was trying to say, but he could

sense the meaning behind the king's words. The Deiusian priests often used meditation to escape their pain, transcending it through blank stillness. However, what the king seemed to be talking about was altogether different. Pei hoped that whatever Atlar was about to ask of him had to do with their plans for revenge.

Seeing the look of determination of Pei's face, Atlar nodded with an austere smile. "You know what I am talking about, don't you?"

"Yes," Pei answered in a gruff whisper, "I think I do."

"Good," Atlar nodded as he put his glass of wine down on the table. "Now, let me ask you something, my friend." There was a hush that fell upon the room. Atlar turned to Pei, looking at him intently, and said, "If you thought there was a way to bring the murderer of your people to justice, how far would you go?"

"Father!" Ona shouted, sounding rather offended. Reese quietly sighed, then sat down on a luxurious looking chair, waiting for the drama to end.

"Let me continue, Ona," Atlar commanded. Pei wondered how close they were as father and daughter. Sometimes, it seemed to him that Ona had no problem defying her father, as if King Atlar were just a common person on the street. However, at other times, they seemed rather affectionate. Being an orphan, Pei had a hard time grasping their parent-child dynamic, but he soon came to the conclusion that their relationship was complex, yet deep. It was something he hoped to one day understand.

Ona shook her head, then sat down on a chair next to Reese who grinned back at Ona, teasing her without speaking.

Atlar then walked over to Pei and stood in front him. "My friend, I'm not asking you to fight or do anything overtly dangerous..."

"But I want to fight!" Pei interrupted the king, much to the surprise of everyone in the room.

Atlar looked stunned, but soon recovered and said, "Pei, you may not understand what it is I'm asking you to do. I simply want you to make your case to The Council. You see, they are having trouble seeing the severity of what has been done to your kingdom, as well as the after effects that will come to us here on Kri. Once it is known throughout the galaxy that a madman killed The Bodanya of Deius, there will be an uproar among the many Shiva sympathizers living on Kri. If word goes out that we, the people's elected leaders, allowed such a tragedy to happen, there will be protests and possibly riots. I highly doubt The Council will want such impending calamity."

Atlar walked to his desk. He then held down a button and spoke into it. "Baran, can you come in here, please?" A few moments later, a strong man with dark, wavy hair entered the room. Pei assumed it was Baran, noting to himself that only someone extremely trusted by the king would have the secret code to unlock the door.

"Yes, my King?" Baran said as he quickly bowed. Pei immediately sensed that Baran and the king had a close friendship.

"Pei, this is Baran, my Second General and nephew," Atlar announced. Baran nodded to Pei, then looked back at Atlar, waiting for his orders.

"Pei, I want you to speak to The Council tomorrow," the king continued. "Baran will introduce you and speak on your behalf. Then, I want you to tell The Council all about how the man named Yol Notama killed your teacher, your Bodanya, and nearly all of your fellow priests. I want you to be explicit, Pei. That's important. I want you to make them understand and feel your pain - your suffering - so that they will see through your eyes, and ultimately, feel consumed with as much guilt as their king does."

The room fell silent. Pei could see the sincerity on Atlar's face. In that somber, quiet moment, Pei vowed in his mind to follow the Krian king before him with all his loyalty and pride.

"Will you do this for me, Pei?" Atlar gently asked. "I know it will be painful to talk about what happened, but I know that if you speak, they will listen."

Pei nodded. "Yes, my King," he solemnly answered. "I will gladly speak to The Council, and I will tell them how that madman sent his assassin to destroy the two most important people in my life. I will make them understand how that loss affects, not just my planet, but the entire Un!"

"Good," said Atlar. "But don't go too much into your religious beliefs. That would probably distance them. Instead, pull at their heart strings, if you can. You see, Pei, it is my objective to gain The Council's consent so that my army can wage a full war against Yol Notama and his followers. As it is, they will only allow a small scale investigation, which Reese here will be leading." Reese nodded.

Atlar put his hand on Baran's shoulder and added, "As soon as we find out more about these terrorists, specifically about Notama, I will send Baran into battle with the full force of my army. For now, if you can convince The Council that what their king wishes to do isn't madness, but justice, then I am certain Meddhi-Lan will finally be at peace."

At the mention of his Lan's name, Pei felt like his heart could break into a thousand pieces, and yet, Atlar somehow found a way to stir something long hidden in his soul. A courage that had been asleep inside him was now awakening, and it roared like a dragon, ready to fly into battle!

"I will do whatever it takes, Your Majesty!" Pei declared. "I will speak to The Council tomorrow, yes. But even more than that, I wish to fight! Let me fight alongside Baran and your soldiers!

Please, let me help take down the man who killed my teacher and brother-in-spirit!" With pleading eyes and heaving chest, Pei nearly broke apart in tears.

Atlar understood Pei's deep sorrow and rage, for he felt much the same. The king walked to Pei and gently laid his hands on the emotional priest's shoulders. "My friend, I know you are in pain," said Atlar, "but you must let the fighting be done by experienced warriors who-"

"No!" Pei interrupted as he threw off Atlar's hands from his shoulders. However, Pei quickly realized his rudeness and bowed his head. "I am deeply sorry, Sire, but I cannot sit still while others fight for my own home!" Determined, Pei looked directly at the king who was a little startled by his passion.

"Your Majesty, with all due respect, I have changed in an irreversible way," Pei continued his plea. "Do you not see that I am no longer a priest? Can you not see that, inside my soul, I have become a warrior? Do you not understand that I MUST fight or I feel my soul will die?!"

Atlar stared at the young man before him, realizing that Pei had indeed changed, not just emotionally, but physically. The king had been so steadfast about his plans, he hadn't even noticed Pei's short, jagged hair. He wondered if Pei had a warrior's spirit after all. *If he could be trained,* thought Atlar, *would he be like Meddhi had been before he became a priest? Could Pei follow in Meddhi's footsteps?*

Atlar turned to Baran who was watching Pei with an eyebrow raised in curiosity.

"Baran?"

"Yes, my king," Baran answered.

"Do you think that there is a Lirhan warrior inside this man?"

Baran looked at Pei for a moment, sizing him up.

"I believe that with enough training, he may have the potential," Baran coolly replied.

Atlar turned to Pei and smiled. "Then, that is your answer, my friend. I leave it to Baran to turn you into the warrior you wish to become. In the meantime, use the last of your priestly skills to make an impression on The Council's conscience. I am relying on you, Pei."

"It will be done, my king" said Pei as he bowed in stoic reverence.

Atlar nodded and gave Pei a firm pat on the back.

Suddenly, Pei felt a sense of euphoria as if the entire Un had been opened up to him in one night. He could feel his soul's true nature, and it was not the soul of a priest. No, he now realized he was a passionate man full of anger and love - like a dragon of ancient myth who is both light and dark, good and bad - the paradox of plasma itself!

Atlar excused Pei and Ona. He then ordered Baran and Reese to stay and discuss what Pei assumed would be secret Lirhan tactics.

As Pei walked through the giant marble halls with Ona, his head reeled. He felt the weight of his new responsibility, but the weight somehow felt right. He could only hope that one day he too would be asked by the king to make secret plans in the dead of night.

Chapter 17: Home Away from Home

As Ayn changed his clothes in the store's dressing room, it made him feel extremely vulnerable. He had never been all that comfortable about his body in the first place, let alone somewhere that was so public and foreign to him.

"Well?" prodded Zin from outside the dressing room. "Are you done yet?"

"No," said Ayn, pouting.

"What's taking you so long?"

At that, Ayn became irate and blurted out, "Nothing fits right!"

"Let me see," ordered Zin.

"No!"

Zin wasn't about to let Ayn act like a spoiled brat any longer. He pulled open the corner of the dressing room curtain and saw Ayn dressed in a blue cotton shirt and a pair of dark blue pants. "Well," Zin prodded once again, "what's the problem? You look fine to me."

Ayn continued pouting and turned to face Zin with eyes full of daggers. "How can you say that?" he replied. "I look ridiculous."

"No you don't," Zin replied, nonchalant. "You just don't look like a Deiusian king any longer, which is exactly the idea. We have to blend in, Ayn, and those royal robes you had on weren't helping us do that."

"Fine," Ayn mumbled as he scratched and pulled at the side of his shirt, "but it feels tight... and the pants are tight as well."

Zin rolled his eyes and assured Ayn that he looked perfectly normal, and that they were supposed to fit that way.

"If you say so," Ayn mumbled once again.

"I *do* say so!" said Zin with a playful grin. "Now... where can we eat? Hmm..."

After Zin payed for their new items, Ayn took his old clothing and folded them nicely inside his rolling suitcase. Zin had a feeling it would take quite some time before Ayn could let go of his past. However, he was not about to stop prodding his new best friend. He hoped, in time, Ayn would come to love his new life, and perhaps even love Zin for giving it to him.

Unfortunately, it wasn't that easy. Not only was Ayn unknowingly suffering from post-traumatic stress, but he was also quite exhausted from the ordeal of walking around a metropolitan city – one that he never could have imagined when he lived in the temple on Deius. Everything on Ayn hurt: his arms, his legs, his feet, his very brain!

Soon he found himself trailing behind Zin who seemed downright perky. This annoyed Ayn even further as he dragged his suitcase on the ground, sluggishly walking a good five to ten paces behind his Ohrian friend.

Zin finally stopped still, muttering to himself about restaurants. He then pulled out a small, metallic looking gadget that Ayn had never seen before.

"What is that?" asked Ayn while a yawn escaped from his lips.

Zin seemed lost in a trance as he stared at the gadget, speaking in Ohrian under his breath. It looked to Ayn as if he were talking to it somehow.

Ayn waited for a response, but got none. He figured Zin was performing some sort of Ohrian ritual.

Bored and tired as well, Ayn slipped into lucid dreaming, a technique often used by The Dei priests to achieve inner peace, as well as to practice stamina and focus. Ayn had been trained his whole life in such techniques, and it was second nature to him. However, the lucid dreaming he fell into was induced by lack of sleep and physical exhaustion, and was more akin to hallucination than meditation. The streets turned hazy and blue, the shops became Deiusian monuments in honor of Adin, and all the while, he could hear the droning hum of The Un.

"Ayn!" shouted Zin. "Are you actually sleeping?"

As Ayn woke out of his trance, he heard the laughter from the people nearby and saw Zin grinning at him, obviously amused. "Come on!" Zin said as he shook his head in laughter. "I found a great place that rents rooms and offers fine dining as well. Now follow me and keep up!"

Ayn did his best to keep the pace even though his feet were aching more than he knew was possible. He wondered how Xenites actually managed to get from place to place in such an enormous city. To him, it felt twice the size of his own Holy City.

Lost in thought as he walked, Ayn didn't notice the strange creature following him. It wasn't until he almost tripped over it that he could see something was there. For only a second, he thought he saw a strange blur of white and gold. It looked like a cat of some kind, but he wasn't certain. One second, the creature was there, and the next, it was gone!

He wondered if he had slipped back into lucid dreaming. *Meddhi-Lan would be so embarrassed about me right now,* he thought, disappointed in himself.

Then, there it was again. The white and gold cat thing — just briefly in focus for a moment on the side of the street. This time, however, it seemed as if it were smiling at him. Now Ayn *knew* he was dreaming.

"Save me!"

Ayn stopped dead in his tracks, then looked around. He had heard a voice speaking directly into his mind!

"Please! Save me!" begged the mysterious, childlike voice yet again.

Ayn looked ahead at Zin who was casually walking without any notice or care about the strange voice.

Ayn gulped and begrudgingly decided to answer back in his mind. "Um… who are you and how may I save you?"

"Well," purred the voice in his mind, "I suppose you could answer me a riddle."

"A riddle?" Ayn silently replied.

"Yes!" said the voice, "a riddle!"

"I'm sorry," said Ayn, "but I'm not very good at riddles."

"Oh, well," the voice said, disappointed, "I guess I'll just be trapped here forever."

Ayn looked around to see where the voice was coming from, but all he could see were street vendors and random passersby.

"I'm over here!" cried the voice in his mind.

Ayn began following the voice, using only his gut feelings. After a few moments of concentration, he could vaguely make out the shape of the white and gold cat creature he had seen before, and it was indeed trapped.

The poor cat-like animal was caged inside of a wooden box that was sitting on the back of a metallic, plasma-powered vehicle. How the creature managed to get inside the box was a mystery to Ayn, but he was trapped there nonetheless.

The vehicle was parked on the side of the street without a driver in sight. Ayn wasn't sure if he should be getting involved, but at the same time, he wondered how often a person is psychically asked for help by a cat.

Ayn looked around to see if anyone was watching him. When he believed he wasn't noticed, Ayn dropped his bag and ran over to the creature. Bending over and gazing directly at the animal, Ayn could see it more clearly.

The creature wasn't really a cat, though it shared similarities, such as its ears, paws, and tail. However, upon closer inspection, Ayn could see that the mysterious animal also had tiny talons on its feet, as well as small wings that were chained together with a plasma-powered lock. Ayn looked into its nearly human-looking eyes and felt sorry for the poor cat-bird creature.

"Don't just gawk at me!" said the strange animal. "Get me out of here!"

"How did you even get in there?" asked Ayn cautiously.

"Weren't you just behind me a few moments ago?"

"No, silly boy," replied the cat-bird as it bent back its ears, "you must have been dreaming! Now help me out of this box!"

"How can I do that?" asked Ayn innocently.

The animal sneered and cocked its head, looking at Ayn as if he had asked the stupidest question in the universe.

"Aren't you The Bodanya?"

Ayn was shocked that the creature knew of his true identity, and he began nervously looking around, wondering if anyone had heard the animal's question.

"Don't worry, Ayn. No one but you can hear me. In fact, not many can even see me... unless I want them to."

Ayn was amazed and intrigued. "How is that possible?" he asked the cat-bird.

"Enough of *you* asking *me* questions! *I* am the one who asks the riddles!"

Ayn shook his head. "Alright then," Ayn replied, "ask me what you want."

The creature smiled, then looked deep into Ayn's blue eyes. "Let's see if you can answer me this," said the cat-bird. "Why is it, with all my powers to control time and space, I am somehow still unable to escape this metal trap?"

Ayn didn't know which part of the riddle to think upon first. His mind immediately jumped to the idea of the creature having powers that controlled time and space, and yet, Ayn's heartfelt sympathy when it came to the cat-bird being trapped in a cage against its will.

The creature stared at Ayn with expectant eyes, waiting

impatiently for an answer.

"Well," Ayn slowly began, "first, I would need to know how it came to be that you were caught inside such a cage."

The creature cocked its head and looked at Ayn with a sneer. "How can you ask me such a silly question?! I was caught by magic, of course!"

Magic? thought Ayn, stopping himself from giggling.

"What's so funny?" asked the cat-bird.

"I... I'm sorry, but I don't believe in magic," said Ayn, matter-of-fact.

The creature snorted, then shook its head. "Well, you're in for a big surprise then!" said the cat-bird with a sarcastic chuckle. "You'll find out how wrong you are soon enough though," the creature purred. "Now, stop asking me foolish questions and solve my riddle!"

Ayn gulped and looked around again, searching for Zin with his eyes. However, Zin was nowhere to be found. Ayn feared he had become separated and began feeling light headed at the thought of being alone in such a big city.

"Concentrate, Bodanya!" commanded the cat-bird.

After a deep breath, Ayn cleared his mind - the way Meddhi-Lan had taught him. He began using a technique that The Dei priests called "Symbol Touching." The technique involved closing one's eyes and imagining a symbol, or an image of any kind, at which point, if you focused on the feelings the image gave you, answers and truths would inevitably come.

At first, Ayn didn't see or feel anything, but when he let himself imagine the cat-bird, and its unfortunate situation in the cage, Ayn's mind began seeing a vast amount of images, almost at once. In his mind's eye, he saw the creature in chains, being lured into the metallic cage with offerings of brightly-colored, sweet tasting fish. However, the image quickly changed to an entirely different setting. It was a planet... a wasteland.

Ayn intuitively sensed that it was the once great, but now mostly abandoned planet of Sirin. He didn't know why he was seeing such a strange vision. Nevertheless, he let his mind wander further into the Symbol-Touching, for he could feel he was close to an answer to the cat-bird's riddle.

Just then, he saw more cat-like creatures, though they were much, much bigger. In fact, they were like gigantic lions, but with wings, and all of them had stoic faces that seemed to Ayn similar to the priests of Deius.

As Ayn saw himself approach the giant cat-birds, they surprised him by turning their enormous heads in one direction at the same exact time - all looking directly at him. Their eyes seemed to glow, and Ayn wondered what they were trying to tell him.

Then Ayn remembered something Meddhi-Lan used to say: "When you want your dream-image to explain its meaning, simply ask it what it wants or feels. It will more than likely tell you. Dream-symbols are always honest, but you have to be brave enough to ask them honest questions."

Ayn took a deep breath and gathered his courage. "Excuse me, magnificent creatures," he addressed them in his vision. "May I inquire what it is you want to tell me?" The giant cat-birds all pricked their ears back at the same time like they were hearing a strange sound they had never heard before. "Do you understand my question?" asked Ayn.

After a moment of silence, he saw them simultaneously open their mouths wide. Ayn wondered if they were going to give out a loud roar. Just in case, Ayn covered his ears, and as he suspected, that's exactly what they did. The roar, however, was even louder than Ayn could imagine. It was so loud that his ear drums felt like they would bleed.

Oh, please stop! Ayn begged in his mind, hoping they'd hear him telepathically. Unfortunately, they didn't stop. The roar became so thunderous that it felt like Ayn would pass out from the intensity of the vibrations. When he could stand no more, Ayn heard something else within the roar; it was almost a whisper, as if a tiny voice was mixed inside the deafening loudness. When Ayn tried to fixate on the whisper, everything seemed to go completely quiet. He then heard what the whisper was saying: "Save us. We are slaves to time. Please... save us."

As soon as Ayn understood the whisper, he felt his eyes open. He was once again standing in the city streets of Xen.

Shaking off the dream-like feelings, Ayn centered on what was real. He saw the wooden cage in the vehicle, but he didn't see the cat-bird creature. *Where did it go?* thought Ayn as he whirled around to see if it had run off somewhere. Sure enough, he saw the cat-bird sitting in the shade under a tree. It seemed to be smiling at him.

"Thank you, Bodanya," it said in Ayn's mind.

"What did I do?" Ayn mentally replied.

"You saw my people, and you understood our plight. I now know there is hope, and soon, I shall be free. That is all I needed to escape that cage. Thank you."

With that, the strange creature ran off – so fast it almost seemed to disappear.

Ayn shook his head and stood in the street, dazed.

"Ayn?!" yelled Zin. "What are you doing? Come on!"

Ayn picked up his suitcase and ran over to Zin. "Sorry," said Ayn, "but that strange cat-bird thing needed my help."

Zin raised his eyebrows. "What cat-bird... thing?"

"Didn't you see it?"

"Uh, no, I didn't," said Zin, looking skeptical. "Ayn, I think you may be more tired than I thought. Just hang on to me, and I'll get you to the hotel before you know it."

Ayn nodded, feeling foolish. Had he dreamt the whole thing? Was there really no caged creature? Had he just been hallucinating the entire time? Despite the vision, something about the whole thing felt so real to Ayn. His instincts told him that he would once again see that cat-bird, possibly in the near future, but only time would tell.

—

"How could he?" Ona asked in frustration. "Does he have no idea what becoming a warrior means? Is he really that naive?"

Frey, Ona's handmaid and best friend, silently shrugged, unable to think of a proper response to the princess' rhetorical questions. Truthfully, Frey wasn't able to give her full attention for fear of accidentally ripping the fine silk of Ona's dress. It was hard enough to undress the princess normally, but when she was agitated, her regal gowns took even longer to unhinge and carefully disrobe.

"Maybe..." Frey said as she unhooked Ona's gown, "the poor boy just hasn't thought things through yet. Maybe he'll change his mind by the morning."

"You think so, Frey?" asked Ona as she slipped out of her

gown, standing half naked in her bedroom.

"Yes, I do," Frey replied in her calming, kind voice. "Just give him time, and he'll come 'round." Ona nodded with a worried face as Frey carefully hung the gown in the closet. Frey looked at Ona and smiled, adding, "You care for him, don't you?"

Ona blushed, then quickly shook her head. Frey's smile grew even wider as she came toward Ona with a light-blue nightgown. Slipping it over Ona's shoulders, she playfully teased the princess with a nudge. "You *do*! You like that priest in a way priests aren't supposed to be liked!"

"Oh stop, Frey!" Ona exclaimed, giving a hint of a giggle. "I don't know if I feel that way for him. But, even if I did, he says he is no longer a priest, so I suppose there is nothing to stop me from liking him. I must admit, Pei is a very fiery man who has a way of making others care for him. He even convinced my father of letting Baran train him to become a soldier, and my father is never easily swayed by anyone."

"Most definitely not," Frey agreed as she began to brush Ona's long, dark-auburn hair. Sitting in the chair, Ona's tired mind wandered. Was she really falling in love with a priest-turned-warrior? Was Pei really the one for her? What about her recurring dream?

"Frey..." Ona addressed her best friend who had always been like an older sister to her.

"Yes, my princess?" Frey happily replied as she gently combed out the hidden knots of Ona's otherwise perfectly shiny strands of hair.

"Do you think Pei is the man from my dreams?"

Frey stopped brushing for a moment and said, "You mean the recurring one you have about the man on the black horse?"

"Yes, that one... the one I've had since I was a child," said Ona, almost as if in a trance.

"Well," Frey said as she continued brushing, "he didn't exactly get here on a big, black horse, but I do think he fits at least a little of what you've told me: the long dark hair, the fiery demeanor. Yes, I suppose it could be him."

Frey looked at her little sister-in-spirit and saw that Ona's face seemed deeply disturbed. "But you know," Frey added with a final stroke of her brush, "dreams are mysterious things... and you never know what they really mean or if they hold any real truth to 'em."

"But... they say recurring dreams tend to be prophetic," Ona stated, her brow knotted with worry.

"Not always," said Frey. "Who can say what the Gods have planned for us?"

Ona nodded again, trance-like.

"What's the matter, my dear?" Frey sympathetically asked as she held Ona's hands.

"I just hope... "

"Yes?" Frey prodded.

"I hope it isn't him."

"Why's that?"

"Well," replied the princess, crawling into her silken bed, "in my dream, the man captures my heart as if it were my very soul. I seem to have no control over myself when I see him. Every time, it's the same. I am in my private gardens and there he is, beautiful as a God with long, dark hair, riding toward me on a black steed. He gets off of his horse and our eyes meet, and as soon as he speaks to me, I am unable to move – as if he is the master of a spell that I am unable to break. It's frightening, Frey!"

"Hush now, Ona," Frey soothed. "It's just a dream. They're supposed to frighten us sometimes." Frey then kissed Ona's forehead, which made the princess smile. "Now, have some more dreams, but have good ones instead."

"That's the strangest part," Ona said with a yawn. "You'd think a dream about a handsome young man on a black horse would be a good dream, and yet, somehow... it's not." Ona looked at Frey with pleading eyes, hoping her handmaid would have the answers. However, Frey had none, and could only give Ona another kiss for comfort. She then turned to leave and said, "Goodnight, sweetheart."

"Goodnight, dearest Frey," Ona whispered in return.

Once Frey had left her room, and Ona knew for certain she was alone in the darkness, the princess' thoughts turned to Pei with his strong jaw and gray-green eyes. She was certain he was not the man of her recurring dream, and yet, he stirred something primal within her.

She was usually rather choosy when it came to men. Because of this, she was still a virgin. Even so, she didn't feel like a child any longer, even if many in the palace still saw her that way, especially her own father.

Spiraling inside sensual fantasies, she wondered if she could replace the man in her recurring dream with this new man of reality. "Pei," she whispered in the darkness, "are you the one for me?"

Uncertain of her destiny, she thought about the man dressed in black and shuddered. *No! I have control over my own fate!* she thought as she shrugged off her fears.

Turning over, she grabbed onto her dark purple covers and burrowed into her pillows. She was determined to have a good dream - maybe even about Pei. There was something about him that gave her hope. His sweetness and strength of will was inspiring, and she hoped they would become close friends, if not more.

Turning off the plasma-lamp in her room by saying the words, "Lights off," she focused on nothing but her mother's gardens and the white flower she was named after. Imagining her mother, Pira, singing her to sleep, Ona found herself forgetting her recurring nightmare. Soon, she was dreaming, but this time about her family and a castle of long ago entirely made of flowers.

--

"I want this man caught!" Atlar demanded. "Then he will pay for the crimes he has committed! Do whatever it takes, both of you."

Baran and Reese nodded and bowed. Even though they were Atlar's closest companions, they were also his subjects, and knew him well enough to know he was not a patient man. When Atlar wanted something or felt passionate about a cause, he would not rest until he accomplished his goal.

In fact, it was his determination and strong will that won him the throne of Kri. Having been born to a brood of six brothers, he learned early in his life to fight for his place among the others. By the time he was fifteen, he was at the top of his class – both in military and in science. However, his father, King Rummund, who was Kri's First General at the time, felt something amiss with his strong, overly competitive sons.

Being a widower who knew little about parenting or tenderness, Atlar's father sent all six of his strapping sons to the planet Deius, hoping they would learn the more metaphysical teachings of Deiusian philosophy. It was Rummund's hope that his sons would become more well-rounded and less competitive by nature.

At first, Atlar was just as bratty and stubborn as his other brothers, wondering why his father had punished him in such a way. In time, however, he became a student of Amun-Lan, and something inside Atlar slowly changed.

He and Meddhi became fast friends, and Atlar's perception of the world had become much broader than that of his brothers. Seeing the universe as a connective thread between every living being, Atlar no longer felt alone or filled with anger. His brothers never quite understood what The Dei had tried to teach them, so they left before finishing their schooling.

While his brothers returned to Kri, Atlar stayed to finish his classes. There, on Deius, he met his true love, Pira, Amya's younger sister, and Atlar changed even more. Love and spirituality guided him in a way his brothers found foolish, and it distanced him away from them all, except for his younger brother, Raifar, who still loved and respected his older brother, despite their misunderstandings.

Knowing he would have to become royalty to win Pira's hand, Atlar vowed to make his dream a reality. As soon as he finished his schooling on Deius, he thanked his teachers, then went home to Kri where he made the announcement to his father, who had been elected King only a few years prior, that he was the only one of his sons worthy to follow in his footsteps.

At first, Rummund laughed, thinking his boastful son was only kidding, but when he saw the seriousness in Atlar's eyes, his face turned cold. Rummund had wanted to educate his sons, but it seemed to him that all he did was make their bloodlust and greed even stronger. Already fed up with his other competitive sons, the king drew out his sword and challenged Atlar to a duel. In doing so, Rummund assumed he'd win, and would teach his son a lesson in the process.

The story, which eventually became famous, was that Atlar had bested King Rummund, but spared his life. Soon after, that daring act made Atlar the new king by popular demand. Rummund was then sent away to live the remainder of his days in exile with his Deiusian concubine.

The truth was a little more complex, however, when Atlar's father later revealed to a select few that he had longed for a quiet life for many years, and was secretly hoping one of them would best him in battle.

He also explained that, after their rigorous duel, Rummund had dared Atlar to kill him, as was the custom on Kri. Atlar, however refused to kill his own father, and threw his sword into the nearby well. Rummund gave a great laugh, then hugged Atlar firmly. He told Atlar he knew Kri was in good hands, then he left, never to return to the palace.

Only Atlar's younger brother, Raifar, and a few of the king's trusted friends knew the truth of what actually happened with his father. Baran and Reese were two such individuals. Neither of them had known Atlar when he was a young man, but they had heard stories from their families, as well as from Atlar himself.

They grew up hearing how Atlar conquered the Ohrian mafia lords of Xen, and how he defended the innocent Sirini women and children when Xen bandits raided their homes during the worst years of The Great Paradox. It seemed to Baran and Reese that Atlar was something of a God – a hero of ancient legend come to life. When Atlar was overwhelmingly voted in as King, Baran and Reese watched as young soldiers-in-training, hoping that, one day, they would have the honor of fighting at his side.

The moment that Baran finally met his hero, and uncle, he

found the king to be even greater than legend. To Baran, Atlar was gentle and loving, much more than Raifar, his own father. Baran soon grew a deep love for Atlar, vowing to be his protector for all time.

Reese' devotion was much the same as Baran's, though more sensual in nature. Many years after Atlar's beloved queen died from plasma poisoning, she found herself giving more than a vow of protection to her king. Reese already loved him as a hero, and when she found him alone one night in tears, she easily gave herself.

At first, she was merely the king's favorite distraction, but soon, she turned into his addiction. Unfortunately, their ongoing affair not only displeased her childhood friend, Princess Ona, but it greatly displeased Baran. Despite his detached behavior, he still yearned for Reese, who was once his true love. If their relationship hadn't ended so terribly, he would have tried to stop her from turning to Atlar, though he had no idea how he would stand against his beloved king.

In time, Baran's need for Reese cooled, and he too found distraction within the arms of many women throughout the kingdom. Much to Reese's disgust, Baran's reputation as a lover almost outweighed his reputation as a Lirhan warrior. Even still, it was Reese's belief that Baran still loved her, just as it was Atlar's belief that Reese still loved Baran. None of them spoke of such things, however, especially not when in the same room.

"Reese," said Atlar, "go to Deius and find out everything you can about Yol Notama. I want to know everything about him: where he goes, what he does, who he speaks with - everything! I want to know what this man eats for breakfast!"

"Yes, my king," Reese quickly replied with a nod.

"And Reese," Atlar added, "be careful. My entire plan hinges on your intel. Don't get caught." Reese nodded with a gleam to her eye.

"Your Majesty," she said with a smirk, "it's me."

Atlar smiled and said, "Yes, I know, but be careful anyway."

"Sire..." Baran interjected.

"Yes?" replied the king.

"What do you wish me to do?"

"Baran," said Atlar, "you must stay here for the time being."

"I beg your pardon, my king?" said Baran, confused and somewhat offended.

Atlar put his arm around Baran and led him a few steps away from Reese.

"Baran, I need you to stay so that you may help convince The Council of my plans," said Atlar, reassuring his disappointed nephew. "Do not worry, though," he added, "when the time comes for a full scale war against Notama and his followers, I will need you to go with me into battle. I assume you will stand at my side when that moment happens."

Baran pressed his fist onto his chest and nodded. "Sire," he proudly replied, "you only need to ask, and I will fight against all who dare dishonor my king and country."

Atlar smiled and said, "Now get some sleep, both of you. I want you at your best for your equally difficult missions."

As they left Atlar's room, Reese walked at Baran's side and grinned. "As if charming blind, old council snakes is a difficult mission," she gibed at Baran under her breath. He smirked and said, "Well, I wouldn't exactly call surveillance work to be all that perilous either, my dear."

Reese smiled, masking her annoyance as well as her attraction for her ex-lover. "At least I have been given a real mission," she taunted back at him.

"Only for now," Baran teased in return. "And when you have brought back the information Atlar seeks to prove his war is just, you can be certain he will hand all future Lirhan assignments back to me." Baran then leaned over Reese and put his arm over her shoulder.

Quickly, she threw off his arm and twirled around, pinning him against the wall. Somewhere between playfulness and anger, Baran and Reese looked at each other with smiling sneers. Surprising her, Baran kissed her passionately. She then pulled back, annoyed, but before she had a chance to speak, he freed himself of her hands and grabbed her arms. This time, he had pinned *her* against the wall, and he wasn't letting go.

Reese smirked. Then, without warning, Baran felt a sharp jab to his groin. Bent over and throbbing in pain, Baran watched as Reese walked past, sauntering down the hall, seemingly proud of her actions. Baran knelt down on the floor, marveling at how beautiful, yet, how deadly she could be.

--

Without warning, Zin stopped dead in his tracks, which made Ayn bump into him and nearly fall over.

"Hey!" Ayn crankily protested.

Zin didn't seem to hear; he was busy staring at something in a shop window. Ayn tried to see what his friend was so enthralled with, but he couldn't be sure since there were so many different objects in the store.

"Ayn..." whispered Zin, "look at it. Isn't it the loveliest thing you've ever seen?"

Ayn looked again through the shop's window, trying his best to see what was catching Zin's eye.

"Um," said Ayn, "what do you see?"

As Ayn looked at Zin's face, he saw a hint of pain in his friend's eyes. Whatever it was that had captured Zin's attention, it was obviously something extremely important to him.

Zin finally pointed at the object, touching his forefinger on the glass of the window. "It's the most beautiful elenon I've ever seen."

"What's an elenon?" Ayn asked.

Zin slowly turned to Ayn, then looked at him as if he had asked him what the sky was. However, instead of answering Ayn's question, he took Ayn's hand and led him into the shop.

As Zin targeted the elenon straight away, Ayn looked around, slack-jawed. He had never seen so many musical instruments! Picking up the eight-stringed instrument, Zin soon began strumming and finger-picking at the same time, which amazed Ayn. He couldn't believe how good Zin was; it was as if he had been playing the instrument his entire life.

The shop filled with sweet harmonics, lulling Ayn into a state of peaceful transcendence. A few minutes went by as Zin played what Ayn assumed to be some sort of old folk music. When Zin finished the song, the last chord he strummed was still ringing in Ayn's ears. The melodic resonance almost made Ayn cry, for it reminded him of the holy songs of his people.

"Zin," said Ayn with a quivering voice, "when did you learn to play so beautifully?"

Gently putting the elenon down on the display window, Zin sighed and gave Ayn a melancholy look. "A long time ago, Ayn," he replied wistfully.

Ayn could feel his soul-friend's sadness as if it were his own.

"How wonderful!" hailed the music shop owner, which caused both Zin and Ayn to whirl around with surprised faces.

"You play like a God, young man!" the owner exclaimed as she excitedly walked over to where they stood. "May I assume," she continued, "that you must have been classically trained as a child?"

Zin looked down at the floor and mumbled something under his breath. Ayn was surprised to see his usually over-confident friend acting in such a way. Still, Ayn could feel how sensitive Zin was about the subject.

"What's that, dear?" asked the bubbly, top heavy shop owner.

Sneering at having to repeat himself, Zin loudly stated, "I said I only trained with a teacher for a short time."

"That's simply amazing!" she giddily replied while clapping her hands. "You were self-taught?!" she added. "How spectacular!"

Zin gave Ayn a thoroughly annoyed look, as if to say, "Let's get out of here!"

"I tell you what, my Ohrian friend," said the buxom woman as she pulled the elenon down from the window. "I'll sell you this rare and authentically hand-crafted elenon for half its worth... on one condition."

Zin raised his eyebrow. "I'm listening," he skeptically said, folding his arms.

"On the condition that you play it at my brother's bar!" she happily replied.

Zin stood silent, dumbfounded.

"You see," she expounded, "my brother, Luceon, runs a very classy club. It's in the city, in the snazzy part of town." The woman then carefully put the elenon in a smooth, black case and said, "I think Luc would love it if you played there a few nights a week. You interested?"

Ayn saw that Zin's eyes had lit up like candles from The Holy Temple, and he felt how much it meant to his friend to play the strange instrument.

Zin swallowed, trying his best to keep his head. "How much are you willing to sell it for?" he asked, cautiously.

"Well," said the woman as she walked to Zin with the elenon in her hand and a gleam in her eye, "I myself came into possession of this rare beauty by the smallest of chances. You see, my brother and I were traveling around the ancient ruins - near the outskirts - where the original Deiusian royal founders first inhabited this planet. Anyway, at the temple for Adin, we came across a band of gypsies who were playing old, religious hymns with this very elenon. They told us that it had been passed down for generations in their family for thousands of years."

She smiled wide, noticing how Zin hung on her every word. "They did not want to part with it, of course," she explained, "but Luc managed to convince them with a good trade. He's a very generous man, my brother. He helped them to get their papers, which would legalize their presence here. They were refugees from Sirin, you see. In return, he and I took this exquisite elenon back home. It is rather rare, but I have a feeling it's finally found its true master, and I have good instincts about these sort of things."

Zin and Ayn were somewhat speechless, and a little winded after listening to her rather lengthy story.

"So, my young Ohrian," she said with a smile, "I'm willing to let you have it for a mere eight hundred. But I really do insist that you play at my brother's club! Who knows? You could be a star!" She winked at Zin, then handed him the instrument in its sleek, black case.

Zin looked as though he was about to cry. He gulped and muttered, "I... I really can't-"

"We'll take it!" Ayn blurted out, much to the surprise of his soul-friend.

"But Ayn!" Zin protested.

"No, Zin," Ayn said, steadfast, "you've gone far too long without music, which I feel is at the heart of your soul! It is *my* money after all, so I will say what we do with it!"

"Yes, but Ayn," Zin argued, "we need that money to stay at a hotel and for food! We have no idea how long we will be staying and-"

"Well, that's not really a problem," the woman interrupted with a grin. "Like I said, my brother is a generous man, and if you are willing to perform at his club, I'm sure he'd set you up somewhere nice. Maybe you can even make it a permanent job. I'm sure he'll be as impressed with your playing as I was."

The full-bodied woman walked to the counter and scribbled something with pen on paper - a rare sight since most used plasma-powered writing tools. "Here," she said as she handed the paper to Zin. "Give this to my brother. Go to Luc's

Lounge in the heart of the city. Play for him like you did for me, and I guarantee he'll set you up."

Zin looked at Ayn who gave him a reassuring smile.

"Thank you," said Zin.

"You're more than welcome, my dear," the woman replied. "And if you ever want to visit me again sometime, my name is Velna. I'd be happy to show you more of my... inventory."

Ayn got the feeling the busty woman was a little attracted to Zin. The idea was slightly alarming to Ayn, considering she looked twice Zin's age. Ayn put his discomfort aside, however, considering how helpful she seemed to be.

"I can't thank you enough, Velna," said Zin. He then reached into his pocket and opened his wallet, handing the woman the eight hundred nex.

"You can thank me by playing that glorious instrument at my brother's bar!" said Velna as she shoved the money into the drawer behind the counter, counting the bills while hungrily placing them inside.

Zin nervously smiled at Ayn, looking for approval.

"It's alright, Zin," comforted Ayn. "I understand how much this elenon means to you. We'll be alright, I'm sure. The Gods will give us help when we need it. We must have faith."

Zin didn't believe in Ayn's Gods, but he hoped Ayn was right. They would indeed need help, and Zin wasn't sure if he could trust Velna or her brother, Luc, or anyone on Xen for that matter.

However, when he looked at the shiny, smooth case with his beautiful new elenon inside, he began feeling as though there might really be Gods watching out for them after all, manipulating their surroundings, and giving them both a new chance at a new life. Unfortunately, the feeling didn't last long as Zin's ever logical Ohrian upbringing snapped him away from such ideas. *I'm being silly,* he thought. *There are no such things as Gods, only chance and will... though I am grateful, nonetheless.*

Ayn sensed that Zin's aura had changed; it was clearer, brighter, more golden-orange. It made Ayn glad, even if it meant they were now down eight hundred nex. Truthfully, Ayn wasn't entirely sure if his statement about the Gods was a correct one, for his faith had been dramatically tested as of late. He was certain, however, that he'd done the right thing in letting Zin buy the elenon.

Ayn suddenly remembered something Meddhi-Lan once told him. It was an old Deiusian proverb that said, "Follow your bliss, and you will become the richest man in The Un."

Ayn smiled, perhaps for the first time since he left Deius. He remembered, not only Meddhi-Lan's warm voice, but the wisdom within his words. "Following your bliss brings pure happiness," said Meddhi-Lan within Ayn's memory, "and *that* is the greatest treasure of all."

"So simple," thought Ayn, *"and yet so true."*

--

"Impossible!" Pei declared as he threw off the silken covers on his bed.

Having tossed and turned more than twenty times since he attempted sleep, Pei was now at the point of completely giving up. How could he rest after such an insane and unbelievably eventful day? His mind was a mix of pain and pleasure with random thoughts streaming into his brain. One minute, he saw Ona's lovely, oval face, and the next, he saw his Lan's blood-soaked body lying motionless before him.

Darting up from his bed, Pei headed toward the large glass doors that loomed on the other side of his room. Frustrated, he opened the doors with vigor, revealing the expansive gardens below. With winding paths of purple and rose-colored flowers amidst the backdrop of tall trees, the gardens overwhelmed his senses. Even in the haze of moonlight, Pei saw its grandeur and was amazed.

Feeling calmer, he became aware that there was something of Ona in the gardens; her aura lingered in the wind. He sensed she had walked in them countless times before. *Perhaps she has felt as lost as I feel now?* he wistfully pondered.

Leaning over the white and gold railing of his terrace, Pei was lost in thought, and didn't hear the knock at his door.

The woman who had been knocking, let herself in, then slyly walked up behind him.

"You know, young priest," she said with a smirk, "it would be all too easy to push you over."

Pei whirled around to see the same red-haired woman Atlar gave orders to in their recent private meeting.

"What are you doing here?" asked Pei as he covered himself up with his robe.

Reese laughed under her breath, then leaned her back against the railing of the terrace, forcing her breasts to protrude slightly from her bronze, full-bodied leather uniform. "Don't get all excited, priest," she said with a grin. "I just wanted to talk with you. May I?"

Pei didn't know what to make of the catty woman in front

of him. There was something dubious about her, and yet, Atlar seemed to trust her, so Pei wanted to as well.

"You may," Pei replied, "but I am no longer a priest so you do not have to refer to me as such. Now, what is it that you wish to talk to me about?"

Reese snickered and said, "My, my... you're so regal and polite, aren't you?"

Pei was utterly perplexed. He could tell she was teasing him, but why? "Well... I..." Pei nervously sputtered.

"That's alright," said Reese as she walked up to him with a wily smile. "What's your name again? Pei? That's alright, dear, don't worry about it. I know you were a Dei priest for most of your life. How could you be anything but diplomatic and... stiff?"

She then gently pressed herself against Pei's body. He could feel his senses reeling uncontrollably as her firm breasts touched his chest.

"Excuse me!" Pei blurted out as he broke away from her closeness. Catching his breath, he quickly walked back to his bedroom. His nervous reaction entertained her as she slowly followed him, grinning like a cat hunting its prey.

"You're excused," she said, laying a hand on her hip.

Pei felt a mix of confused disgust and guilty pleasure. Everything about the woman seemed wrong to him, yet he found her intriguing. From the way she moved to the way she spoke; it all made Pei far too excited to even think.

"What... um... I mean, what is it you wanted to talk to me about, Lady Reese?" he asked, swallowing his nerves. She looked at him and smiled for a moment. She then folded her arms and leaned against the dresser of his room, lifting her right leg up onto a nearby chair.

Pei was certain she was fully aware of her sexual power, though he was determined to act as if he didn't notice. However, as she stood gazing at him with her green cat-eyes and her slightly exposed bosom, it seemed an impossible task.

"Please... just call me Reese," she finally replied.

"But," asked Pei hesitantly, "aren't you a lady of the royal court?"

To that, she gave a hearty laugh and shook her head. After she stopped laughing, her focus centered again on Pei, this time with even more fiery determination. Then, much to Pei's surprise, she walked to him and wrapped her arms around his neck, pressing herself so closely against him that he was certain his body would betray his mind.

"You are just the most adorable thing," Reese cooed as she tickled his mouth with her full, rosy lips.

Pei knew he had to stop the strange, oversexed warrior-woman pressing herself against him, but how? All he could think about was her red lips and curvy, yet muscular body.

Just then, he had a sudden flash of fear. *What if she was sent here to kill me?* he thought in his racing mind. Unable to control his paranoia, he suppressed his excitement and pushed her away.

"I asked you and will not ask again!" he shouted. "What do you wish to talk to me about?"

Reese looked at him with a raised brow. "Oh, I see," she replied in a low voice.

"You see what?" asked Pei, frustrated and confused.

Reese folded her arms and said, "I heard you have a little crush on our dear princess, and I see now that the rumor is true.

So I suppose someone like me just isn't good enough."

Unable to fathom her in the slightest, he curtly replied, "I really don't see how that is any of your business."

Reese grinned and said, "Oh, but it *is* my business, dear priest. You see, you are going to be trained by General Baran himself to become a Lirhan soldier."

"I am?" Pei replied, shocked.

"Yes, dear priest, you are," she said with a smirk, "and when Baran is called to fight, Atlar will probably ask me to continue your training. Now, if I'm going to make an elite soldier out of you, then everything you do from this point on is of interest to me: what you eat, how you sleep, who you desire - everything."

Pei stood silent with his mouth slightly open. He was both frightened and excited about becoming a Lirhan warrior.

Ignoring his state of shock, she added, "Now, I feel I have to warn you, dear priest. Trying to bed Kri's most perfect little princess is tantamount to climbing the highest mountain of Deius... without a rope!"

Releasing a hearty laugh, she annoyed Pei immensely. Refusing to let her teasing get to him, he calmly said, "Lady Reese, I am most appreciative for your concern, but I assure you, I am aware of my own actions, and I know what I am doing."

Reese's smile slowly turned to a look of contempt. "Oh, you pathetic boy," she said with a low, guttural voice, "you have no idea what you're doing. You're a commoner! You think Atlar will allow you to be with his only daughter? And even if he did, that picky little princess is going to take your heart and throw it on the ground where it will crack into a thousand pieces. Just let her go, priest, if you know what's good for you."

Pei shook his head in denial, suppressing his anger.

"Please," he said as he pointed toward the door, holding back from shouting, "just... leave now."

Reese smiled again, but this time with a hint of pacified amusement. "Alright, I'll go," she said as she walked to the door. Stopping before she left, Reese turned back around and said, "but do me a favor and re-think your future, not only about your silly desire for that spoiled princess, but also about becoming a Lirhan. We are an elite group who live and breathe for the truth of Krian morals. We live and breathe and DIE by those morals, and if you aren't willing to put your entire body and soul into the training you're about to receive, then you will fail... and probably die."

With those icy words, Reese swiftly left his room, leaving Pei to feel as though he had just been hit by a tornado.

Will this day's raging storm never cease? he silently asked the Gods.

Exhausted, he locked his door, then flung himself on his bed. His thoughts raced, but soon turned into nothingness inside a deep void where only dreams were welcome.

Chapter 18: Topsy Turvy

*L*uc's lounge wasn't as far as Ayn feared it would be. They had hailed a hover-car that took them directly into the heart of the city, and it had arrived at the club in less than fifteen minutes.

As Ayn and Zin walked up to the arched entrance, they saw a big sign above that read, "Luc's Lounge." Walking inside the club, they saw a few locals exiting at the same time. Ayn had to look twice at the appearance of one of the people walking by them. The creature was a woman, but she looked a little like a lizard with protruding eyes and green skin. She made Ayn wonder what sort of strange beings lived on X-314.

They slowly entered the smoke filled club and saw a circular room with a round stage in the center of it, giving the entire place a feeling of intimacy, especially between the patrons and the performers who played there. At that particular moment, there were five musicians playing on the stage with instruments Ayn had never seen. The musicians looked exotic and new to him as well, and they seemed similar to the lizard-woman who had walked past him on the way in.

Is Xen an outpost for these lizard people? Ayn thought, somewhat frightened. *Where did they originally come from? Were they born on this planet? Why didn't the priests teach me about these types of people?*

Zin turned with a big smile on his face and said, "This place is fantastic!" He had to shout above the loud, upbeat music that the lizard-like musicians were playing. Ayn shook his head, confused and uncomfortable. "I wonder where Luc is?" Zin shouted again.

They looked around, seeing a myriad of beings, many Ayn never knew existed. There were men with faces like horses, complete with tails and hooves. There were even women with multi-breasted bosoms. Looking at them, Ayn became quickly embarrassed, so he instead looked over at Zin who was obsessively staring at the bizarre women.

"Stop it!" Ayn said as he nudged Zin's shoulder.

"What?" Zin replied, feigning innocence through a devilish grin.

Ayn nervously smiled in return. Looking around the club, they both couldn't believe the variety of patrons. *Where did they all come from?* wondered Ayn.

"Can I get you two boys a drink?" came a voice from behind. They turned around and saw that the voice came from a young woman who looked to Ayn to be of Deiusian origin. She had two arms and two legs, and Ayn was comforted by her normality.

"Sure!" said Zin, happily.

"Do you want to sit at a table or at the bar?" she asked, smiling at Zin in particular.

"A table would be wonderful," Zin replied flirtatiously. Ayn rolled his eyes, but followed behind as the Deiusian girl led them to a round, clear-colored table. When they sat down, she gave them a menu showing prices for drinks and food.

"Take your time," said the waitress, "and I'll be back to get your order." She winked at Zin, then walked away. Both boys uncontrollably watched her as she walked away, mainly because her bottom was noticeably peeking out from under her skirt.

"Do you think that's the normal attire on this planet?" asked Ayn.

"I hope so!" replied Zin who was smiling from ear to ear.

Just as Ayn was about to scold his friend, they were distracted by a man who jumped onto the stage. He had shaggy, blond hair and was dressed in a purple vest with a silky blue shirt and pants.

"Ladies and gentlemen!" the shaggy-haired man announced. "I have the deepest pleasure to bring you the one, the only... Lady Raven!"

The crowd seemed to know the Lady Raven woman because they erupted into eager applause and whistles. Ayn and Zin both looked at each other, wondering what sort of entertainer was about to take the stage.

As the lights went down, they heard a voice; it was eerie, yet lilting and calm. The voice then became louder and turned into a smooth, pleasing tone. When the lights rose on the stage, they saw her; it was Lady Raven, and she was gorgeous. She had a black satin gown draping down her lithe body with the shoulder straps half falling off her pale shoulders.

As they listened to her sing, they found themselves intoxicated by her soothing, tantalizing voice. There was only one thing that distracted Ayn about the singer; she had wings. He didn't know if they were part of her dress, but they appeared to be coming from her back and hovered over her like looming, black clouds. Even with such an oddity, however, Ayn thought she may be the most beautiful creature he had ever seen. Zin seemed smitten as well.

Neither one of them could think about food or drink while listening to Lady Raven's voice, but as soon as her set ended, and the roaring applause finally died down, Ayn's stomach grumbled loudly, reminding him of his hunger. Ayn then glanced at the menu's prices and found them a little high. He didn't really care though; he was desperate.

"What should we have to eat?" Ayn asked Zin who was still looking at the remaining musicians on the stage, mesmerized. Distracted, Zin replied, "What?"

Ayn shook his head. He knew Zin was lost in the music and couldn't be bothered at the moment with food.

When the Deiusian waitress came back to their table to take their order, Ayn took it upon himself to order for the both of them. He ordered something called a "Wet Wonder" for Zin and a "Teal Tornado" for himself. He had no idea what kind of drinks they were, but their pictures on the menu looked fun and tasty. As for dinner, he ordered "Blue-fin Salad" and "MahMah Stew." Both were Deiusian, vegetarian dishes he had dined on as a child when he would visit his mother at The Royal Palace. It gave him comfort to have a tiny bit of home, at least for the moment.

As Ayn was about to tell Zin how he felt, he noticed his Ohrian friend was no longer seated at their table. He looked around the club, but couldn't see Zin anywhere.

Just as a dread panic was beginning to take hold, filling Ayn's head with irrational, fearful thoughts, such as being all alone in the city at night, he saw his silver-haired friend standing at the foot of the stage. Ayn was immediately relieved, though he wondered what Zin was doing.

The waitress brought the drinks to their table, and as Ayn took a sip of his strangely bitter, yet surprisingly refreshing drink, he saw Zin standing next to Lady Raven. Zin seemed to be flirting with nothing but his body language. Ayn had to laugh at his friend, for he reminded Ayn of when Pei was younger and would behave nervously in front of their Lan during a difficult lesson. The memory made Ayn so homesick that he almost felt like throwing up his intensely strong drink. Would he ever see Pei again? Was Pei even alive? Ayn had no idea.

Just then, Zin turned around to face Ayn and held up his thumb, as if signaling some sort of assurance. Ayn's thoughts started swimming, which made him unable to process whatever Zin was trying to tell him.

Baffled and drunk, Ayn watched Zin step onto the stage with Lady Raven. Holding his elenon in his hand, Zin smiled like a child on his birthday. Ayn smiled along with him, moved by his friend's happiness, and for a few moments, Ayn was briefly taken away from his own moody, pensive mind.

As Ayn ate his salad, he listened to Zin play the elenon to perfection. The music was an elegant piece Ayn had never heard before. It was slow, soft, and sensual. Mixed with Lady Raven's smooth, bewitching voice, the music filled the room with a mellow, nearly liquid mood. Ayn could feel his spirits lift while watching Zin play his new elenon. It seemed to Ayn's woozy brain as if he were watching a God in The Un who was creating a new star in the heavens.

"He's amazing, isn't he?" came a booming voice. Ayn looked around and saw a man sitting backwards in Zin's seat.

He was the announcer with the shaggy, blond hair. "Now THIS is the kind of musician I've been looking for!" he loudly said over Zin's music. "Sorry," said the shaggy-haired man, "let me introduce myself. I'm Luc and I run this joint." The man reached over and shook Ayn's hand firmly. "You're not from around here, are you?" asked Luc as he smirked at Ayn with squinty, blue eyes.

"No, not really," replied Ayn.

"I didn't think so!" laughed Luc. "You must be from Deius."

Ayn nearly spat out his drink.

"Ha! It's alright, kid," added Luc, highly amused, "I won't hold that against you."

Ayn looked at Luc, confused. He was relieved that Luc didn't seem to know he was The Bodanya, but he also wondered how Luc knew he was from Deius, and why he would hold anything against someone if they were. The man seemed odd to Ayn and just as alien to him as Lady Raven with her black, curved wings.

"Anyway," Luc continued as Ayn and Zin's dishes arrived, "don't you agree?"

Ayn took his first bite of the delicious MahMah stew, and then, with a mouthful of stew, he burbled out, "Agree? About what?" He then swallowed what felt like the most satisfying food he'd ever eaten.

"About your friend up there!" Luc exclaimed with a laugh. "He's fantastic! The best musician I've seen in a long time! And he's handsome as well, which is definitely a plus when drawing in the crowds."

Ayn nervously nodded and smiled, hoping Zin would be done playing his music soon so that he would come and talk with this Luc person himself. There was something about him that made Ayn feel rather itchy and anxious.

The song finally ended as Lady Raven bowed to Zin, gesturing with her hand to the audience to show who had been playing the beautiful music. Zin proudly bowed with an exuberant smile. He then rushed to the table where Ayn and Luc were sitting.

"Did you see that, Ayn?" gushed Zin. "My father would be shocked!" Zin was about to say even more, but when he saw that Ayn was not alone at the table, he quickly stopped himself.

"Congratulations, my silver-haired friend!" said Luc as he stood up to shake Zin's hand. "You really are a fine elenon player."

"Um," Zin nervously muttered, "thank you."

"Sorry," said Luc, laughing as he stood. "I suppose you want to eat now. Where are my manners? I really can be an old Sirin-fish."

Ayn couldn't help but giggle.

"I was just so caught up in your musical talent!" Luc exclaimed as he pulled up another chair. Zin, who was rather confused, and somewhat skeptical of the strangely jovial man, placed his elenon carefully down beside the table, then sat down in his chair. He took a look at the stew and grimaced. By Zin's reaction, Ayn gathered MahMah stew wouldn't have been Zin's first choice in entrees. Ayn didn't understand. *Anyone who doesn't like MahMah stew is clearly out of their minds!* thought Ayn.

"So, you liked my performance?" asked Zin as he took a bite of his salad.

"Liked it?" replied Luc. "I loved it! You are a gifted young musician, my boy!"

Ayn noticed that Luc had a few rings on his fingers, as well as a necklace made of what looked to be rubies and emeralds. Ayn didn't know if Luc's affluent appearance meant he was rich or if his jewelry were merely fancy-looking fakes, giving him the appearance of wealth.

Either way, Luc seemed to appreciate clothing and had a flair for fashion. Ayn noticed Luc had on black, Ohrian style boots, which were made out of some kind of smooth skin, perhaps whale or Tokani, though most Deiusian sea mammals were endangered, so he doubted Luc would be wearing their skins. Then again, he didn't know what sort of man Luc was. *Perhaps he is exactly the type to wear the skins of an endangered animal,* Ayn mused. He then bit into a mushroom, trying not to think about it further.

"Thanks, my friend," said Zin. "Hey, you wouldn't happen to know a man named Luceon, would you?"

The shaggy-haired man gave a hearty laugh. "Yes, my boy," he giddily replied, "I think I may know the fellow!" Luc again laughed, stomping the floor with his boots.

Ayn looked at Zin and nudged his head to the left, attempting to communicate to his friend that the man sitting there was actually the owner of the club. Zin seemed to understand the signal and smiled nervously.

"I am the man you're looking for, and I am completely at your service," said Luc as he scooted in toward Zin. His somewhat dramatic, overtly friendly behavior didn't bother Zin all that much, but Ayn became more and more uncomfortable. *Is this man physically attracted to Zin?* Ayn wondered, a little shocked. Having no experience with other cultures or laws other than those of The Holy City on Deius, Ayn felt clueless and naive.

Unfazed by Luc's closeness, Zin reached into his pants pocket and pulled out the letter given to them by Luc's sister, Velna. He handed it to Luc, smiled at Ayn, and then continued to munch on his salad. Ayn couldn't help but marvel at his friend's nonchalant confidence.

"Ah! Great minds think alike!" exclaimed Luc after reading Velna's note to him. "My sister and I are twins, you know. 'Course, I'm the better looking one!" Luc gave another hearty laugh, then threw his arm around Zin's shoulder. "Alright, my young Ohrian wonder," Luc continued, "here's my proposition! Since I'm a generous man, and I've also been blessed with the gift of knowing a good thing when I see it, I'll hire you for two nights a week with free room and board at my extended stay hotel as your starting pay. If you do well, which I'm sure you will, I'll add you to the lounge's regular roster of performers, and you'll get a handsome salary! So, what do you say, kid? Does that sound good to you?"

Trying his best to seem aloof, Zin paused, took a sip of his drink, then replied, "Sounds... promising."

"Wonderful!" Luc practically shouted as he stood up and clapped.

Ayn wondered if the bar owner's dramatically flamboyant behavior was common on Xen or if it was just him.

"Now, do you play anything else or just the elenon?" Luc asked excitedly.

"I can play any instrument set in front of me," Zin replied, cool as a winter night's breeze.

Luc howled in amusement. "Marvelous!" he exclaimed. "I expect you to start tomorrow night! You'll open for Lady Raven and play as her soloist! Just you wait, kid, the crowds will come from everywhere to see you!"

"How much will he be paid?" asked Ayn, unaware of the impropriety of his question.

Luc laughed his boisterous laugh and grabbed Ayn and Zin's shoulders, which made Ayn wince a little. "I simply adore the both of you!" Luc wailed. "I tell you what," he said as he caught his breath from laughing, "how about we discuss those details tomorrow before you play? You go ahead and enjoy your dinner, which is on the house, by the way. Everything will work itself out like the very Un does in heaven!"

He winked at them and turned to leave. However, he didn't leave. Luc snapped his fingers and turned back around. "Oh!" he dramatically shouted. "I almost forgot to tell you where my cousin's hotel is! You honestly can't miss it. Just turn right once you leave here, and go a few blocks down. It's within walking distance, and the sign is hard to ignore! It's the only one with those big, blue waves on the top. It really is the best hotel in the city! Just check your pretty selves in, and I'll arrange everything else." With that, Luc winked at them once more, then finally left their table.

Ayn raised his eyebrows at Zin with a mix of confusion and fear. Zin smiled at him in return. "Don't worry," Zin said between sips of his drink. "Like the man said, everything will work itself out... like The Un does in heaven."

Ayn gazed at Zin who was happily eating his dinner. Unable to understand his friend's carefree attitude, Ayn sighed and shook his head, which was still reeling from the Teal Tornado. Everything felt like it was spinning: the room, his whole entire life.

--

Reese didn't like the idea of her best friend from childhood playing with a sweet man's affections like that. How could Ona be capable of such cruelty? There was just no way that a Krian princess would be allowed to court a Deiusian priest, and Reese was sure Ona knew of that fact.

Unless... thought Reese, *Ona has truly fallen in love and is willing to fight her kingdom's conventions, and perhaps her own father, just to be with him.* Reese wondered if Ona had finally grown up and forgotten that silly dream about the man on the black horse.

Walking down the hall, deep in thought and unsuspecting of any danger, Reese didn't notice the man's hand aiming for her mouth. In a flash, she felt herself being dragged away and shoved into a corner behind a pillar.

She was about to bite the man's hand off when she realized whose hand it was. Baran quickly gestured for her to be quiet with his finger against his lips. He then pointed to two men who were down the hall dressed in hooded robes and looking around them, as if wary of being caught. She soon realized that Baran had been watching them, and he wanted her to witness the secret meeting of these men as well. As Baran slowly released his grip from her mouth, she smirked at him, then joined him in carefully spying on the suspicious men in robes.

"Did anyone follow you here?" asked one of the men with a gravelly voice. In an instant, Baran and Reese recognized the voice; it belonged to Octian. The eldest of the councilmen, Octian's voice was distinctive in its low, scratchy tone.

"No, I don't think so," said the other man, whose voice was much younger and unrecognizable.

"Good," replied Octian, shifty-eyed. "We need to be as discreet as possible."

Taking one last look to his sides, Octian gestured for the other man to follow him. He then put his hand on the knee of the statue of the Goddess Verlo, which was located behind them. Much to Reese and Baran's surprise, the statue turned and revealed an opening to a secret passageway. They both had known of such passageways, but were shocked that someone like Octian would be aware of them as well.

"In there?" asked the young man, alarmed.

"Don't worry, Darvis, my boy," said Octian. "It is safe... and more importantly, it is extremely private."

Darvis... thought Baran. He remembered the young man, but only vaguely from his youthful school days. Baran was older than Darvis by a few years, but Baran remembered him to be mild mannered and polite with an attraction to the arts. *Why in the world is Darvis following a man like Octian into a secret chamber?* he questioned silently. Baran knew there was only one way to find out.

As Baran prepared to follow them, Reese held him back by his arm. "Do you ever think before you move?" she hissed in a whisper. Baran sneered at her. "Give them some time to think they're alone," she advised, "and then follow. When they are discussing their plans, record whatever you hear." She smiled wickedly as she tapped the black button that was usually concealed by her collar. It was times like these Baran remembered why he had once allowed himself to fall so madly in love with her.

Baran waited a few moments, then carefully pursued Octian and Darvis into the secret passageway. Reese followed close behind him, silent and quick like a thief in the night.

Their Lirhan training prepared them for moments like this, and they were ready for any situation, even at home when all seemed safe. As they quietly weaved through the dimly lit passageway, they could barely see the figures of Octian and Darvis, who seemed to be exiting through a secret door. As Baran and Reese approached where they had last seen the two men, all they found was a stone wall. Reese knew better, however, and grinned at Baran with her catty smile.

"Fold your hands and give me a lift," she said in a low, hushed voice.

"What? Why?" he whispered in reply.

"Just do it," she ordered.

Baran shook his head, then folded his hands together tightly with his palms upward. He had done such things before with Reese when they were in the Xen war together, as well as all throughout their Lirhan training days, but it had been a long time and he had forgotten how capable Reese was when executing acrobatic stunts.

She placed her foot on his folded hands, then jumped into the air. Grabbing onto the top of the stone wall, she pulled herself up and stood on the narrow ledge. Smiling with pride, she winked at Baran and began searching with her hands for something on the wall above the ledge.

Baran had no idea what Reese was up to, but he knew her well enough to trust she knew what she was doing. Reese wasn't Atlar's top Lirhan spy without good reason.

Sure enough, she seemed to find what she was looking for: a knob of some kind. As she slowly turned the knob clockwise, Baran noticed that a triangular shaped window was becoming visible near Reese's head. The clear window had not been there before, at least not that Baran had seen.

Reese looked out the window for a moment, then quickly took out a rolled up twine from her pocket and began lowering the twine down to Baran. Grabbing onto the sturdy twine, he was pulled up by Reese, and was soon able to stand on the ledge next to her. As he stood there, balancing, he marveled at her talent and skill. She never ceased to amaze him.

Reese pointed to the window. "This is an ancient peering window," she whispered.

Baran had read of peering windows in stories as a child, but never believed they were real. According to legend, a person could see and hear the objects on the other side, but couldn't be seen or heard in return – mainly because they were made of crystals that were enchanted by the ancient "magic" of the legendary Krian elders. It seemed ridiculous to Baran to think that these magic windows were real, but the window they were now peering through seemed to fit the description in the stories perfectly. The only question was if the people on the other side could see them in return.

Reese pointed at the window once again, this time showing Baran that the men they were following were now in a secret room on the other side of the window. "Oh, look," she said with a catty smirk on her face, "it's good old Octian and that poor Darvis fellow. Hmm... I wonder what they're talking about?"

Her smirk grew into a full blown grin as she turned the knob from before, but this time, just a sliver counter clockwise.

Baran could now hear their voices, clear as bells.

"Brilliant!" he exclaimed. Baran immediately worried that Octian and Darvis would hear him, but that didn't seem to be the case since they kept on talking, as if they were entirely alone.

"But don't you see, Darvis?" said Octian. "The king only does what *he* wants without thought for his council or even his country! In fact, if it suits him, he freely sends young men to their deaths, simply because he wants to win!"

"That isn't true," Darvis replied in his soft-spoken manner. "I know that you are speaking from a place of great pain, considering what happened to your son. Believe me, I was Leif's friend so I feel your pain, but..."

"He was my ONLY son!" Octian passionately interrupted.

"Yes... I know," Darvis replied like a dog who had been scolded by his master. "Forgive me, wise elder. I realize what a terrible ordeal his death must have been for you. But how can you, in good conscience, blame King Atlar for Leif's death?"

"Easily!" Octian shouted as he crossed the secret room,

which looked like a small library, barely lit by the plasma-candles hanging on its stony walls.

"I am sorry if I offend, Councilman Octian," said Darvis, biting his lip, "but I was under the impression that your son willingly joined the war of his own volition?"

Octian slowly turned around to face Darvis. With a snarl, the gray-haired councilman lifted his chin proudly and adjusted his Krian broach, which clasped to his shoulder, as if the act of doing so could somehow hold back the rage deep within him.

"I'm afraid you don't quite understand, my dear boy," Octian calmly replied. "My son believed in Atlar's convictions the way a child follows a God - a mighty Warrior-God - without flaw. But that is far from the truth, for I know the king too well. He is my younger brother after all."

"You are brother to the king?!" Darvis asked in shock.

Baran was almost as shocked as Darvis that his secretive, distant uncle, who usually kept his royal relations to himself, would tell Darvis the truth about his family. Reese was not as shocked, but she found it strange as well.

"Yes," Octian answered in a glum voice, "I was even designated to be the next in line as First General, and possibly king, like my father before me. But that all changed when Atlar fought my father for his title. Such ego! Such impudence!"

Darvis nodded and listened with genuine interest.

"All my life, I've watched as Atlar simply took what he wanted," continued Octian, "without care how it may hurt those around him. First, he took the throne by defeating our father, making The Council believe he was some kind of hero, which he was most certainly not. I refuse to deem a man a hero by how many wars they have won. Then, he took his wife by threatening Deius with war if they did not allow the marriage to proceed."

"That is untrue," said Baran, incensed. "Queen Pira fell in love with Atlar. Everyone knows that." Reese smirked, then shushed him, patting Baran's shoulder.

"Finally," said Octian, "he took my son's life, as well as many more Krian sons, when he declared war against the Ohrian mob who controlled Xen. It was a useless, shameful, stupid war that we never should have entered. I even warned him that Kri would fail to conquer Xen! But did he believe me or even listen to my advice? Of course not! He is a foolish, brash brute and always has been since he was a child!"

Darvis didn't seem to know how to respond to Octian's ranting. Instead, he stood, thunderstruck and speechless. Baran, however, was appalled by Octian's charges and was doing his best to control his anger.

"I am very sorry for your loss," Darvis said in a soft voice.

"I don't want you to be sorry," Octian replied, "I want you to be loyal."

"Loyal?" Darvis repeated, confused.

"Yes, loyal - loyal to Kri, to your people, and to me as well, for I am your mentor and your true friend. You were always there for my son, and now, I will be here for you."

Darvis stood for a moment in perplexed silence.

"What..." Darvis slowly replied, "do you want me to do, Octian?"

The old man smiled. He then took out an Ohrian transmitter from a pocket inside his robe and handed it to Darvis.

"I want you to keep watch... and I want you to listen and learn everything you can about what the king has planned." Octian motioned for Darvis to hide the transmitter on him somewhere. "Don't let anyone see you using this mechanism. It is Ohrian made, and there would be wagging tongues about using such technology while Ohr is suspect in helping overthrow the Deiusian royal line."

Darvis nodded, hiding the transmitter inside his robe.

"Good. You've always been a clever, good boy, Darvis. That is why I've chosen you as my protegee. That is why my son loved you so, and that is why you will help me expose Atlar as the greedy, blood thirsty, unfit king he truly is."

Darvis' face looked plagued with a mix of guilt, pain and sadness. It was clear to Baran that he was not a bad person, but young and full of sorrow, which Octian preyed upon.

"I will do my best to honor you and the memory of Leif, your beloved son and my most treasured friend," Darvis said, fighting tears.

Octian nodded stoically. "Yes, I know you will," he replied, giving his apprentice a tender, fatherly hug. Baran turned to Reese and saw that she was twisting the curls at the ends of her wavy, red hair. It was a habit of hers and one that used to make his heart pound with love... back when he allowed himself to feel that way for her. Now, however, he took it as a sign that she was hatching a scheme. It brought a smile to Baran's face as he thought, *Some things never change.*

--

They couldn't believe what they saw. Luc hadn't exaggerated; his cousin's hotel was the most beautiful and luxurious that either of the sheltered princes had ever seen. There was a grand entrance with a huge fountain in the shape of a Sirin-fish, which periodically spit out rainbow-colored water. Even more impressive was a giant, crystalline, plasma-powered lifting machine that took them to their spacious rooms. All of it was a glorious feast for their young, inexperienced eyes.

When they entered their rooms via their swiping cards made of smooth silver, Zin instinctively ran to the balcony. He opened the aqua, seashell-shaped doors that seemed made of the same smooth type of material as their entry cards. He then stood on the balcony and took a deep breath of Xenite air, which he commented to Ayn was much cleaner smelling than that of Lesnia, his own city on Ohr. Ayn too could smell the difference, although Deius had reduced their plasma use in recent years. He remembered that his mother had made plasma reduction one of her final decisions before passing. The memory made Ayn sad, yet proud as well.

"Can you see it?" asked Zin as he motioned for Ayn to stand with him on the balcony.

"See what?" asked Ayn who couldn't really see much now that it was nighttime.

"Look! It's that old Xen temple in the distance! Remember, Ayn? We saw it as we took The Chord into the city."

Ayn leaned over the silver railing and squinted. As his eyes adjusted to city lights ahead, he saw the temple as well and felt a surge of warmth in his soul.

"I see it now," Ayn said with a smile, "and if I remember correctly, it was called Hithra Temple."

"That's right," added Zin with a smile as pleased as Ayn's. For a moment, they both felt at peace.

Unfortunately, Ayn's fragile heart couldn't allow the good feeling to last. Unable to suppress his memory of Meddhi-Lan's death, he frowned, distracted by the pain. Trying his best to focus on the moment, Ayn looked at the abandoned temple in the horizon and wondered about its origins.

"Zin," Ayn said in a somber tone, "why do you think my people built a temple here?"

"Well, it was a long, long time ago, Ayn," replied Zin as he sat down on a balcony chair and took out his elenon. "Who knows what their reasons were," he added as he began fingering the strings, "other than their usual reason: to spread their so-called enlightenment."

Ayn hated when Zin talked that way about his people - with such condescending sarcasm. Why couldn't he respect and appreciate all the different views and religions of The Un? Why couldn't he view their diversity as being part of the great knowledge of life? Ayn shook his head, telling himself that his new friend just didn't know any better and that he should try to feel pity for him.

Ayn relaxed, listening to Zin play the elenon for a while until both of them became exhausted - Ayn especially so. When Zin stopped playing, he noticed Ayn had fallen asleep in his chair. Zin couldn't help but smile, tickled by the sight.

Zin scooped his sleeping friend into his arms, which surprised Ayn who had entered the early stages of dreaming. He then lay Ayn down on one of the two beds in their room. The blankets were soft and warm with the texture of smooth, downy fur. It made Ayn feel somewhat comforted, despite his still aching heart.

Zin pulled up the covers and tucked Ayn in, much like he would if Ayn were his own little brother.

"Zin..." said Ayn with a tired voice.

"Yes, Ayn?"

"Can you stay with me... till I fall asleep?"

Zin smiled, nodding his head. He was reminded of how mentally young Ayn could still seem, which Zin believed was entirely the fault of The Dei priests.

Zin then opened the covers and lay next to his sleepy friend. "Everything will be alright, Ayn. You'll see," he said, trying his best to comfort his new soul-friend. "Our lives will be better than before, I promise."

Ayn pouted and turned away from Zin, curling his knees toward his chest. "That is quite a promise, Zin," he sadly replied. Ayn waited for Zin to say something, but he did not. Ayn looked behind him and saw that Zin had fallen sleep. Looking closely at the sleeping Ohrian prince, Ayn watched how the gills on Zin's neck opened and closed ever so slightly in unison with his breathing. It fascinated Ayn and put him in a trance-like stupor.

Soon, they were both fast asleep, forgoing the pain of waking life for the soothing calm of the subconscious void.

--

"It is not for you to decide!" yelled the man with white hair and sharp jawline. "How DARE you make such decisions for the people without consulting us first?!"

Ayn didn't know where he was or who was shouting, but he knew that the man was shouting at him, and yet, not him. Was this a dream?

He looked around and saw familiar faces, though none he could immediately name. Everything seemed like his old palace, and yet, it was vastly different. The walls were blue instead of white, and the ceiling was triangular instead of oval. There were plants in every corner, giving the palace a tropical feel. It all seemed foreign to Ayn, but familiar as well.

He looked down at his hands and could see they were bigger than his own, manlier and more defined. Even stranger, he saw that the top side of his hands were tattooed, inked in blue and gold. They looked like images of a winged, feline creature, much like the cat-bird he recently encountered. *Was that real or was that a dream?* thought Ayn as he began losing grip on reality.

Panicked, he searched for a mirror to determine who he was and where he was located. He could hear the white-haired man shouting about rules and traditions and other things that Ayn didn't want to hear.

Racing to find his old room in the palace, he nearly knocked over one of the man-sized vases that held the over-sized, green, alien-looking plants.

"Watch yourself!" scolded a woman who was wearing a white dress with a white wreath of ona flowers on her head. She was familiar to him, but he didn't know why.

He apologized, then continued searching for his old room. It HAD to be there!

He finally found it, but when he opened the door, all that remained was ash and rubble. Then he remembered that his home had been blown apart, and someone had murdered his beloved father... or teacher. He wasn't sure.

"You shouldn't be here," said a familiar voice coming from the doorway. It was a priest in a black robe.

It was Pei! He had come to rescue him!

No... wait. It wasn't Pei. it was someone else, but with Pei's eyes. *Is he someone Pei used to be?* thought Ayn, utterly confused.

"Please!" Ayn begged as he grabbed the man by the arm. "Please help me!"

The man with Pei's eyes shook his head, taking a step backward. "You should have asked me for help before," he replied, emotionless.

Ayn felt the man's coldness as if it were a blast of cool air from the legendary mountains of Sirin.

Sirin... The planet's name suddenly gave him a jolt.

"Pei," Ayn addressed the cold priest, "what happened to Sirin? Where are all the mountains and plants that used to grow there like weeds? What happened to the rushing oceans and the giant trees? Pei! Why did you never tell me what happened? You're my Lan now! I demand that you tell me!"

The man with Pei's eyes merely looked at Ayn with a melancholic, deadened glare.

"You should have asked me about all that before," said the man, stoic and unfeeling.

"How could I?!" Ayn shouted in tears. "How could I know that my training would stop short like this? How was I to know that Meddhi-Lan would die?! Why do all the priests think I'm the one who can stop this insane universe from doing what it wants to?! What do you think I am, a God?! Well, I'm not! Do you hear me, Pei?! I'm not your Bodanya, and I can't stop The Un from dying! I can't!"

Ayn stood with tears of frustration streaming down his face, his shoulders heaving after screaming at the man with all his anguish.

As he waited for a response from the man with Pei's eyes,

he noticed that the man's ears were bleeding, and not just his ears, but his eyes too! *Is this my doing?* Ayn asked himself, trembling in fear. *No! I couldn't have done this!* he silently told himself. *I couldn't be capable of such an act of evil!*

The man with Pei's eyes slowly collapsed and began bleeding from every orifice on his body. It was grotesque and horrific, shocking Ayn to his core.

"Oh dear Gods, what have I done?!" shouted Ayn. He looked down at his tattooed hands and saw that the cat-birds were moving with their claws extended, as if they were trying to scratch their way off his hands.

"Help me! Help me, Gods, please! Help me!"

Ayn darted up from his bed, his heart racing. Droplets of sweat fell down his forehead as he came to his senses.

It was only a dream, he thought. *Thank The Gods!*

He threw off his blanket, and then stood up, fumbling around in the darkness. After hitting the night table with his knee, which tempted him to curse, he finally found the bathroom.

The water from the faucet felt like the cooling sensation of the Sirini plant, Oonwa, when applied to a sunburn.

Had he dreamt something about Sirin plants? Yes, it was something about how they used to be abundant, unlike the barren drylands of modern Sirin. *Was there something else?* wondered Ayn. *I'm forgetting something important, I can feel it.*

As he ran his hands under the water, Ayn felt his stomach turn with an uncomfortable, subconscious knowledge. There had indeed been more, far more, but he didn't want to remember. He could sense it was an awful dream and didn't want to recall it.

Once he had splashed his face with water a few times, Ayn

clumsily walked back to the bed. Zin was still fast asleep, which made Ayn glad for his friend's sake, but also a little sad that he was alone in the dark with no one to talk to.

Ayn hated being alone, now more than ever. He decided not to bother Zin and crawled into the bed nearby. His mind kept on racing, forcing him to amuse himself with other thoughts so that he wouldn't remember his horrible dream.

Desperately needing distraction, Ayn picked up a gadget of some kind that was sitting on the night table near his bed. It was smooth, oval shaped, and obviously Ohrian, as so many machines and gadgets seemed to be on Xen.

Ayn played with the object until it became activated by something he had pressed, though he wasn't sure how it happened. Lights twinkled around it and a feminine, yet machine-like voice said, "Command, please."

Ayn was afraid the voice would wake Zin, but he didn't budge.

"Command, please."

"Uh... um," said Ayn, nervously, "I would like to fall asleep."

Ayn noticed that the gadget itself showed the word "processing" in Deiusian letters. *How strange*, he thought. Why would an Ohrian device have its language set for Deiusian?

"Would you like suggestions to help you sleep?" asked the gadget.

"Yes, please," said Ayn, amused.

"Do you wish to watch a serenity hologram?"

"Um... sure," Ayn replied in a shrug.

Again, it showed the word "processing."

Finally, it said, "Please designate your desired setting."

Ayn didn't know what to say.

"Please designate."

"Okay!" he loudly whispered, trying not to wake Zin, "I want to see my home. I want to see Deius!"

Again, it read, "processing."

After a few moments, Ayn was amazed at what he saw. Directly in front of where the doors to the balcony were, an image appeared. It was The Royal Palace of Deius. It wasn't just a picture, however; it was the most realistic hologram he had ever seen. It was as if he could reach out and touch the golden stones that covered the palace of The Holy City.

Ayn became breathless and burst into tears. He knew he'd never see his home again, and even if he did, it would never be the same. Its beauty was in shambles. How could it have survived?

Just then, as he was wiping his tears with his hands, he felt something move on the bed near his feet. He focused his eyes, but couldn't see anything there.

"Don't cry, young Bodanya," purred the cat-bird creature while slowly becoming visible. "When you are king, all will be restored to your home, and peace will return once again to your people."

Ayn couldn't believe that the cat-bird was now in his room. *How did he get in?* thought Ayn.

"I can go where I please... when I feel like it anyway," said the creature as he licked its paws, looking like he was calmly grooming himself.

"But... how? And how did you know what I was going to ask you?" questioned Ayn.

"Oh, it's just something I was born with. Same as how you were born with your natural abilities."

"What natural abilities?" Ayn asked, pouting.

The cat-bird frowned at him and said, "Why are you so unaware of yourself, Bodanya?"

"Can you please stop calling me that!" blurted Ayn, raising his voice, just above a whisper.

"Fine then," said the creature, who nonchalantly climbed on Ayn's chest, nestling into him like a real cat would, "but if I'm to call you by your birth name, then from now on, you must call me Axis."

"Axis? Is that your birth name?"

"Well, it's as close to it as you Deiusians could understand."

Axis began purring louder and lightly scrunched his paws, one after the other into Ayn's chest.

"What are you doing?" asked Ayn.

"I'm getting comfortable," replied Axis.

Ayn didn't understand this creature, but he enjoyed his company nonetheless, and was grateful for it. Despite his slightly alarming, foreign appearance, Axis was warm, soft, and somehow familiar. It was what Ayn desperately needed at the moment.

"Alright," said Ayn, "you can sleep on me, I guess."

"Of course I can," replied Axis in a yawn, "and I will. Now be a good boy, and get some sleep too. Tomorrow is a new day."

"That is true," said Ayn, also yawning, "but what if it's an even worse day than today?"

Axis picked up his head with his ears back and looked at Ayn.

"Listen to me, Ayn," he said with a serious expression, "we are linked, and from this point on, I will tell you when you are in danger. You won't have to worry, for you will always be protected. Is that understood?"

Ayn didn't know what to say. He wondered how that would even be possible. He also wondered if this was just another hallucination. Was he truly losing his mind?

"And tomorrow," continued Axis, "it will be difficult, yes. I won't lie to you, Ayn. But you will survive it, and when it is over, you will find true bliss."

Axis yawned long and hard, then put his face down into Ayn's chest.

"Now go to sleep," he purred, "and this time, dream of much happier moments in time."

Ayn yawned uncontrollably, feeling as though Axis had control over his mind. He now felt comforted, calmed, and he wanted nothing more than to follow this strange creature's commands.

"Thank you," whispered Ayn, finally able to slip into a peaceful slumber.

Chapter 19: The Art of Battle

Atlar loved the way she dug her nails into his chest, like a wild animal, yet gentle enough not to break his skin. She truly was the best lover he had ever experienced — even better than his beloved departed wife, Pira, had been. If only Reese could claw her way into his heart the way his wife had done... so long ago.

However, Reese could only give him physical satisfaction, as his heart still cried out for his wife's loving, gentle soul. Reese understood she would never be able to replace Queen Pira. In fact, it was one of her conditions: that he would still treat her as his best Lirhan soldier, even if they became intimate.

It wasn't easy for Atlar to hold that promise though. He often yearned to keep Reese safe and all to himself. However, he knew it would be impossible to stop her from going on missions or fighting for her country. Reese's honor was everything to her, and he respected that vital part of her personality.

Reese, on the other hand, felt entirely different about the situation. She enjoyed making Atlar feel good, but she also used the act of pleasuring him to escape her memories of Baran who still haunted her heart like a demanding ghost.

She had always been desperately in love with Baran, beginning from the time they were children. He was a few years older than her and had protected her from the bullies at school. She had many due to being an orphan with bright red hair, a characteristic uncommon on Kri. As a child, she couldn't help but look up to Baran and found herself falling for him, deeper and deeper.

During their Lirhan training, they were merely good friends. Soon, however, a romance bloomed, and despite being younger than he, she believed with all her heart that he felt the same intensity she did for him. She had heard about his flirtatious reputation, but she trusted him all the same. In her mind, she knew the real him, and the others were just jealous, or so she told herself.

Everything changed when she was fifteen years old and found him with another girl. He was openly kissing her in the courtyard. Reese was crushed, and when she confronted him about what he had done, he laughed and told her that the girl was "nothing" to him. She wanted to believe him, but her own fears and issues with trust held her back.

From that moment on, she vowed to change. She promised herself that she would stand on her own, never expecting anyone to love or protect her; she would only protect herself and demand the same from others.

So she spent all her time training to become the toughest, fastest warrior in all The Lirhan, which seemed to annoy Baran at first. He slowly changed his attitude, though, when he realized how strong she had become. He then became even more attracted to her in a way he hadn't quite shown before. Unfortunately, it was too late. Reese was done with men.

Then Atlar happened. The king wooed her with unexpected fierceness, making her feel as though she was the most voluptuous, valuable treasure in all the galaxy. She loved the way he seemed to need her. Atlar was much older than Reese, enough to be her father, but she didn't care. He was handsome and lion-like, full of vigor, and had been her hero growing up. What more did she need? Even if he wasn't her true love, she had left that fantasy behind years ago and was no longer looking for romance.

Their hidden love affair quickly became an obsession, for both of them. Atlar needed her sex and she needed his. It was a mutual and consensual affair. Still, Ona never approved of her childhood friend's relationship with her father.

Reese had met Ona when they were small children. After Reese's parents were both killed in the Xen war, she was adopted by Frey's older sister, Mair, whose husband had also died in the war. Mair had been unable to have a daughter, though she had always wanted one. Mair had also been friends with Reese's mother and had promised her that she would take Reese in if anything happened to her. No one objected to the adoption, except Reese, who spent her first years with Mair and Frey completely mute.

It wasn't until Reese met the princess that she began speaking. Ona and Reese had an instant bond and played together often. Eventually, they became as close as sisters, laughing and sharing their dreams. When Baran broke Reese's heart, it was Ona she turned to for comfort.

Ona had always been there for Reese, despite the differences in their social class, and they loved each other like true sisters. However, when Reese became her father's mistress, it was a betrayal in Ona's eyes, especially since she confided in Reese how much she and Atlar had missed Pira. Knowing how much Reese felt for Baran, Ona just couldn't understand what Reese was doing.

In truth, Reese knew all too well what she was doing. It wasn't a betrayal in her mind, it was survival - for both her and Atlar as well.

"I wish you didn't have to go," Atlar moaned as Reese pulled away from his arms.

Standing up, she turned her head to the side and gave him a grin. "You're the one who ordered me to leave," she teased, sliding into her tight, bronze-colored uniform.

"That is true," said Atlar as he slowly stood up and stretched his arms, "but only because you're simply the best."

Reese raised her eyebrows, and in return, Atlar smiled wide. This was how they both preferred their relationship: light, sexy, fun.

As Atlar put on his favorite, velvety, Deiusian style robe, he waved his fingers at Reese, signifying for her to come. She walked to him, smiling, and wrapped her arms around his neck.

"Yes, my king?" she purred.

"Listen to me, Reese," said Atlar as he buttoned up the front of her uniform. "When you get to Deius, I want you to blend in perfectly. To get close to that madman, you'll have to make sure Notama trusts you."

Reese nodded.

"To do that," Atlar continued, "I'm afraid you're going to need the War-Ruse."

Reese groaned.

"I know," Atlar said sternly, "but there isn't any other way."

"You know how much I hate that stuff!" whined Reese as

she placed her hands on her hips.

"I know, but-"

"No, Atlar, I don't think you do. After I took that vile stuff, I was sick for weeks. I almost died!"

Reese turned away, then angrily put on her boots. Watching her get dressed, Atlar fell silent.

Sometimes, Reese wondered whether her beloved king even cared if her life was in danger. She knew him well, and once he had a mission in mind, he would do anything to accomplish it.

"Reese," Atlar cooed, breaking the silence. He approached her from behind, putting his hands on her sides and added, "My dear, listen to me, the War-Ruse is necessary for you to become a Deiusian, not only by acting the part, but looking it as well. Now, after the drug wears off, remember to take the antidote this time. It will be different from the last debacle, honey, I promise."

Reese broke from his arms and turned to face him. "I didn't forget to take the antidote! It was Baran's fault! If he hadn't tried to kill everyone on the premises, and had been quicker, we would have escaped the Ohrian's hideout, and would have made it to the antidote on our ship. It wasn't me who screwed up - it was that jerk whom you give far too much authority."

Atlar shook his head, slightly smirking. Her still present attraction for Baran was obvious to him, and he couldn't help but be amused by it.

"My dear, it doesn't matter to me whose fault it was," he replied, holding back his true thoughts. "All that matters is this time you do not fail to use the War-Ruse properly."

Reese wasn't happy. She wasn't afraid of much in the world, but her near-death experience after taking the War-Ruse made her more than a little uneasy. She hated the bitter taste too.

Despite her hesitance, she understood the drug's power and why it was still being used by Lirhan spies on occasion; it was the only drug that could physically alter the user's body into a different appearance entirely. The drug could change eye color, hair color, skin color, and even facial shapes, if the dose was large enough. How this "sorcery" was achieved was an absolute secret. Only The Lirhan alchemists possessed the secret knowledge of how to manipulate the chemicals that produced the War-Ruse, and they told no one, not even the king.

She knew Atlar was right. If they wanted to fool Yol Notama, she would have to take the ancient drug, like it or not.

"Fine," she said, turning to him, "I'll do it. But I swear, Atlar, if I get as sick as last time, I'm making you dress up as my nurse maid and forcing you to wait on me hand and foot."

Atlar grinned, embracing her. "My dear, as long as you come out of this alive, and with valuable information on Notama, I'll do whatever you want."

"Oh really? Is that a promise, Your Majesty?" she teased as she grabbed his manhood.

"You have my word," Atlar responded, instantly aroused.

"No," Reese corrected him, "I have your everything."

"Yes, indeed," agreed the king as he passionately kissed her, possibly for the last time.

--

Ayn could feel tiny licks of wetness on his cheek and brow.

In between the shadows of sleeping and waking thought, he realized that it was his new friend, Axis, who was licking his face like a house cat who wants his master to wake in hopes of getting fed milk or fish. Ayn smiled at that idea, and then slowly opened his eyes.

For a brief moment, he thought he saw his new cat-bird friend with his nose to Ayn's nose, grinning. However, just as Ayn was about to pet Axis' short coat of golden hair, his furry friend had vanished, as if in a dream.

Soon, other senses took over Ayn's mind, like the smell of enticing food wafting in the air. He sat up and rubbed his eyes as Zin walked in and out of the room with plates in his hands. Setting a plate on the table, he smiled at Ayn and gave him a wink.

"Well, good morning, sleepy eyes!"

"Good morning," Ayn replied in a yawn. He slowly got out of bed and made his way to the table, which called to him with its delicious aroma.

On the table, Ayn saw a variety of baked breads, as well as many other strange, yet tasty looking offerings. There was something that looked like Paya-na fruit, which was a favorite Deiusian fruit of Ayn's. This fruit, though, looked slightly different in color; it was redder and more round. There was also some kind of pink meat present on the table. However, Ayn was not a meat eater and had no interest.

Fortunately, there was much more food on the table, such as hard boiled Anko bird eggs. Ayn didn't like to eat the flesh of animals, but eggs were another story. In fact, he loved them. Anko birds tasted the best, in his opinion, especially when the yolks were slightly raw, which they seemed to be at present. *What a feast in front of me!* thought Ayn, happily.

All of it had been provided by Zin, which made Ayn

incredibly grateful. Swallowing down his emotions, he held back tears as a lump swelled up in his throat.

"Thank you so much, Zin," he said to his friend in a quiet voice.

Zin sat down in the chair next to him and smiled. "You're more than welcome, Ayn," he replied. "Now eat!"

They sat at the table, enjoying the good food and each other's company. As the sunlight peered through the window, Ayn felt its warmth shining on his face, allowing him to feel a much needed sense of comfort.

Then, Zin began telling Ayn all about the hotel, and how amazing it was. According to Zin, there was, not only a free buffet of baked goods and fruit, which was available each morning in the lobby, but there was also free Konaka brew. In addition, the hotel provided a free Virtu-Pod with the daily news, which they placed at your door.

Ayn had absolutely no idea what a Virtu-Pod was, but Zin sounded so excited that he made Ayn feel the same. Ayn nodded along happily while eating sweet breads and listening to his friend's exuberant words. For a moment, all seemed calm, simple and good.

Zin showed him what a Virtu-Pod was, and it changed everything. The device itself didn't matter to Ayn, but what it did made his heart stop. The small, black, circular object was much like the tool that controlled the holographic screen he had watched with melancholia the night before. Instead of playing atmospheric images of landscapes, it projected images that told the galactic news. Shockingly, Ayn's face was now three-dimensional and floating above the table. Ayn found himself looking at his own face with sad eyes and in full Bodanya costume. Ayn dropped his fork as an Ohrian voice narrated along with the images displayed in virtual format.

"The child, known to his Deiusian followers as The Bodanya, Shiva the Fourteenth was killed yesterday morning when the anti-religion organization, The Tah, attacked the Deiusian Royal Palace during what would have been the fourteenth coronation of a Shiva-born king. According to witnesses, The Bodanya was shot at by an unknown gunman. Dei High Priest Meddhi-Lan, who was a good friend and ally to King Atlar of Kri, was then brutally shot down while protecting the child. According to King Atlar, The Bodanya had been quickly taken to a safe room while he and the Deiusian priests, as well as the Ohrian king, Lod Enra, assessed the situation. However, The Tah had planted a plasma-bomb in the palace, which went off in multiple explosions. Unfortunately, The Bodanya was inside the palace when it exploded. Having just barely escaped with his life, King Atlar described the tragic event as 'brutal and horrific.' His daughter, Princess Ona, was also present, but was unharmed."

Ayn could barely breathe as familiar, terrible images flashed in front of him, forcing him to relive the nightmare of the day before. They showed the remains of his palace, then Atlar's image, followed by Meddhi-Lan's dignified, solemn face. Then, they showed a man Ayn didn't know, though his image somehow bothered him. The man's face made Ayn feel as though he'd been punched in the stomach.

"The man being held accountable for the attack on The Bodanya, as well the Deiusian Royal Palace, is Yol Notama, the current leader of The Tah. There isn't much known about him at present, but we will keep you updated as soon as more information becomes clear. We now bring you King Atlar's speech as it comes to us live from his palace on Kri."

Ayn and Zin watched with wide eyes as they saw the virtual version of Atlar sitting at his desk. He seemed to be looking directly at them with tears in his eyes.

"My fellow Krians, Deiusians, and all who are watching the news unfold this very sad day, I greet you with a heavy heart, for this day will be remembered as the day the galaxy lost a great spiritual leader, as well as a potentially great king." Atlar sniffed and then changed his hurt expression in a matter of seconds. Now, he was angry, and it showed.

Continuing his address, he added, "I was there, my friends, and I can tell you the attack on the Deiusian temple was nothing short of extremist terrorism! And to those who claim that the Deiusian priests had this coming to them, I say to you that no matter what you believe about their religion, or even their government, they were our allies and friends, and did not deserve to be brutally attacked! As for The Bodanya, I am deeply saddened he is no longer with us. It was a senseless killing, and I am outraged that The Tah would stoop so low as to kill a child who had not even reached adulthood."

Atlar took a deep breath and then continued with a stoic fierceness, completely capturing Ayn and Zin's attention.

"As I speak to you now, my friends, only one Deiusian priest remains alive. Only one! He was like an older brother to The Bodanya and has been forever changed... and so have I. With that in mind, I say this now, directly to Yol Notama, the leader of The Tah: you can pretend your actions are true and just, but they are not, and I will not stand for the crime you have just committed. I will not stand idly by while you get away with murder! And if you do not surrender, you should now consider Kri to be your biggest enemy. Remember this: I am King Atlar, leader of The Lirhan and I WILL use all my strength to capture you and bring you to justice for your crimes! Consider yourself forewarned!"

Then, the image of Atlar's enraged face morphed into the news anchor's serene, Ohrian face.

Ayn and Zin sat in their chairs, speechless.

"And there you have it," said the Ohrian anchor. "You have just seen King Atlar's response to the tragedy on Deius, which occurred yesterday, Deiusian Time. We have also heard that, shortly before his speech, The Council of Kri held a meeting with the lone survivor of The Royal Dei. His name is being kept private, but we did capture this video of him as General Baran spoke to our reporters."

As the Virtu-Pod played the image of Baran, Ayn stood up, pointing, his mouth agog. He was shocked to see the hooded priest who stood near Baran.

"It's Pei!" he shouted. "I can't believe it!" Ayn was now breathing out of rhythm, feeling faint.

"As far as I'm concerned," said Baran, calm as a shallow pond, "if King Atlar were officially to declare war, it would be completely justified."

Ayn looked at Zin with crazed eyes. It made Zin slightly nervous.

"We have to go to Kri," Ayn declared, determined.

"No," replied Zin.

"Yes!" Ayn shouted.

"It's not a good idea, Ayn!" Zin argued.

"I don't care! Pei is alive! And he thinks I'm dead! They all do!"

Ayn stood breathing hard for a few moments. He shook his head, folding his arms. Ayn then broke the silence with a voice Zin had not heard before; it was piercing, deeply throaty, and somewhat terrifying.

"I have to go, Zin! Are you listening to me?! I hereby *command* you to take me to Kri!"

Shocked, Zin nodded and fell to his knees, bowing, almost

against his will. He had no idea what was making him cower like that, other than something in Ayn's voice and demeanor; it was awe striking, like he had suddenly been possessed by an ancient spirit of war and death. Not that Ohrians believed in such myths, but Zin knew of them and secretly loved the romance of their ancient songs and stories. Yet, the idea of Ayn becoming one of those spirits frightened him and made him wonder, even if just for a split second, if it was somehow possible Ayn truly did have the power of The Bodanya... whatever that was.

Zin quickly shook off his fears and stood to his feet, returning to his logical, Ohrian self.

"Alright, if you really feel that you must go back, I'll take you to Kri," Zin said with a grimace. "However," he added, "I'm not going back. I can't. My father has probably disowned me by now."

"You don't know that," said Ayn, back to his normal, soft-spoken voice.

"Yes, I do," Zin replied. "I know my father. He's probably fuming that I ran away... once again."

"I have a feeling," said Ayn, "he'd be happier about your return than angry at you for leaving."

Zin shook his head in disagreement. "Look," he said as he began packing his beloved elenon, "I will take you to Kri, but then I'm coming back here to Xen where I finally have a way to play my music and live freely without expectation or pressure to be someone I absolutely am not! And if you were smart, Ayn, you'd do the same."

Ayn watched Zin head to the bathroom. "I'm taking a shower, and then we can go as soon as you're ready," said Zin, somberly as he shut the bathroom door. Ayn felt empty, wondering if he was doing the right thing. He loved Zin like a brother, much like he loved Pei, but he knew in his heart that Kri was calling to him, and going there was the right thing to do.

"Are you sure?" said a cat-like voice as Ayn was re-packing his clothing.

"Yes, I'm sure."

"But you could remain unknown if you stayed here," said Axis as he pounced on top of the bed, "and appear as a normal, average person."

"What would you know about normal?!" snapped Ayn. "You magically disappear every time someone else is around!"

Axis sneered, then licked his paws. "Well," he purred, "that's because most people are strange and wouldn't accept that I even exist."

Ayn groaned. "Ha! *I* don't even accept it! In fact, I'm probably just suffering from some sort of mental breakdown and have invented you to deal with the trauma of what happened to Meddhi-Lan."

Ayn started to giggle at the thought of it: their Bodanya gone crazy!

Axis frowned as he jumped down from the bed, and then onto Ayn's suitcase. "Stop it!" he demanded.

"Why?" Ayn replied with a wild, sarcastic smile. "Why should I even care anymore?"

"Well, you're going to have to care," Axis said, "if you go to Kri and attempt to reclaim your throne!"

Ayn looked into Axis' deep blue eyes. It felt as though he was looking into his own reflection.

"You're right," said Ayn, "I have to face what happened.

And I have to help King Atlar do what is just, yet without causing a terrible war."

"Good luck with that," said Axis, rolling his eyes as he licked his paw.

Ayn watched his new cat-bird friend for a moment, taking in how strange, yet wonderful he seemed. Could Axis really have been created in his mind? Ayn didn't want to believe that he had truly gone insane, but at the same time, it was almost comforting to think he was as normal as everyone else with as many psychological problems and fears as the rest of them. He wondered what Pei would think of him now.

Pei had seemed so sad in the news clip, and it caused Ayn to feel nervous, yet excited twitches in his stomach when imagining their reunion.

"Must you really go back to being The Bodanya?" questioned Axis while curling up next to Ayn.

Nodding decidedly, Ayn sat on the bed while waiting for Zin, occasionally petting Axis, as if he were a mere house cat.

"Yes... it's my destiny," affirmed Ayn.

Axis sighed as he tried to enjoy the petting despite being rather displeased with his friend's answer.

Yawning, he mumbled, "If you say so... but my people don't believe in destiny."

"Really?" Ayn asked, curious. "What do your people believe in?"

"Time."

"Time?"

"Yes, time... and love. Nothing more, nothing less."

Ayn had no clue what Axis really meant, but he found it surprisingly comforting.

"I like that," said Ayn.

Axis snickered in between purring, "Yeah, you would."

Ayn smiled and found himself glad to have Axis at his side. Even if he really was insane, at least he wasn't alone.

--

The news reporters swarmed the steps of the great palace like flies swarming the carcasses of fallen soldiers in battle. As they tried to get another glimpse of the king, or perhaps attain one more interview with one of the councilmen, the security forces patrolling the area wouldn't allow it. Atlar's orders were strict and followed with loyal diligence.

Baran, however, was ordered by Atlar to give an official statement to the media; it was something he found unnatural, despite possessing the natural talent. Even as a child, he was able to command the attention of just about anyone he came in contact with. Baran had no idea why he was able to speak so easily and with such charm, but he assumed it was a gift from the Gods, and one that should be utilized for a grand purpose. He could only hope he was justifying the Gods' generosity in moments such as these.

Pei had also been asked by Atlar to make an appearance with Baran, not only in front of The Council, but for the press as well. It was a completely foreign and uncomfortable world to Pei, and he secretly counted the seconds until it would all be over.

"Come with me, Pei," ordered Baran while motioning with

his right hand. Pei didn't know where Baran was leading him, but if it was away from the news reporters, he was glad to follow.

Down the white marble corridors of Atlar's palace, Baran led Pei to a large room with sleek, wooden floors. The walls were crystalline blue, yet trimmed with some kind of ancient text which was written in gold; a style that reminded Pei of Deiusian design.

"Where are we?" he asked Baran.

"This is the training room for The Lirhan."

Pei couldn't believe it. Baran was actually serious about training him to become a Lirhan soldier.

"Will you begin my training now?" Pei asked with cheerful, boyish glee.

"I don't know," Baran replied coyly as he threw his blue jacket and outer shirt, onto a chair in the corner. He then cracked his knuckles and grinned at Pei. "What do you think?"

Pei was suddenly nervous. He had never fought a man, nor had he even thought about fighting. He had no idea what was expected of him.

"Don't just stand there," Baran commanded. "Take off those priestly robes, and show me what you've got!"

Pei was mortified. He had no idea what he had to show Baran or to anyone.

Unfortunately, Baran didn't wait for Pei to figure it out. The next thing Pei knew, Baran's powerful fist was smashing into his left cheek. The combination of pain and shock was quite different from anything Pei had ever experienced.

As Pei fell hard onto the wooden floor, Baran let out a hearty laugh. Pei desperately attempted to regain composure, but the world seemed to be moving by him in slow motion.

"Get up!" ordered Baran.

Pei stammered to his knees, trying to follow the general's orders. He was moving slowly, however, as he was still rather dizzy from the punch.

"I said, get up!" Baran shouted as he grabbed Pei by the collar of his robe. "And what are you doing still wearing this Deiusian costume?"

Costume? thought Pei, angered. How could Baran dare call his holy robes a 'costume?' It was Meddhi-Lan who gave Pei the robe he was wearing. Didn't he have any respect for the man who died trying to protect The Bodanya?

"It's not..." grunted Pei as he stood to his feet, "a costume!"

Baran smirked, amused. *Perhaps this young priest has promise after all*, thought Baran. However, he knew he'd have to push him much further if there was any chance of erasing The Dei training in his mind.

"Then why do you still wear it?" asked Baran. "Are you not done with being a holy man of Deius?"

Pei didn't understand why Baran was teasing him about his robes, especially after having hit him across the face like that! If this was a test, Pei couldn't figure out how to pass it.

"But..." Pei muttered.

"Speak up!" ordered Baran as he held his hands in a fist, looking like a snake coiled to strike. Pei was terrified Baran would throw another surprise punch at his face, so he instinctively moved back and to the side. This made Baran smile.

"You yourself told me to wear the robes so that it would seem more convincing to The Council when we made our plea to them this morning!"

Baran nodded with a slightly amused sneer, then replied, "That's true, but you seem a little too attached to your old life for my liking. Now take off your robes, and forget about your past! You're not a priest anymore, are you?"

"No..." said Pei, motionless.

"Then stop acting like one!" Baran shouted as he grabbed Pei by the collar. "Come on! Give it your best shot and punch me!"

Pei stood still, unable to think straight. *He really wants me to punch him*? thought Pei. Unfortunately, as angry and confused as Pei was, he just couldn't do it!

"I see how it is," Baran said with a sarcastic smile, circling Pei like a vulture with its dinner. "When it comes down to it, you're just like the rest of those pathetic Deiusian priests who were so weak they got themselves killed! No wonder your own teacher wasn't able to save your Bodanya's life! He was a weakling, and so are you!"

Pei was breathless and on the verge of red-hot tears. He wanted to scream, but his voice felt locked up, as if it were trapped inside of a bottomless well of pain.

Then Baran did something Pei was completely unprepared for. In one fell swoop, he grabbed the front of Pei's robes and ripped them off, leaving Pei in nothing but his shorts. Laughing, Baran threw the robes across the room, and then looked at Pei with intense, dark blue eyes.

"No wonder you couldn't save your Bodanya!" Baran growled. "You're a frightened, little excuse of a man! You really believe you could be a Lirhan soldier, you pathetic coward?! You weakling! You-"

"Stop!" Pei screeched in pain.

"Make me," Baran coldly replied.

Pei couldn't take it. He was crumbling inside, unable to stop the tears he had been so desperately trying to keep from pouring forth.

Baran shook his head, and then surprised Pei with another earth-shattering punch to his face, then again from the other side. Pei didn't even have time to think about the pain. All he could feel was the shock of the impact. Then, just as Pei regained his senses, Baran's fist was smashing into his stomach.

Pei doubled over, spitting blood uncontrollably. With his head spinning from the pain, he caught a glimpse of Baran's fist as it was on its way to slam into his face once again.

Baran's fist was stopped, however, unexpectedly by a hand of rage: Pei's hand. Out of a subconscious and unknown depth within Pei's soul, he had grabbed onto Baran's fist, acting in a deep, primal need for survival.

Baran stood silent, grinning at Pei. "Now," said Baran, "what shall you do, Pei-Lan?"

Baran's last remark triggered something inside Pei's brain causing him to fly into a wild rage he had never before experienced. Screaming, Pei punched Baran repeatedly in the face and sides. Over and over again, his fists flung into the general's body as fast as lightening, yet as hard as a pillow. For a man like Baran, who was possibly the strongest warrior within The Lirhan, Pei's punches didn't inflict much damage, and so Baran took it, letting Pei release his full anger. In truth, however, it wasn't the strength of Pei the general was testing, it was his will.

Finally, when Pei had let out as much of his rage on Baran as he possibly could, he stopped and looked at the general, out of breath and with tear-soaked eyes.

"So," said Baran as he wiped his own blood from his lips, "are you still a priest?"

Pei shook his head and cried. "No," Pei softly replied, "obviously, I can no longer be one."

"Do you regret that?" asked Baran. "Because, Pei... you must understand that you can't regret giving that old life up if you are to become a Lirhan warrior. There is no room for doubt! A Lirhan soldier lives and breathes fighting for justice, and if you don't want to fight, then you cannot be Lirhan! Do you understand what I'm saying to you?"

"Yes!" Pei shouted defiantly.

Baran nodded, pleased with Pei's response. "Good," he said, "now we can begin your training."

"What?" asked Pei, shocked. "Wasn't what you just did part of the training?"

"No," replied Baran, "that was just a test... to see if you were even worth the effort!" Baran gave a slight chuckle, and then wiped his mouth with a towel, which he threw to Pei after he had used it.

Pei couldn't believe the nerve of this general. Who did Baran think he was beating him so severely while calling him weak, and then forcing him to go into such a rage? Yet, Pei felt better somehow: more released and powerful. He was starting to feel hunger for the fight. In fact, now that he thought about it, there was a burning inside him he never realized was there before, and it was a thirst that needed quenching. Unfortunately, it seemed to Pei that the only way to calm his thirst was through violence. This new, primal side was both wonderful and disturbing to Pei, but he couldn't wait to learn more.

Following their initial test-fight, there was much more Baran taught him that afternoon, not just about how to throw harder punches, but where to land them and the places on the body that are more sensitive than others. Pei learned The Lirhan was somewhat like The Dei in the sense that it was almost a mystical religion, having supposedly been started by The Great Adin himself.

"Now, the key to The Lirhan fighting style," said Baran, "which you will learn at some point later - when you're ready - is to think and react in multidimensional ways."

"What do you mean?" asked Pei.

"Well," said Baran, "loosely based on Adin's philosophy, The Lirhan technique involves seeing that which cannot be seen, meaning you must always be aware of what is around you, even if you can't see it in your direct view. You must begin relying on all of your senses to detect what is truly there. This is the first and foremost lesson every Lirhan soldier learns when we are being trained."

"Who trained you, Baran?"

The general crossed his arms and subconsciously twitched his muscles. "I was trained by my king," said Baran, "but considering Atlar had been trained by your Lan, I consider Meddhi-Lan to be partly responsible for my training."

Pei was confused. "Meddhi-Lan... trained King Atlar?" he asked Baran, completely bewildered by the idea.

"Yes," Baran replied, "when Atlar was a young man, he'd been schooled on Deius at the Shiva Palace. He and Meddhi-Lan became close friends. Up until then, Atlar had been given a military education and had gone through some training within The Lirhan, but..." Baran suddenly fell silent.

Deeply curious, Pei impatiently asked, "What then? What happened?"

"Well," Baran hesitantly answered, "you see... Atlar had never gotten along with his father, my grandfather. So Atlar quit early and... failed his Lirhan training."

Pei was shocked. The idea of Atlar failing anything seemed ludicrous.

"So, King Atlar is your... uncle?" asked Pei, a bit confused.

"Yes," Baran replied stoically.

"And Atlar's father," Pei added, "declared Atlar a failure?"

"Yes, that's true," Baran continued, "but to be fair, my grandfather, King Rummund, was a hard, and sometimes cruel man... especially with Atlar. I don't know if my grandfather really wanted Atlar to pass his training or even to become a Lirhan soldier."

"Why wouldn't he?" Pei asked, even more confused.

"It's hard to explain," sighed Baran, "but their relationship was often rocky and difficult... to the point where Atlar felt he had no choice but to learn everything on his own, including fighting techniques."

Pei didn't understand the intricacies of Atlar's relationship with Rummund, but he could definitely empathize with feeling separated and distant from a father. Having never known his own father, Pei had always felt the sting of isolation; it was something both he and Ayn had in common. Luckily, they had grown up under Meddhi-Lan's care and could look to him for fatherly guidance.

Deep in thoughts about his past, Pei felt the agony over losing his teacher and his spiritual brother. He tried to shake the feeling, but the all too familiar lump in his throat began to ache.

"You're thinking about the past again, aren't you?" Baran

astutely observed.

"Yes," Pei replied solemnly.

Baran sighed, then shook his head. "Here," he said as he handed Pei a bottle of water. "You can rest. However, even though we are taking a break, we're not done. Rest for now, and tend to your wounds. You're going to need your wits for what I'm about to teach you."

Pei was curious and a little frightened. Mostly, he was just thirsty and glad to be drinking the ice cold water Baran had given him. He felt like he had sweat more than he'd ever done in his entire life.

"What will you be teaching me?" Pei asked before taking another gulp of water.

Baran flashed Pei a wicked grin. "I'll be showing you how to think and move like The Great Adin, which is what Meddhi-Lan taught Atlar back when he was young. Trust me, Pei, it will change your life."

Pei couldn't imagine how learning a few fighting maneuvers could change his life, but if Meddhi-Lan had known such knowledge, then he wanted to learn it as well.

"Baran," said Pei in a soft voice, "how did Meddhi-Lan know the fighting style of The Lirhan? Isn't it a secret knowledge only known to a handful of Krians?"

"Well," Baran said after guzzling down his bottle of water, "from what I've heard, and from the little Atlar has told me, your Lan wasn't always a holy man. In fact, he began his life as a Deiusian rebel, and then later, he studied the secret arts of Adin, which is actually rather similar to the fighting techniques of The Lirhan."

Pei was mystified by the idea of Meddhi-Lan as a Lirhan

warrior, and one who was perhaps so skilled that he was able to turn Atlar into the strong fighter the king had become.

"But if Meddhi-Lan was a rebel in his youth," said Pei as he wiped his sweat-drenched back with a towel, "does that mean he was once part of The Tah? No, that can't be true. That's impossible!"

"Pei," replied Baran, "some things aren't what they seem. That's what I'm trying to teach you with The Lirhan philosophy. Some things are true, even if the truth has yet to be revealed. I'm telling you the truth about Meddhi-Lan, Pei. He was indeed part of The Tah; that is fact. However, he eventually became their harshest critic, and in time, he helped his own teacher, Amun-Lan, completely disband them."

Pei stood in shock, trying to process the words Baran had spoken. Was it possible? Could his own mentor and father figure have done such radical things? He couldn't imagine it, but that didn't mean it wasn't true. Pei began thinking about the many possible ways he could bring up the subject of Meddhi-Lan's past with King Atlar.

"Now," said Baran as he cracked his neck and shoulders, "as I was saying about the philosophy of The Great Adin, it's all to do with seeing what is unseen. You must train yourself to use senses you don't usually rely on."

"Like hearing?" asked Pei.

"Yes, that's one of the senses that can help you see without your eyes, but Lirhan technique utilizes more than the obvious senses. For example, what do you feel right now?"

"What do I feel?" said Pei, awkwardly.

"Yes. What do you feel right now? And I don't mean physically."

Pei folded his towel and placed it on the table in the corner of the room. He pondered Baran's question while drinking another sip of water. What did he feel? How could he answer such a question when he felt entirely too much?

"Well?" Baran prodded.

"I... I feel too much!"

Baran smiled. "Good," he replied.

"That's a good thing?" Pei asked, surprised.

"That's a very good thing," said Baran. "When you start to lose feeling, that's when you have to worry."

"Can that happen?"

"Yes," said Baran, "but it's only an illusion, telling your mind that your feelings are gone. One must keep The Lirhan understanding that there is always an emotion behind the self-made veil of coldness. Again, seeing in multidimensional ways is the key. Pei, you must remember, from this point onward, there is always more to know, more to learn, more to see."

As Baran finished speaking his last word, Pei saw Ona out of the corner of his eye – or he thought it looked like her anyway. He had no idea, however, why the princess would be in the Lirhan practice room. He wondered if Baran's punches had pushed him too hard, causing him to hallucinate.

Pei slowly turned around and saw that his eyes hadn't deceived him after all. Ona was indeed standing by the entrance, looking to him like a Goddess in a green, flowing gown. She had a concerned look on her face, and it made Pei's heart ache with love.

"Ah, greetings, Princess," Baran addressed Ona with a smile and a half-bow. Pei suddenly remembered that Ona was royalty and gave her a bow as well. When he returned to an upright stance, he could see her face hadn't changed; it was still wrought with worry.

Baran crossed the large training room with a confident stride, then stood in front of Ona, folding his strong arms, which seemed to Pei a habitual mannerism of his.

"What brings you to the training room, Your Highness?" Baran asked, smiling.

The princess raised her stoic, royal chin and looked directly at Baran, as if to accept some sort of hidden challenge. "My father wishes to speak with you, General, as soon as you have the free time to do so." She then gave Baran a sarcastic smile. It seemed to Pei to suggest something far different from what she was actually saying, and this confused him greatly. Pei didn't understand why he suddenly felt jealous, yet he couldn't shake the feeling.

"Thank you for relaying the message, Princess," said Baran with the same sarcastic smile she had given him. "As long as it is not an emergency, I shall speak with your father as soon as I am finished giving my new student his first lesson."

Ona's brow turned downward and transformed her face back into the worried appearance Pei had noticed from before, except it now had a twinge of anger as well.

"Fine," she snapped, "finish your lesson. When you are done, however, you are to meet my father in the green marble room. The location, I assume you know."

Baran nodded, then thanked her again for giving him the message. He then bowed to her as she turned to leave.

Pei wanted to stop her and ask why she looked so upset. He also wished to talk to her about more personal matters. However, she was gone before he could speak, and his heart ached even more than it did before.

Baran sighed. Speaking with Ona had exhausted him. Turning to face Pei, he grinned, which made Pei rather confused: a feeling he was beginning to get used to when in Baran's presence.

"That princess of ours is quite the ball-buster, wouldn't you say?"

Pei's jaw hung open.

"What," teased Baran, "did my blunt tongue offend that delicate, priestly sensibility of yours?"

Pei didn't know how to react. He was angry, yet enthralled by Baran's every word and gesture. Pei had never in all of his life encountered a man so arrogant and cocky. Even so, Baran's confidence, as well as his graceful, yet manly demeanor, impressed Pei to the point where he couldn't help but admire the Lirhan general, though it seemed against his better judgment.

"Hmm," said Baran as he folded his arms with a devilish grin, "I think it's going to take a while longer to break that Dei's training inside your head."

Pei grimaced and proudly stated, "But I don't want it fully broken!"

"Really?" said Baran as he walked over to a hidden closet in the wall. Reaching inside, he pulled out two weapons that looked to Pei to be some kind of ancient swords. They were slightly curved with silver and gold hues to their metal, and Pei was absolutely intrigued.

"I would think you'd be glad to get rid of all that nonsense," added Baran.

Pei clenched his teeth. "It wasn't all nonsense," he said, firmly holding his ground.

Baran sensed Pei's seriousness and respected him for it. As playful and teasing as Baran could be, he knew when a man meant business. Pei's entire aura was now radiating with pride and it made Baran smile.

"Here," said Baran as he handed Pei one of the silvery-gold swords. "Let's see if your Dei training can help you trust your senses when handling a Viha."

Pei carefully held the sword by its golden hilt and immediately felt a warm, tingling sensation travel from the hilt all the way to his shoulder. He shivered and looked at Baran for reassurance. "I... I feel... What is this feeling?" asked Pei in desperation. "Is it supposed to be so..." Pei couldn't finish his sentence for the strange sensation was now making him lose grasp of his senses.

"Yes, Pei," assured Baran, "what you are feeling is quite normal. The Viha is a very old weapon that The Lirhan have been hand-crafting for thousands of years. Its shaft is lined with plasma, you see, and it emits a power similar to that of lightning, well, when it is used by a skilled Lirhan warrior anyway. But even when a novice holds it, they can feel its power coursing through them. Since I plan on training you how to fight with one, I suggest you get used to it."

Pei had no idea how anyone could get used to such a weapon. The sword was causing his entire body to become stimulated... in every way possible, and it was making Pei exceedingly nervous. It was also causing him to think uncontrollably about Ona: her beautiful, pouty lips and the smooth, perfectly curved outline of her soft, feminine body.

"Oh, my Ona," escaped from Pei's lips in a whispering moan.

Realizing what he'd just said, he opened his eyes and saw Baran laughing at him — rather loudly. Pei felt his face flush with embarrassment. He hadn't meant to speak her name, but it felt as if he were no longer able to control his deepest desires, and that feeling frightened him.

"Ona?!" blurted Baran as he chuckled. Clearly amused, he shook his head and grinned. "So... you have a thing for the princess, eh?"

Pei swallowed hard and shifted his weight, utterly embarrassed.

"And what if I do?" he responded, defensively.

The general's face quickly changed from amused to troubled.

"Well," replied Baran, "if that was indeed the case, I'd tell you that such a desire is a lost cause and that you should find another flower in the garden to take delight in."

Normally, Pei would have allowed Baran's rudeness to slide off of him like water, but for some reason, he just couldn't do it. In fact, Pei had never felt more anger in his entire life. It felt to him like a wild, burning fire had begun to ignite deep inside his gut and he had absolutely no control over his emotions.

"What did you just say?!" Pei shouted.

Baran smirked, amused yet again by his new protege. "Calm down, my excitable friend," he said as he reached for the Viha held firmly in Pei's right hand. "I think, perhaps, you aren't quite ready for weapons training," Baran added

Carefully, Baran removed the sword from Pei's hand. He could feel the raging, sexually repressed energy Pei had unknowingly planted inside of the Viha's plasma, and for a moment, his own head reeled with dizziness. Catching himself, before Pei's energy affected his own, Baran quickly sheathed both of their Viha. He then took a deep breath, exhaling the tension out of him.

Pei didn't understand what had just happened, but he felt a strong sense of relief once the Viha's plasma was no longer coursing through his body.

"I'm... sorry," said Pei.

"No," Baran replied, shrugging, "you have nothing to be sorry for. I should have prepared you for how powerful these ancient swords are. Truth be told, not even the most skilled among The Lirhan can fully control their energies once they are able to bond with the Viha." Baran smiled at Pei. "You should actually be proud of yourself, my friend, for only someone with great potential would be able to bond with this kind of weapon so intensely, and so quickly."

Baran's words were flooding through Pei's mind like a rushing river. He felt both honored and frightened by the idea of being someone with great potential for power.

"Baran?" he asked while still recovering from his first encounter with the Viha.

"Yes, Pei."

"Why did you say that about Ona? Do you think I'm not good enough for her?"

Baran let out a small laugh. "No, Pei, that's not at all what I meant."

"Well, what did you mean?"

Baran sighed. "Calm down. All I was saying, is that Ona – Princess Ona – isn't exactly allowed to socialize romantically with just anyone. Commoners, such as yourself, would never be able to become intimate with the princess, and I doubt Her Highness would be seeking such intimacy with a Lirhan warrior anyway being how much she is against fighting of any kind."

Pei's heart began to sink. "Do you mean to tell me, Baran, that even if King Atlar consented to her marrying a commoner, she still wouldn't want me because I am training to become Lirhan?"

"That would seem to be the case," sighed Baran, "from what I know of her, that is."

"But that doesn't make any sense!" Pei blurted. "How can she hate the very army that her own father is the leader of?"

"That's a very good question," replied Baran, "but one that may not have an easy answer." Taking another deep breath, Baran stretched and cracked his neck. "Listen to me, Pei... I'm going to tell you an absolute truth about women: they are creatures of mood and hardly ever make any sense."

Pei wanted to laugh, but merely cracked a smile.

"And they never know what they really want," Baran continued. "One moment they are praising a man. The next, they are attacking him for the very things they previously praised him for! Ona is no different from any other woman. She is fickle, Pei, trust me about that. As beautiful and proud as she may seem, underneath that perfect exterior, she is a woman like any other, and all women are unable to make up their damned minds! It's the curse of their gender, if you ask me, which is why there are so few women within The Lirhan. Their weakness isn't just physical – it's something inside their core. They just don't have the ability to fight with any real-"

Before Baran could finish his sentence, he was completely thrown off his guard by the lunging hand that had silently surprised him from behind.

Pei soon realized it was Reese, and she had grabbed Baran so fast it seemed as if she had appeared out of thin air.

Baran struggled with all his might, but it was useless. Reese had Baran in a stronghold, and it was impossible for him to break free.

"What was that you were saying about women being weak?" she growled with a grin.

Baran grunted and again tried to break free, but was unable to do so. Pei wasn't sure how she was doing it, but it looked to him as if Reese had maneuvered the fingers of her right hand into the back of Baran's neck, and when she pressed her fingers harder, he could only wince in pain.

"I... didn't... mean... you," grunted Baran.

Reese flashed a wicked smile, and then finally released Baran from her powerful grip. "Of course you didn't," she said, sarcastically. Coughing and rubbing his throat, Baran looked at Reese with contempt.

"You really want to kill me, don't you?" said Baran.

Reese grinned and rolled her eyes. "Don't be ridiculous," she nonchalantly replied. "If I really wanted to kill you, you'd already be dead."

Baran gave her a smirk to which she gave right back.

"Look, I hate to spoil your male-bonding party," she teased, "but I need to speak with you, General... alone."

Baran grimaced, then nodded, reluctantly following Reese as she led him to a far corner of the room. Pei didn't know what to make of what was going on between them, but he didn't feel it was his business, so he quietly practiced a few Lirhan moves Baran had shown him.

"What is it?" Baran asked her under his breath.

She smiled, and then playfully pouted. "Aw, are you angry

at me for pinning you, and in front of your new pet to boot?"

"He's not my pet," he replied. "In fact, he's quite promising. I think he may turn out to be one of the most talented Lirhan warriors we've seen in quite a long while." Reese raised her eyebrow in skepticism, and then looked over at Pei, contemplating the general's assessment of him. "Now," said Baran with crossed arms, "what did you want to talk to me about?"

She took a breath, then leaned close to Baran's ear. "I need you to keep an eye on that fiendish old Octian for me while I'm gone," she whispered.

Baran nodded, slyly. "Of course," he replied in a low voice, trying not to become excited by the nearness of her mouth.

"And you must do it without being seen or heard," she added. "I'm trusting you, Baran. Don't let that boorish impatience of yours make you clumsy."

He gave her a sarcastic smile. "Yes, dear. Anything else?"

"Well," she playfully grinned while wrapping her arms around his neck, "you could miss me while I'm gone."

"That, my dear, would be asking far too much," he replied, just as playfully.

She pouted in jest, teasing him with the closeness of her body; a maneuver Baran was all too familiar with. Carefully removing her arms from his neck, as if she were a snake curled upon his shoulders, he pulled away. Baran then gave her a stern, serious look.

"Is there anything else?" asked the general.

"Not really," she replied with a hint of genuine sadness. "I just wanted to say goodbye."

"Oh, for heaven's sake, Reese, why the drama? It's not as if we'll never see each other again."

She looked at him with a raised brow and said, "Are you certain of that, my dear general? I am, after all, having to use the War-Ruse once again."

Baran's face turned white. "What?! You've got to be kidding me!"

"No, I'm not kidding," she replied. "Atlar wishes me to use it so I can completely convince Notama I am genuinely Deiusian and to gain his favor."

"That's insane!" shouted Baran. "You can't use it, Reese! There has to be another way!"

Reese gave Baran a sweet smile, one that she hadn't shown him in many years. "It's kind of you to care, my dearest general, but I agree with Atlar on this matter. There just isn't any other way."

"Well, I absolutely disagree with my uncle!" Baran angrily replied. "Has he gone mad?! Doesn't he remember how we almost died the last time we used that toxic poison?! There is a reason it's been outlawed! The Lirhan shouldn't even be using it anymore, in my opinion."

"Well, unfortunately, it's not your opinion that matters in this case, dear Baran," she said, deadpan. "You should know better than anyone that the king's word is law. Therefore, I'm going to use the War-Ruse for as long as I can. So, you see, Baran, this may indeed be our last meeting."

Shocked and bewildered, Baran stood in front of Reese, looking at her with a mix of deep concern and defiance. He wanted to grab her by the shoulders and shake some sense into her. If that didn't work, he wanted to kiss her passionately and beg her not to do such a mad, extreme sort of mission. He remembered what the effects of the War-Ruse had been like the last time they had taken it, and the pain was something he would not soon forget.

Unable to hold his feelings back, Baran grabbed Reese by her shoulders. "Please," he said, his voice slightly cracking, "I'm begging you, silly girl. Don't do this!"

She smiled, comforted by the feel of his strong hands and by the knowledge that Baran still cared for her. "It is already done, my love," she cooed. "I took it about an hour ago and I am now awaiting the effects. So, as you can see, there's no use fighting it now."

He winced, and then gave her a hard, passionate kiss on her lips. Reese had forgotten what his kisses felt like: strong, sensual, warm and full of hunger. Being caught in a momentary spell, his full, but masculine lips reminded her of why she had fallen so hard for him when she was younger. After their kiss, she sighed and played with the back of his dark, wavy hair.

"Oh, you eternal charmer," she said with a contented, catty grin.

"You don't have to go," he whispered softly. "I can speak with the king and make him change his mind. I'll tell him I can go in your stead."

Reese smiled wide, truly touched by Baran's foolhardy, heroic tendencies. "No, my love," she said as she slowly pulled away from his arms. "It has to be me. You could never pass as a Deiusian, nor could you fool Notama into believing that you're on his side."

"Yes, I could!"

"Baran, you may be a great warrior and a mighty leader – worthy of Atlar's inheritance even – but you are no good at spying. You are far too honest for this side of The Lirhan's battle.

There is nothing wrong with that either. It's who you are, and this... is who I am. Please, just respect me for what I am good at. I can do this, Baran. You must believe me."

Baran wasn't happy about what she was saying to him, but deep inside, he knew she was speaking the truth. "I do believe you are the most suited for this job, Reese, but... "

She smiled and patted his chest. "Don't worry, dear, I won't get myself killed. You have my word." She then gave Baran a small, gentle kiss goodbye on his lip, leaving him with a yearning sensation throughout his body.

Watching her saunter out of the training room, Baran felt his heart drop with heaviness. *Damn it!* he thought as he hit the wall with his fist, *I still love her!*

Chapter 20: The Lurking Shadow

*T*he sky was a perfect shade of pale blue, without a cloud in sight. Ayn couldn't help but smile at its beauty, and he took it as a sign from the Gods that he was indeed doing the right thing by traveling to the kingdom of Kri.

"Zin, can I ask you something?" said Ayn, cheerfully, while the two of them walked along the dock, heading toward their parked ship.

Zin quietly nodded, still sore about Ayn's decision to leave X-314. "Well... I was wondering," Ayn continued, "where on Kri is Atlar's palace? Is it big? Is the Krian kingdom bigger than my own kingdom? Is the royal city also its own country, like it is on Deius? Have you been there? Do you know?"

Zin sighed, rubbing his forehead. The way Ayn could go on in such an excited, little boy type of way amused, and yet, exhausted him. "Yes, I've been to Kri," Zin replied. "When my father was first elected king, he brought my mother and I there so he could make a good impression on King Atlar who had just been elected king as well. I suppose he wanted Atlar to believe we were a close family." To that, Zin gave a small, sarcastic snicker and then folded his arms.

"Oh!" said Ayn, playfully hopping over the painted lines in the street. "You hold elections to determine your royal line on Ohr - just like they do on Kri?"

"Yes, although, on our planet, it's more of a Dynastic government," said Zin with a yawn.

"So, your people don't just elect certain people as their rulers," said Ayn, trying to understand, "but the entire family who will rule them?"

"Yes," replied Zin, sluggishly, "and then there's the Prime Minister, who is also elected, but that's a whole other part of our government."

"Hmm, that's interesting," said Ayn, "because on Deius, we don't have elections, we have successions. I mean, The Dei may hold private elections about which law should pass or fail, but for the most part, everything is decided by divine right."

"Yes, I know," Zin replied, not only sluggish, but motionless as well.

"What's the matter?" asked Ayn, noticing Zin's lack of movement as well as the strange look on his face. "Does it bother you that Deius is run that way?" added Ayn. "It's not my fault, you know. I didn't decide these things."

"No, it's not that, Ayn."

"Well, what's wrong then?" Ayn asked with a confused pout.

Zin's silvery-thin brow knotted as he scratched the back of his neck, his gills slightly enlarged while turning a reddish hue. "Oh, I'm just wondering where my ship is, that's all."

"Huh?" said Ayn, even more confused.

Zin pointed ahead of him and shrugged. "It was docked right here. I know it was."

Ayn looked at where he was pointing and saw the dock was completely empty with not a ship in sight.

"That's... odd," said Ayn, mystified. "Where did it go?"

Zin shook his head, annoyed. Just then, he remembered something and began searching through the items in his blue-colored bag.

"What are you looking for?" asked Ayn.

Zin's brow was now sunk inward toward the bridge of his nose. Searching frantically through his bag, he became more and more agitated.

"Zin?" repeated Ayn.

"I'm looking for the receipt the man at the dock gave us when we landed yesterday!" Zin blurted.

Ayn could tell Zin was far too annoyed to answer any more of his questions, so he decided to just let him be, taking the moment to sit on his suitcase for a small rest.

In the distance, Ayn could see blue-green waves appearing to belong to an ocean. He was entranced, thinking of a time when docks were once harbors for actual ships that sailed seas instead of flying ones that now sail the sky. He wondered if men had to work extra hard in those ships, catching fish or buried treasure. Ayn smiled as he daydreamed, staring off into the serene, blue sky.

"HA!" exploded out of Zin's mouth. "I found it!"

Bounding up from hunching over his bag, Zin raced over to the dome-shaped office nearby where he had received the docking receipt. Ayn completely trusted his friend's ability to handle these types of things and continued sitting on his luggage as he watched the clouds roll by, still happily caught up in his wistful, dreamy state of mind.

"Excuse me," Zin said as he approached the man sitting in the office. The man was lanky and middle aged, leaning back in his chair with his feet up on his desk.

"Excuse me, but I can't seem to find my ship," explained Zin, "which I had docked here yesterday... around late afternoon."

Zin took out the receipt, which was a rectangular, opaque card with a long amount of Ohrian numbers listed on it. He then handed it to the man in the office.

The man sniffed and wiped his nose with the back of his hand. "Yeah, um," he said with a nasal voice, "I remember the ship being docked here yesterday. It should be there... in the East section."

"I've already looked there!" Zin shouted. "I've looked in *all* the sections!"

"No need to get excited, kid," the man in the office replied, a little defensively. "I'm sure your ship can be tracked. What is your tracking number?"

Zin cocked his head, confused. "What tracking number?"

The man in the office gave a slightly frustrated sigh and then explained, "Every ship comes with a security alarm that has a tracking device. If you have the number, you can enter it into your security stick. Do you have the stick with you?"

At this point, Zin was becoming so agitated and perplexed that Ayn thought he might fall over in a dizzy fit of rage. Coming to his rescue, Ayn walked up to the man in the office and said, "We don't have any security stick... I don't think. Our ship didn't come with one."

"I don't think that's possible," said the lanky man. "As far as I know, all ships these days come standard with them."

Zin looked at Ayn with a face that begged for silence. Ayn decided it might be best to let Zin handle the situation, so he sat back down on his suitcase.

"Look," said Zin, trying to keep calm, "my father didn't install a security device, so I don't have a tracking number... stick... thing!"

"Well, that wasn't very wise," said the man.

Zin's face turned a shade of reddish purple, his gills becoming so inflamed Ayn worried his friend might dehydrate from his own anger. Ohrians were known to require a lot of liquid, especially if they became agitated or excited. Ayn wondered if Zin was going to need a nice, warm bath after talking to this man.

"I don't have time to explain things to you!" blurted Zin. "I just want you to find my ship! Is that understood?!"

There was an uncomfortably quiet pause as the man in the office looked taken aback by Zin's outburst. He then re-checked the receipt's number on his data-desk, swirling his fingers on the touch screen in a rapid motion. "Nope, it's no good," he said dryly. "My program isn't detecting the ship on the motion sensor whatsoever. I'm sorry, young sir, but it looks like someone may have stolen your vessel. I can run a scan, if you'd like, to see if the motion sensor detected movement in that area between the time you docked and now, but that's all I can do."

Zin looked as if he were about to cry, but nodded and stoically said, "Yes... I would appreciate that." Turning around to face Ayn, Zin took a deep breath and sighed. "I'm so sorry, Ayn. I know how much you wanted to go to Kri."

Ayn shrugged, nonchalantly. He then patted Zin's shoulder with a comforting smile. "That's alright, we can take another ship.

They must have ships to buy or rent around here somewhere. It's not really such a big problem, Zin. No need to get so upset."

"I don't think you understand, Ayn. We can't afford to get another one. All my money was kept inside a safe on my ship. All we have left now is what we received when we sold your medallion, well, minus the amount it cost for the hotel and food."

Ayn stared at Zin, trance-like and yet focused. He heard Zin's words, but wasn't processing what Zin was telling him.

"Sir?" said the man in the office.

Zin turned around and faced him. "Yes?" Zin replied.

"It appears there was indeed motion in that area where your ship was docked late last night. Would you like to make a report to the authorities? I could even save the footage to a virtu-pod as evidence for their inspection."

"No," Zin said abruptly, "I... don't wish to contact the authorities."

The man in the office nodded with a knowing look on his face. "I fully understand," he replied.

"Is this all you can do for me?" asked Zin with a pleading expression. "Can't you at least compensate us by refunding the money it cost us to park here?"

The man sighed. "Yeah, alright... but it's not really allowed by my supervisor being that we aren't actually liable for theft."

"I'd appreciate it," said Zin.

As the man gave Zin the refund, the realization of what was happening finally dawned on Ayn. He got up and walked over to where Zin stood, ready to scold him for not having the sense to install a security device on his ship. Even if it was his father's ship, Ayn figured Zin could have installed one anyway. The whole situation greatly annoyed him.

"Thank you," Zin said to the man in the office and then turned to face Ayn. "Well, it's not nearly enough for a new ship, but it's enough to stay at least a week more at the hotel. Then maybe Luc will pay me soon for performing at his club, and we could buy a decent ship, though it most likely won't be half as prime as mine was."

Ayn's face was stern and stony. After a few moments, he slowly shook his head at Zin. "No," Ayn firmly stated, "we are NOT staying here any longer! Don't you understand? I HAVE to get to Kri! I have to stop King Atlar from waging war on Deius and putting thousands of lives in danger! They all think I'm dead, Zin. I have to tell them I'm alive and that war is never an answer. It's my duty as The Bodanya! Don't you understand that?!"

Zin could feel the desperate, emotional flooding of pain rising inside of Ayn, and it made him want to cry along with his soul-friend. What worried him more, however, was how loudly Ayn had declared his own identity. Zin quickly looked around the dock nearby to make sure no one had heard Ayn's words.

"Look, Ayn," said Zin, "I understand your concern, but..."

"What about a public transport?" Ayn curtly interrupted. "There must be some kind of ship the common people use to get on and off of this Gods-forsaken planet!"

Zin looked at Ayn who was now fully agitated, seeming close to despair. Zin wanted to soothe his beloved friend somehow, but didn't know what to do. Sighing, Zin tenderly embraced Ayn. "I'm so sorry," he whispered. "All of this is my fault... and I wish I could make things right somehow. If I could, I'd go back in time and change everything bad that happened. I wouldn't even have brought you here with me. I don't know what I was thinking. I just... wanted you to be safe, and I guess I selfishly wanted you with me. I thought it was the right thing to do at the time, but now I know I was wrong. Please try to forgive me. I really do love you, Ayn. I swear it."

The two young men held each other and shed reluctant tears. Time seemed to pass by them for a moment as the sky changed from pale blue to pale gray.

"It's going to rain," said Ayn softly.

"I know," replied Zin.

Slowly pulling away from each other, they wiped their faces and sniffed, adjusting to the reality of their situation. "We should go back to Luceon's club," said Zin as he nodded. "I was already scheduled to play there tonight, so I might as well do that. Then maybe he can pay me in advance for any future shows I play this week. It might be enough for a public transport, like you suggested. That was a good idea, Ayn. We should find out what our options are, and then you can fly to Kri as soon as possible."

Ayn cocked his head and asked, "What do you mean? Aren't you going to fly there with me?"

Zin rubbed his forehead with his long, graceful musician's fingers. "Ayn..." he said in a sigh, "I'm not going to lie to you. I hate Ohr. I always have. I have no intention of going back."

"I'm not asking you to go back to Ohr!" snapped Ayn. "Why should that matter when it comes to flying with me to Kri?"

Zin once again worried they were speaking much too loudly. He then gently pulled Ayn aside hoping to keep their voices away from prying ears.

"Because, Ayn," whispered Zin, "my father will be notified of my presence the minute I set foot on Kri, especially if we are to seek an audience with Atlar at his palace. And the truth is, I'd rather die than go back to my previous life on Ohr. I was miserable, Ayn. I was trapped in a sterile life of endless repression and pretense. Don't you understand? It nearly destroyed my soul."

Ayn nodded, sadly. "I do understand," he replied, "but you should still come with me. Once we're on Kri, you can seek asylum with Atlar and stand up to your father, if you must. I don't think I can do all this without you, Zin. It's your destiny to help me... I think."

Zin shook his head and smiled. He couldn't help but be touched by his soul-friend's honest, albeit demanding plea for help.

"Alright, I'll come with you to Kri," said Zin, "but once you're there safely, I'm heading right back here to Xen. I'm a musician in my core, and this is the only place I can be one without being judged or caged. If my father had his way, I'd be in training right now to become a cold king and strict scientist like he is. I won't become a puppet to my father, Ayn, I just won't."

Ayn nodded in understanding. "Just go with me to Kri," Ayn replied, "and then you can come back here. Please, Zin, I need your help."

They hugged as rain fell lightly from the sky. "We'll make it there, Ayn," said Zin, swallowing his tears. "Trust me."

Ayn smiled, assured and calmed by Zin's words. "Yes, we will!" he happily replied, returning to his child-like self. "Now, let us go to Luc's bar," Ayn added. "I'm hungry anyway, and I was rather looking forward to hearing you play again."

Ayn then picked up his suitcase and stood facing Zin with an energized glow about his entire being. Zin smiled at him in return.

They walked along the street, heading for Luc's bar. From the corner of his eye, Ayn saw that Axis was grinning at him while lying under a parked vehicle on the street. The cat-bird then licked his paws and yawned. Ayn wondered if he had been there the entire time.

"Zin?" asked Ayn.

"Yeah?"

"Do you think maybe I've gone a little crazy?"

"What?" said Zin, perplexed. "Why would you ask me that?"

"Well, it's just that I... I think I may be seeing things that aren't there."

Zin snickered a little and said, "Isn't that your job? I had heard that The Bodanya is supposed to have visions so he will understand the universe, curing the ills of the world through meditation... and all that nonsense."

Ayn frowned and muttered, "It's not all nonsense."

Zin sighed and folded his arms as he walked. "Sorry," he replied. "But to answer your question, no, I don't think you've gone crazy. I just think you're upset. You've lost so much in these past few days, and despite what some may believe, you're mortal. Anyone would be feeling a little insane if they went through what you've been through."

Ayn hoped Zin was right and that his visions of Axis would eventually cease. If not, he was sure he'd have to seek help from The Un. It's not that he minded Axis' company – he quite liked it actually – but the idea of The Great Bodanya talking to a cat-bird whom no one else could see wasn't something Ayn wanted anyone knowing about. Visions were one thing, but delusions were another, and Ayn wasn't altogether sure which category Axis belonged.

As it lightly rained, Zin and Ayn casually walked until they reached the Chord Station. Ayn felt good walking in the rain, feeling like it was a rebirth of some kind. He no longer felt as angry or anxious as he'd been after seeing that small glimpse of Pei on the news. He was aware that he needed to stop Atlar from declaring war, but he also remembered Meddhi-Lan's teachings: you cannot fight the flow of the river, but instead, you can move along with the current, thereby influencing its direction. Ayn felt certain he and Zin would reach their destination, and at the precise time they were supposed to reach it. The Gods themselves would have it no other way.

The ride on The Chord seemed more enjoyable to Ayn than he had experienced the day before. He guessed it was because he felt a little less shaken and exhausted. Passing by the wondrous sights, he marveled again at the old, abandoned Hithra Temple and found himself daydreaming about the ancient Dei priests who first explored this exotic outpost planet. Were they much different from the modern priests of Deius? When had they first discovered Xen? So many questions swirled in Ayn's ever curious mind.

Before he knew it, the ride was over. Soon they were walking into the heart of the city, and this time, the merchants in the shops didn't scare Ayn like before. He and Zin passed by the music shop that Luc's sister, Velna, owned, and for a moment, it seemed to Ayn that Zin wanted to stop inside. He resisted, however, as they continued walking to Luc's club.

When they got to Luc's, Ayn's feet really hurt. He wondered why Zin had rejected his suggestion of taking a public hover-car when they were at the Chord Station, though he had a feeling it had something to do with Zin not wanting to spend the money. Being that Ayn had been raised unaware of the material world and didn't really understand the whole system of money to begin with, he kept quiet about it. Walking, however, was not Ayn's first choice of transportation, and he planned on doing the least amount of it when they finally did reach Kri.

Much like the previous night, Ayn sat down at a table near the stage and watched Zin perform alongside the beautiful and mysterious Lady Raven. With her long, silky black hair and her soft, black wings, she intoxicated everyone in the room. It was an effect she seemed to have every time Ayn saw her perform, especially on the men, some of whom he recognized from the night before. Clearly Lady Raven had a following.

Zin was truly in his element, closing his eyes while fingering the elenon, as if he were making love to the instrument. Watching the way Lady Raven responded to Zin made Ayn slightly angry, yet he had no idea why. He wondered if it was because he was used to being the center of Zin's attention, but it didn't quite feel like that.

Sipping his paya-na fruit drink, Ayn tried to dig deeper into his emotions to find the answer. The only thing he could come up with was that he wished he himself could be like Zin: graceful with music, charismatic, and flirtatious with women. Ayn's whole life, he fantasized about being a romantic, heroic figure from an ancient love story. In reality, he was only ever fated to become The Bodanya. It was something he was proud of, but his destiny did not seem to match who he felt he was inside – just like the paradox of his body.

Becoming moody and melancholy, Ayn ate his dinner. Instead of MahMah stew, he chose to have something different. It was a vegetable based steak bathed in an unfamiliar, yet sweet glaze. Ayn thought it was rather excellent, and he had to hand it to Luc; not only did Luc's lounge present great entertainment, but it had some of the best food Ayn had ever tasted.

Shortly after their last song ended, Zin and Lady Raven joined Ayn at his table. Zin held the chair out for her, and then sat down next to Ayn. Introductions were made, and even though Ayn was nervous, he couldn't help but be fascinated by Lady Raven's every word and movement. She was so different from any woman he had seen growing up at The Dei's temple. She was beautiful and glamorous, and reminded him a little of his mother, which saddened, yet warmed his soul.

Ayn watched Lady Raven as she pulled out a long, fancy looking smoking pipe. She then elegantly lit the end of it with an oval, red lighter. She completely fascinated Ayn, but when she looked at him and smiled, he quickly looked away, turning almost as red as her lighter.

"I've got good news, Ayn," said Zin, wiping the beads of sweat that had formed on his brow while playing his elenon. "I talked with Luc right before going on stage, and he said he'd be willing to give me half of my earnings tonight and the other half by the end of the week."

Expressionless, Ayn shrugged and returned to eating his vegetarian steak. Zin hated when Ayn did the silent routine, but he figured Ayn was just being moody about the ship being stolen. "Oh," added Zin, "and Luc also said there is an opening for a bus boy, if you want the job."

Slowly, Ayn's head rose to look at Zin. His expressionless face turned to one of bewildered disgust.

"Or... maybe not," said Zin, grinning.

"Ayn... That's your name, isn't it?" Lady Raven said through an exhale of smoke. Ayn nodded nervously in response, noting right away how smooth and silky her speaking voice sounded – much like her singing one. "Well, Ayn, do you have any talents? Perhaps you could join Zin and I on stage."

Vigorously shaking his head from side to side, Ayn blushed. "No, Lady Raven," he shyly replied, "I could never do that."

"Why not?" she asked him.

Ayn didn't know how to respond. Her deep, burgundy-colored eyes made him want to tell her anything she wanted to know, but he was well aware that he couldn't freely talk to her, or anyone for that matter - certainly not about anything too personal for fear they might realize he was actually The Bodanya. Ayn knew there were unsavory people on Xen, not just from Zin's description, but from his own gut instinct, and he didn't want to divulge too much to the wrong person. He decided to act like he didn't understand the question. He shrugged, and then went back to eating his food.

"Ayn," said Zin, "I'm just going to go speak with Luc for a moment about my payment, and then I'll be right back. You'll be alright, won't you?"

Shooting Zin a look of desperation, Ayn quickly shook his head, silently begging him to stay.

"Don't worry, Zin," said Lady Raven with a gentle smile. "I'll keep your friend company."

As Zin got up to leave the table, Ayn found himself alone with the most beautiful woman in the room. He didn't know what to say or do, so he sat still, looking off to the side, fidgeting with his napkin.

Even with his head turned away, he could still feel her burgundy eyes staring at him. Ayn didn't know whether Lady Raven was just curious about him or if she thought him strange, or worse, if she somehow recognized him from the news.

Taking a deep breath and gathering his strength, Ayn turned to face her. He found her smiling at him as she delicately took a sip from her fruit cocktail.

"How old are you, Ayn?" she asked, still smiling.

"Four- er, I mean... sixteen," he replied, sweaty-palmed.

Grinning and clearly amused, Lady Raven took another sip from her drink. "Sixteen, huh?" she said. "You look quite handsome and manly for your age."

Ayn immediately blushed as red as a rose. "Stop," he protested, suppressing an embarrassed giggle, "you're just teasing me."

"No, my dear boy," said Lady Raven, "I meant what I said. If only I was ten years younger. You and Zin are both delectable."

Ayn was now squirming. He nervously smiled, and then gulped down his drink, silently praying to The Great Adin for guidance.

Finally, after what seemed to Ayn like an eternity, Zin returned to the table with a big smile on his face. He was holding a card of some sort in his right hand, and Ayn had a feeling that Luc had paid him in credit.

"Did you miss me?" teased Zin.

"More than either of us could bear," replied Lady Raven, smirking at Ayn.

This kind of flirtatious banter was entirely foreign to Ayn, and he wished someone would just say what they actually meant for at least five minutes – just long enough for him to regain his equilibrium.

Unfortunately, the two of them continued their flirty exchange for far longer than five minutes. After Zin had eaten a hearty meal of Zeewah flank and sauteed Ohrian root vegetables, he and Lady Raven had conversed about their favorite music, instruments, and contemporary singers – all of which Ayn was sadly lacking knowledge.

"Can we go now?" asked Ayn abruptly.

Zin and Lady Raven stopped mid-conversation and looked at Ayn.

"Sorry," said Ayn, embarrassed, "I would like to leave now, if that's alright. I'm very tired."

Zin cracked a smile, half amused and half annoyed. He turned to the elegant Lady Raven and kissed her hand. "I'm sorry, my dear," said Zin, "but we'll have to carry on this fine conversation some other night. It seems my friend is rather spent, and I must help him find lodgings for the evening. Perhaps we might continue our extremely enjoyable discussion in private sometime later, say, tomorrow night... over dinner?"

"Wow, thought Ayn. *How did Zin learn to be such a smooth talker with women?*

Lady Raven subtly smiled and nodded at Zin with restrained approval. Both young men understood that her body language meant they should play their cards right when dealing with such a fine, sophisticated woman.

Walking to The Blue Wave Hotel - the same hotel they had stayed the night before - Ayn marveled at how easily Zin charmed Lady Raven with his romantic words and demeanor. He wanted to ask Zin how he did it, but felt too embarrassed to even approach the subject. Zin, however, could feel his soul-friend's eyes upon him, and he had a feeling Ayn desperately wanted to talk about something.

"What's on your mind?" asked Zin as they walked, dragging their rolling suitcases behind them.

Ayn shrugged, trying to act as if nothing was bothering him.

"Come on, Ayn, you've been much too quiet," prodded Zin, "and that's not like you. Are you angry with me?"

"No," Ayn replied.

Zin looked at his uncharacteristically quiet friend, and then stopped walking. "Ayn, is this about the ship being stolen?" he asked. "If so, I promise I'll get us a new one as soon as I've made enough money. Then, you can go to Kri and be The Bodanya thing... and I'll no longer be a burden to you, I promise."

Ayn stopped walking and looked at Zin, annoyed. "You're not a burden," he said, frowning. "I just... I sometimes feel... I mean..."

"What? Just spit it out," Zin interjected, agitated and tired.

Ayn took a deep breath and tried to focus his jumbled-up thoughts.

"Well, it's just... how are you so good with girls, I mean, women?"

"Women?" asked Zin, confused. "All your pouting and silence is about... women?"

At first, Zin stood still, a little stunned. Finally, he burst into laughter. Ayn didn't like the idea that his friend was laughing at him for something he was so sensitive about. He folded his arms in brooding protest.

"This isn't funny," said Ayn.

"No," said Zin, suppressing his giggle fit, "of course not."

"You're being rude," Ayn replied, pouting with knotted brow.

Calming down, Zin shook his head and took out a long smoking pipe. He then lit it with an oval plasma-lighter, much like the one Lady Raven had. He took a small puff, then held it in his mouth for a moment. "Oh Ayn," he said as he exhaled, "you're so funny sometimes."

Ayn failed to see the humor in what he said. He also didn't like the idea that Zin was now smoking a pipe.

"Where did you get that... thing?" asked Ayn.

"Lady Raven gave it to me," replied Zin

"I thought so."

"You don't like her, do you?"

Ayn was starting to get more annoyed.

"I like her quite a lot, actually!" Ayn defended.

Zin's face slowly changed from skeptical to illuminated. "Oh!" said Zin, "You *like* her! You little devil!"

Ayn shook his head and tried to repudiate Zin's claim, but all that came out of his mouth was a small giggle through a red face of embarrassment.

"You do! You like her!"

"No!" Ayn shouted with a wide, irrepressible grin.

Zin smiled in return. "Oh, Ayn, it's alright. Just admit it. She's very beautiful."

"Well, yes... I admit that she is indeed rather beautiful," Ayn said bashfully, "but that doesn't mean I like her... like *that*."

Zin smirked at Ayn with a doubtful eye, then slung his bag over his shoulder as he continued walking, dragging his suitcase behind him. Ayn quickly responded by grabbing his own suitcase, running up to walk by Zin's side.

"Why are you asking me about women if you're not attracted to Lady Raven?"

"I didn't say I wasn't attracted to her," Ayn mumbled under his breath.

"To be honest," Zin added, "I'm surprised you even

noticed. Most of the time you seem so... oblivious."

Ayn looked at Zin, confused and slightly offended. "What do you mean 'oblivious?' I am The Bodanya. I'm never unaware of anything!"

"Shh, Ayn," said Zin with a slight laugh, "don't say that so loudly, and don't get so upset. I didn't mean you were oblivious about normal, everyday things or even about the universe. I meant about... love or sex. It just didn't seem like something you were interested in."

Ayn didn't know what to say or how to respond. Did Zin really think he had no interest in love? Ayn couldn't believe that someone who seemed able to feel his feelings so easily wouldn't realize how often he had thought about love.

"I'll have you know," Ayn rebutted, "I have many times fantasized about the romantic stories I've read involving the Gods and Goddesses of heaven, especially between The Great Adin and his most beloved consort, Sri Unda!"

Zin snickered and said, "Oh you have, have you?"

"Yes, I have!"

"How often have you... fantasized?" Zin said through a giggle. "How many times a day, Ayn?"

"I... I don't know. Why?"

Zin laughed, trying to stop himself from further teasing his naive friend.

"What's so funny?" Ayn innocently prodded Zin.

"Nothing," Zin replied, "I just hope you're not making the Gods in heaven go blind with how many times you fantasize about them each day." Zin couldn't help but giggle even more.

Ayn didn't get his joke, but he could sense Zin was teasing him. The stories about the heavens of Deius meant a great deal to Ayn, and he wished Zin was taking it more seriously.

"Wait a minute," said Zin. "Wasn't Sri Unda the scientist who discovered plasma?"

"Yes, she was," replied Ayn, matter of fact.

"Well," said Zin, "correct me if I'm wrong, but doesn't your religion look down on science and even blame it for the inconsistencies of The Un?"

"Not really," said Ayn with a shrug.

"What do you mean?" Zin asked. "I thought being anti-science was the main reason The Tah rebelled in the first place, and ultimately, why our two home planets have been at odds so often throughout history?"

"That might be true about our planets," said Ayn, "but it is untrue to say that my people's religion is based on distrust of science. We more so believe spirituality is the driving force behind all sciences."

"Yes, well," said Zin, "same thing really."

"No, it's not," Ayn quipped.

Zin laughed and said, "Alright, you win... as usual. I have to address your claim, though, that Sri Unda was Adin's consort. That's just impossible, considering Sri Unda was a real person in history, and Adin was most likely just a mythic legend - made up to soothe your people's hope for a savior."

Ayn stopped walking, then crossed his arms and looked at Zin with an angered face.

"Oh come on, Ayn," said Zin, "just admit that your people made up most of what is in your holy books. For example, there is no way 'The Great Adin' crossed The Un when he died, and then magically came back the next morning, fully alive and healthy! That's just ridiculous and completely unscientific!"

"Clearly you do not understand the meaning of symbolism," said Ayn, stoic and deadpan.

Zin shook his head and angrily replied, "Yes, I understand symbolism, Ayn, but your people take it all as if it's fact! That's why they've now got The Tah at their heels."

Ayn cringed at Zin's second mention of the ones who murdered his beloved teacher. "Please stop saying their name," he said, frowning at Zin.

"I'm sorry," Zin said, rubbing the back of his neck. "Look... let's not argue about any of this. The fact of the matter is there is no historical evidence or documentation that suggests Sri Unda was Adin's lover. I don't know where you're getting that. Did you read that in some ancient scroll somewhere?"

"No," said Ayn sheepishly. "Well, yes, but... even if I hadn't, I feel it to be true."

"You feel it?" teased Zin. "You're basing all this on your... feelings?" Zin snickered, then shook his head.

"Actually," said Ayn, "it is a little known fact that Adin was a co-writer of the sacred book called 'The Pure Light of The Un.' Having written it with Sri Unda, they wrote the scientific, yet spiritual book that would define and shape the way all people everywhere imagined The Un's creating force."

Zin looked at Ayn intensely. It was times like these he felt he didn't really know who Ayn was. Half the time, his friend acted like an innocent child, always in wonderment about everything and teetering on the edge of an emotional breakdown. The other half of the time, Ayn seemed to Zin as if he were some sort of ancient, wise priest from long ago, channeling through a boy's body.

Zin shook his head and rubbed his eyes. His thoughts felt muddy, making him feel too stupid for such a heady conversation. Zin figured it was due to lack of sleep and walking all day. Looking around, Zin realized they had taken a wrong turn somewhere; The Blue Wave Hotel was nowhere to be found.

"Ayn..."

"Yeah?

"Where are we?"

"Um... I don't know."

The young men giggled at their own foolishness. "I guess we shouldn't talk and walk at the same time," said Ayn, still giggling.

"Yeah," Zin replied, smiling, "especially not at night time. I can't see very well, to be honest."

"Really?" said Ayn. "That's strange. I thought Ohrians had excellent vision."

"Not me," Zin said with a slight grimace. "I have terrible eyesight actually. I can't see objects that are far away or at night, for that matter. It started when I was about seven years old. Father wanted me to have an operation, but I refused. I didn't want plasma in my eyes. That stuff has been overused, in my opinion, and the last thing I want is to die before I even... um, well, you know... fully become a man."

Ayn laughed and nodded, understanding what Zin meant.

"Anyway," Zin continued, "the only other option given to me was the use of lenses, which are specially made on Kri. They work wonders, actually, and unlike plasma-based lenses, they're all natural, though they do wear out easily. My last pair was on the ship... so I have to admit, I'm a bit blind right now."

Ayn nodded, and then pursed his lips together, thinking. At first, Zin wondered if Ayn was making fun of him. Even though it seemed entirely out of Ayn's character, the puckering of lips, like a fish, was something non-Ohrians – especially Krians – would do when making fun of his people. Zin had been bullied as a child by a Krian boy when he briefly attended an inter-planetary boarding school, but the bullying stopped once his father had the bully's father threatened with a royal court order. Sometimes it was good to be a prince.

"I've got an idea," said Ayn, breaking Zin's meandering thoughts.

"What is it?" asked Zin.

"Well... I... um... it's hard to explain," Ayn replied, "but I think I may know a way to figure out where we are and how to get back to the hotel."

"Really?" asked Zin, happily surprised.

"Yeah," said Ayn, "just, um... stay here. I have to, well... just trust me."

Slightly embarrassed, Ayn turned away from Zin, and then went off a little to the side. Zin had absolutely no idea what in the universe his friend was doing, but he was amused nonetheless. He decided to take advantage of his moment alone and took out his gift from Lady Raven. Even just a small taste of the pipe reminded him of her scent and the fullness of her lips. Soon, Zin was in a happy, dreamy haze.

Looking back, Ayn saw his friend smoking. Zin seemed preoccupied with his own thoughts, allowing Ayn the chance to call for help.

"Axis," he whispered. "Axis, are you here?"

There was no answer.

"Axis?" Ayn whispered louder.

Ayn didn't know why his cat-bird friend wouldn't be responding to him, considering he always seemed to be everywhere Ayn was, popping up, even when Ayn least expected. If Axis was imaginary and only in his mind, Ayn assumed he should be able to conjure the animal at will whenever needed. So why wasn't it working?

"I need you, Axis!" Ayn loudly whispered.

Not a sound was heard, and nothing seemed to be in sight, except for a few parked hover-cars, which were made visible from the light of nearby plasma-powered street lamps. The silence made Ayn feel exceedingly uncomfortable. He didn't know if it was because he had gotten used to having his imaginary friend always with him or if it was something else entirely, but the stillness of the night was making Ayn feel strangely uneasy.

Ayn turned around and hurriedly walked back to Zin who was now sitting on his suitcase on the sidewalk, smoking his pipe with his eyes half-closed.

"My Gods, are you smoking a hallucinogenic pipe?" asked Ayn, annoyed and a little offended at Zin's behavior. Taking drugs was strictly prohibited at The Holy Temple, unless it was necessary for vision quests. However, Ayn had always been told by Meddhi-Lan that a real, honorable holy man didn't need drugs to have vision quests, and Ayn believed Meddhi-Lan's words to be solid truth. The idea that Zin was now using a vision-drug just for fun seemed a travesty, especially when Ayn was feeling so vulnerable. Why couldn't Zin sense his feelings and comfort him the way Pei would have done?

Ayn cringed when thinking about how much he missed Pei. Feeling alone and lost, Ayn broke into tears.

Not entirely oblivious, Zin saw Ayn's tearful face and tried to comfort him by offering Ayn a puff of his pipe.

"No, thank you," said Ayn, wiping his tears, then defiantly folding his arms.

"So..." sighed Zin as he took another inhale of his pipe, "I take it you didn't figure out how to find our hotel."

"No, I did not," Ayn quietly replied, ashamed.

"I guess your great Bodanya powers don't work with directions," said Zin with a teasing smirk.

Ayn frowned and said, "You doubt everything about me, don't you?"

"No," Zin replied as he stood on his feet, putting out his pipe, "I just doubt everything about your religious upbringing, and I doubt The Dei priests who forced you to believe such a giant lie."

Ayn shook his head and sighed. "You don't have to believe what they believed," said Ayn, "but... if you really are my friend, you should at least believe in me."

"Ayn," Zin replied as he walked up and put his hand on his friend's shoulder, "I do believe in you, and I think you have the potential to be a great leader, but I also think you're still so caught up in the web of their well-spun illusion. You are not a God, Ayn. You know this to be true. You're just flesh and blood like the rest of us. Hell, you're still just a boy who gets easily frightened and lost. You can't expect yourself to have the answers to the entire Un if you can't even use logic to figure out which direction to go when lost on a city street."

At his wit's end, Ayn began tearing up. He knew his blunt friend was right. Ayn had no idea what he was doing, and he felt completely useless. "Fine! I'm not The Bodanya!" cried Ayn. "I don't know what I'm doing, Zin. Please, help me!"

Zin embraced Ayn, hugging him tightly. "Don't worry, my brother-in-soul, I will always be here to help you. I won't ever leave you."

"That's what Pei said!" Ayn blurted in tears as he grabbed onto Zin's back with pleading fingers.

"Yes, I know, Ayn, but I'm not him," Zin replied while picking up Ayn's face with the tip of his forefinger. Giving Ayn a comforting smile, Zin playfully added, "I could never be a priest. I'm far too lusty. I'm also an Ohrian. We're naturally smarter than most, so... there's that as well."

Ayn released a slight laugh. He wanted to thank Zin for calming him with his warmth and humor, but the words wouldn't come out; they were caught inside his throat, stilted by too many emotions.

Zin simply nodded, sensing Ayn's feelings. "It's alright, Ayn," he said. "Everything will be alright."

Hugging, they stood on the street corner and looked into each other's eyes. Zin felt as if he could see deeper than ever into Ayn's sky-blue eyes. He wondered if it was the pipe that was making him receptive or if it was Ayn's immense spirit. Either way, something was causing him to feel pulled, and his heart thumped loudly inside his chest.

Ayn didn't know what was happening. It felt like he was caught inside Zin's mysterious spell – the same one that emitted from Zin's music when he played the elenon.

Feeling the weight of Zin's slanted, aqua-colored eyes, Ayn felt pulled against his will. Shaking himself out of the spell, Ayn noticed how much it looked as if Zin was going to kiss him. Slightly panicked by the idea, Ayn cracked a nervous, confused smile, and said, "Um... what are you doing, Zin?"

"I..." mumbled Zin, "I don't know."

"It... seems like you're trying to kiss me," said Ayn awkwardly.

"I guess I am," quietly replied Zin, trance-like. He closed his eyes and slowly leaned in closer to Ayn's face.

Ayn didn't know what to do. He hadn't thought he felt romantic feelings for Zin or for any boy. However, his heart was beating fast, and he wondered if he actually wanted to be kissed. Having no previous experience in love, he wasn't really sure.

Breathing slightly out of rhythm, Ayn closed his eyes. Not long afterward, the softness of Zin's lips touched his, and Ayn felt the warmth of Zin's strong aura, like a wave of protective energy, covering Ayn during a mighty storm. Zin's kiss was neither lusty nor rushed, but romantic and sweet.

The two young men kissed gently in the moonlight, and for a moment, they were lost in the feeling of their sudden intimacy. Afterward, they opened their eyes and looked at each other with bewildered wonderment.

"What just happened?" asked Ayn.

Zin slowly shook his head and nervously smiled.

"I don't know," said Zin as his smile turned impishly wider, "but truthfully, I want to do it again."

"Wait!" said Ayn with his hand raised, covering his own lips.

"Why?" Zin replied, slightly offended.

"Because! I don't understand why you're doing this."

"Um... because I want to," said Zin, shrugging.

"Well, that's not a good enough reason," said Ayn, scowling.

Zin sighed and said, "What other reason should I have?"

"I don't get you at all," replied Ayn as he rubbed his forehead, confused. "Why did you kiss me? Do you think I'm a girl or something? If you do, you're quite wrong."

"No, Ayn," said Zin with a laugh, "I don't think you're a girl."

"Then why did you do it? I mean, is that normal on Ohr – boys kissing other boys?"

"Boys... girls... anything in between," Zin calmly replied. "Why wouldn't it be?"

Ayn didn't know how to respond. In The Holy City on Deius, such couplings were looked down upon, and had even been illegal before Ayn's mother became queen. The Dei raised Ayn to believe that romantic unions were only meant for a man and a woman; anything else was sacrilege.

"But I thought you liked Lady Raven!" blurted Ayn, trying his best to process the situation.

"I do like her, Ayn... but with you, it's different. You're special. You're... like my other half. I can't explain it, but I want to be close to your very soul. I need you, Ayn... and I think you need me too."

Before Ayn could gather his thoughts enough to reply, Zin bent down to kiss him again, which made Ayn feel extremely uneasy. He just couldn't understand. Only a short time ago, Zin had teased him for not seeming sexual in the slightest. Yet here he was, kissing him like some romantic hero in one of the old Deiusian love poems.

The truth was, Ayn had always secretly wanted to be the hero in those poems and had usually imagined kissing a beautiful princess - not a prince. It all seemed so strange, and yet, it was still somewhat enjoyable. Ayn felt loved and alive, but more lost and confused than ever before.

"Aw, look at these two little love birds. Ain't it sweet?"

The unexpected, condescending voice instantly broke the tenderness of their kiss, making Ayn and Zin feel disoriented and almost naked.

"It's just picture perfect!" shouted another sarcastically cruel voice.

Ayn's senses began overloading with fear and confusion. He couldn't see them fully, but Ayn could tell he and Zin were surrounded by three or four men who had auras as dark as night. *Who are these men approaching from the darkness?* thought Ayn, panicked. *What do they want? And where in Adin's name is Axis?!*

Jumping in front of Ayn, a young man with buzzed, dark hair and pierced lip grabbed Ayn by his right arm. He also had a tattoo on his forehead: a red dragon. Ayn was fascinated by it, yet too frightened to care.

"Oh, lookie here! This one's got hair like a girl!" the red dragon-tattooed man yelled to the rest of his gang who were starting to emerge, one by one, from the darkness. Ayn tried to escape, but the man was too strong and was now pinning both of Ayn's arms together behind his back. The gang members laughed as they cheered, whistling and hollering.

"Let him go!" Zin sharply demanded.

The gang laughed at his words.

"No," said the man holding Ayn by his arms, "I don't think so. I think I'm gonna keep your little princess all to myself. What you gonna do about it, fish-boy?"

Zin sneered, and then put down his elenon case, laying it

carefully on the side of the street, next to their luggage. He cracked his neck, then stood directly in front of the gang member who had Ayn by the arms.

"I should warn you," Zin calmly said, snarling his lips, "I have been trained in the art of The Lirhan fighting style."

All the gang members mocked sounds of awe.

"I'm so scared," said the man holding Ayn.

"You should be," Zin replied.

In what appeared like a flash, Zin punched the man in the right side of his rib cage, then immediately kicked him in the right side of his knee cap, causing the tattooed man to release Ayn, falling to his other knee. He wailed in pain as Zin pushed Ayn away. "Run!" Zin yelled.

Ayn was in shock, but listened to Zin's command regardless. However, as he turned to run, he found himself blocked by two other gang members, both with the same type of buzz haircuts and piercings.

"Please, go away!" begged Ayn.

They laughed and grabbed him. One of them held Ayn's left arm while the other held Ayn's right. Zin was busy fighting off another member of their gang, but when he saw Ayn was in trouble, he quickly reacted by knocking his opponent down with a high kick to their throat. Ayn saw Zin's fighting ability and was amazed; it was something Ayn had no idea Zin could do.

However, Ayn was too terrified to think about Zin's fighting skills. All he could do was scream and yell for help. In the back of his mind, he prayed for Axis to rescue him, but only if Axis was indeed real and not just in Ayn's mind.

"Get away from my friend!" Zin once again demanded.

The two gang members holding Ayn laughed. Zin saw that their eyes seemed to be reacting to something behind where he was standing. He quickly spun around and saw the man with the red dragon tattoo holding a plasma-gun, pointed right at Zin's chest.

Within the span of about fifteen seconds, Zin's entire life flashed before his eyes: playing with his favorite toys as a child, holding his mother, arguing with his father, playing his elenon with Lady Raven... holding Ayn. Was it all going to end so quickly?

A low-pitched resonance was heard, quickly followed by a thunderous shock wave and a beam of light hitting Zin's chest. He immediately fell to the ground.

"NO!" Ayn yelled at the top of his lungs.

The gang members all cheered as the man who shot Zin grinned, then mocked being an entertainer, taking a bow. He was obviously their leader, the man with the red dragon tattoo, and Ayn wanted him dead.

Anger upon anger was rising inside Ayn like a tsunami of rage. It was so intense, he felt he could pass out from the feeling.

"Don't worry, my little princess," the tattooed man said as he came up to Ayn, grabbing him away from the other men who had held him before, "my gun ain't set to kill. That's not how I like to play. What's the fun if you kill 'em before you've taught 'em any lessons? Nah, don't worry, your fishy boyfriend ain't dead, he's just sleepin'. He's gonna have one hell of a headache though."

Ayn wanted to strangle the man, but he couldn't move. He hated how weak he was and how much stronger they were. He hated his body more than ever before.

"I hate you!" Ayn screamed with red-hot tears streaming down his face. "Leave me alone!"

"Oh, but yer so pretty," said the red dragon-tattooed man as he licked his lips with a vicious grin.

Swiftly, he yanked Ayn to the side of the street and pushed him down.

"What you doin, boss?" said one of the other gang members.

"Nothin!" the tattooed man shouted. "Just go and mind yer own business! Make sure that crazy fish-boy don't get back up and cause trouble. You can take his money and that weird instrument while yer at it."

The other gang members nodded nervously, then went back to where Zin was laying, scavenging him for valuables.

Ayn squirmed and struggled underneath him, but the tattooed man had pinned Ayn firmly to the ground.

Gods, please, Ayn silently prayed, *if you can hear me, please, I need your help! I was The Adin! Please, hear me and come to my aid!*

Ayn was distracted from his praying, however, when the man began ripping off Ayn's clothing. With one hand, he had both of Ayn's arms pushed down and was tearing his clothes with the other. It felt to Ayn like being violated by a giant monster made of stone – the very opposite of a red dragon.

"You have no right to wear the holy Siya Dragon on your skin," Ayn said as he snarled through his tears.

"Shut up!" the gang leader snapped as he tore down Ayn's pants. Reaching between Ayn's legs, his face changed from determined anger to a look of amused shock. "Well, what do we have here? You *are* a pretty little princess after all!"

Laughing wildly, the man with the red dragon tattoo

shoved his fingers inside of Ayn's body – into the place that Ayn himself had never wanted to touch. It was his female part, and it was something Ayn never wanted to acknowledge even existed, let alone have it penetrated in such a violent, horrific way.

Then, the man did something even worse. Quickly removing his fingers from Ayn, he replaced them with the vile hardness that was between his legs, forcing himself into Ayn's tender, previously untouched body.

It hurt beyond any pain Ayn had ever known. It hurt so much that he could barely think any longer. The dizzy, lifeless haze of defeat was starting to take control of his being, and he felt that any more of this horrendous pain would crush his very soul.

Everything was going white, though he could still faintly hear the red dragon-tattooed man laughing and grunting. Ayn didn't want to leave his body. He wanted to stay and fight, but the pain was making him lose consciousness.

Just then, through the haze in his mind, Ayn saw The Great Adin, wearing white and gold, appearing stoic and strong.

"Get up and fight!" Adin ordered him.

Ayn felt too weak. He tried to do as Adin commanded, but all he could do was cry.

This seemed to make Adin intensely angry. He raised up his mighty arms, outstretching them into the heavens while lightning struck through the clouds.

"I SAID GET UP!"

Gasping, Ayn woke from his vision and found himself awake, though not entirely. It was a state of mind he had never experienced before: aware of everything, yet unaware of his own consciousness.

The red dragon-tattooed man who had been selfishly thrusting into Ayn's body without even looking at him, suddenly felt an overwhelming need to look directly into Ayn's eyes.

Blue... so blue. Unable to stop looking at the blue, thought the gang leader who was now caught within Ayn's power.

Ayn stared at the tattooed man with a fierce intensity. His eyes appeared to the gang leader like they were on fire: a blue fire that made the man feel itchy and like he couldn't breathe. The more he looked into Ayn's scorching eyes, the more uncomfortable the itching became - to the point where he felt his entire face was going to burn up and explode.

Flying backwards, the man with the red dragon tattoo grasped his neck, as if something was choking him. His nose was bleeding, and he looked like he had seen a ghost.

Ayn felt like a spirit and moved like one as well. Slowly getting to his feet, he pulled up his pants and gracefully walked over to where the other gang members had crowded over Zin's body.

They immediately felt the intense sensation of Ayn's aura and turned around to face him. Looking into his glowing blue eyes, they ran away like wild dogs, fleeing in fear.

After a few moments had passed, Ayn began feeling like himself again. He saw Zin's bloody and lifeless body lying on the street and bent down to hold his friend in his arms. He could tell the gang had beaten Zin while he was unconscious. Their depravity was beyond Ayn's comprehension.

"Please wake up," he softly begged his soul-friend. After being met with a few seconds of silence, Ayn couldn't help but cry. "Please!" he shouted through his tears. "I can't go on without you, Zin! Please, wake up!"

Zin grunted with his eyes still shut and put his hand over

Ayn's mouth. "Alright, alright," he groaned, "I'm awake. Just stop yelling at me, will you? My head is killing me."

Ayn gave a slight laugh, relieved, albeit mixed with a great deal of pain and sadness. "You're going to be fine," Ayn softly replied through his tears. "I'm going to protect you."

Zin opened his eyes and laughed, but quickly stopped when it hurt his ribs. "You're going to protect me, huh?" Zin teased with a smirk on his blood-stained face.

"That's right." Ayn replied, gently smiling as he wiped his tears.

Zin smiled and reached for Ayn's hand. Their moment of calm was broken, however, when they heard a frightening, familiar sound: a low-pitched, resonant sound that only comes from plasma-powered machines.

Turning around, they stood up and saw that the man with the red dragon tattoo was in front of them with his plasma-gun cocked in his hand and aimed directly at Ayn's head.

"You're a freak!" he yelled at Ayn. "And this time, I've got my gun set to kill! You're gonna die for what you did to me!"

Instinctively, Ayn held up his hand. *Please, Great Adin,* he thought, *help me once again.*

A deep sense of calm grew inside Ayn's mind, unlike any other type of meditation he had ever experienced. He knew it was Adin's calm, and Ayn had no choice except to let Adin's power take full control of his mind and spirit.

Ayn stood with his hand raised and blue eyes glowing. Within a matter of seconds, there was an explosion, followed by a deafening sound, and then a bright light refracting, displaying a prism of colors.

Between the loud, resonate sounds and the blinding lights, Zin could barely make out what was actually happening. All he knew was neither he nor Ayn were dead. Yet, the man with the red dragon tattoo had somehow completely disappeared.

Exhausted after Adin's power left him, Ayn swayed. He then passed out cold, falling backward. Just in time, Zin caught him and held his beloved friend tightly in his arms.

It's all my fault, thought Zin.

He then dropped to his knees with Ayn still in his arms, and felt the need to weep. Unfortunately, there wasn't any time to mourn or digest the horrific experience they had just gone through. Zin could hear the sirens of police cars in the distance, and though he was badly beaten and felt he would pass out any moment, he knew they needed to flee from the scene. He shuddered when thinking about what would happen if the police found them. Not only would his father be alerted to his whereabouts, but if the police were as corrupt as he had heard, Ayn might be sold to the very people who wanted The Bodanya dead: The Tah.

Zin didn't know if the gang that attacked them had anything to do with The Tah, but he wasn't taking any more chances by being found by the mafia-run police.

He took a deep breath, holding Ayn firmly in his arms and then tried his best to stand on his feet. The pain of his crushed ribs, however, was dragging him downward, against his will.

No! he yelled to himself. *I MUST do this!*

He slowly got back up, but then felt his back snap. The pain was entirely too intense as blood rushed to his head. Then, everything went white.

Time seemed to slow down as Zin saw aqua-skinned Ohrian angels singing to him with white elenons in their rainbow-colored, scaly hands. There was a river of emerald-green cascading behind them, and everything felt serene and warm. It was the paradise Ohrians used to believe in... so long ago before the complete conversion to science, and it made Zin happy to know it indeed existed.

As the angels took his hands, he was sad about leaving his soul-friend behind, but at the same time, he felt ready to enter the ancient afterworld of his people.

"Zin," whispered a voice that seemed to purr. "Zin, wake up. This isn't your time to cross over the river. Wake up."

Then, there was a wetness upon his cheek. He slowly opened his eyes and thought he saw a cat of some kind, licking his face.

However, the image disappeared as he fully became conscious. Everything still felt hazy, but he felt much better. Miraculously, his cracked back and busted ribs had somehow been healed.

Zin then got up with the strength of a lion, running down the shadowed corners of the street, carrying Ayn in his arms. He didn't know where he was headed, but he felt guided somehow, as if the angels in his vision were telling him where to go.

"Hessen's Emergency Hospital," read the sign up above.

As Zin ran inside, Axis knew he had done all he could to heal and guide him.

Watching from outside the hospital, under a parked hover-car, Axis felt consumed with guilt. He hated himself for not having the courage to face the evil he knew was coming into Ayn's path. He had sensed the terrible auras of the gang members all that afternoon, and it had made his paws quiver with fear.

It's too difficult being one of you! he shouted in his mind to his long-dead ancestors. *How am I supposed to know when to warn him and when to let him make his own choices? I don't like watching him suffer! This isn't fair! I don't want my powers anymore! Take them back!*

There was no response from his ancestors – there never was.

Axis cried, feeling full of doubt and shame. The only thought comforting him was the idea that Ayn would soon be healed and they'd be cuddled up in a bed, warm and safe, dreaming together about playing in the green fields of the gardens of ancient Sirin.

Looking upward at the night's starry sky, Axis prayed once more to his ancestors. "Can you hear me?" he whimpered. "Do you care at all if my soul lives or dies? What about Ayn? Don't you care about him?"

Again, there was only silence.

"Fine! Don't answer!" he shouted through his tears. "You give me no choice but to stop believing in any of you! Gods, or whatever you are, I deny that I even come from you! I am just a weird cat thing... and I'm all alone in the darkness. No one cares if I even exist!"

Sobbing, Axis wondered if he was actually just another side of Ayn's psyche. *How strange that would be,* he thought, weeping as he curled into a little ball under the car. He wondered if he would die there, and if anyone would even notice.

As his tears fell on his furry face, he felt his body rock gently back and forth. At first, he thought he was doing it instinctively to give himself comfort, but he soon realized it was not his own movement; it was something else rocking him.

Looking up, confused and tired from crying, Axis saw a sight that both amazed and frightened him. It was a cat-bird creature like he was, but much bigger. It was golden like him too, and it was holding him in its huge, but warm and loving hands.

"Wha... what are you?" sputtered Axis as he stood to his feet.

Smiling, the giant, golden God lifted Axis closer to his face and said, "I am... your ancestor. You called to me, did you not, little one?"

Amazed that his prayers actually worked, Axis giddily jumped up and licked his ancestor's paw, which was cradling around him like a warm bath of smooth fur.

"Oh yes! I did indeed call you!" Axis said as he purred. "I just can't believe you're here! What took you so long to come to me? Don't you know I've been so alone?"

"I am sorry," the giant cat-bird replied. "I have traveled through time to find you... and it wasn't easy. I am here now though. Would you like me to take you to another time and dimension where you will be safe?"

Excited he might be reunited with his family, Axis jumped around in the God's paw and said, "Oh, yes, please! Are my parents there?"

"Yes, of course they are," said the giant cat-bird, "as we all are when we are spirits."

"Wait..." said Axis, confused. "Are you a spirit?"

"I am a spirit, yes, but I am also flesh. You see, Axis, this is not my time to be here, so I can only remain in this dimension for a few moments. It will cause a paradox if I stay too long."

"I don't understand," said Axis. "Where is my family? Are they in another time? Are they alive or dead? Why did they leave me here all alone?"

Smiling at Axis, the God purred and said, "All your questions will be answered, little one... in time. The only question you need to ask yourself right now is if you wish to stay here with your friends or if you wish to come with me. You cannot do both. You must choose what your path is, and then, you must accept whatever consequences come from your choice. That is the way it has always been and always will be."

Axis shook his head and felt utterly conflicted. He wanted nothing more than to be with his own kind, but he also couldn't imagine leaving Ayn's side.

"What will happen to Ayn if I go with you?"

The golden God sighed and said, "The power of The Bodanya has yet to awaken within him, and I fear he never will without you as his guide."

Axis felt sad, but also a twinge of pride. "You mean..." said Axis as he looked up to his ancestor with bright eyes, "Ayn needs me?"

Nodding his giant head in the folds of the starry sky, the golden God smiled and said, "Yes, Axis, he needs you, more than you know."

Axis smiled, despite his aching heart. "I can't leave him then!" he shouted. "If he needs me, then I must stay and help! He is a part of me, and I am a part of him. I see that now."

"Yes," said the giant God in the sky, "and you will guide each other on a journey that is full of adventure and pain, light and dark, happy and sad. Do not lose hope, my little one. It is your destiny to become great alongside your bonded friend. You may not remember having chosen this path before now, but you did. Time and time again, you have chosen to stay with him. It is your undeniable destiny to help each other find the light within the darkness so that you may spread that light amongst the universe, and it is a destiny you should be proud of, just as it has made your family proud, watching you from the stars."

Axis burst into tears and gently pawed against the giant God's furry face. Purring loudly, Axis looked up into the bright blue eyes of the God who held him, and then smiled.

"You're right," replied Axis. "I need to stay and help Ayn no matter what! He will live through this, and I will help him from now on! I will be strong, I promise! I won't give up! I won't lose hope! I will be his guide, and I will make sure that he becomes The Bodanya!"

Smiling and nodding, the great cat-bird said, "Yes you will, my little one, but first, you must become great yourself."

"Oh, I will!" said Axis, jumping in place. "You'll see! All of my family will see too from the stars... or wherever it is you watch from. I will become a great being of light, like you are, and I will help Ayn to become strong too! He will be even greater than Adin was! I promise!"

"I believe in you," said the giant cat-bird as he slowly placed Axis back onto the ground. "Now, all you have to do is believe in yourself... and nothing will be impossible."

"Right!" Axis replied in a cat-like yelp.

"I will always be with you," said the golden God as he levitated up into the clouds.

"Wait! Where are you going? Can't you stay a little longer?" Axis begged.

"No," he replied as he drifted further away, becoming one with the plasma in the stars. "I must return to my time. Goodbye, my little one... and remember, you are very important, and you are very loved. Until we see each other again..."

Axis felt sad watching his ancestor drift into the stars, but at the same time, he felt stronger than ever, full of new-found confidence and hope.

Hang on, Ayn. I'm coming! he thought as he ran to the hospital. *I won't give up, so you can't either!*

Knowing now that he was connected to his family within the universe, Axis beamed with the energy of an ancient being of light, and he was determined more than ever before to share that light with Ayn and the whole galaxy.

Axis felt his soul flying inside of the hospital through walls and even through people. He felt he could go in and out of time, though he wasn't quite sure how he was doing it. All he knew was he was going to heal Ayn, even if it took his entire soul to do it.

Finding himself hovering over Ayn's sleeping body, he made a silent vow. *You will become The Bodanya, Ayn! I swear to all the Gods of The Un, you will!*

With those words, he curled up next to his beloved friend and quietly promised to face the future with him for all time, for good or bad, come what may.

End of Book One

If you've enjoyed this book, please consider leaving a
<u>Review</u>! Thanks!

<u>Book Two: The Veil of Truth</u>

<u>available on Amazon</u>

<u>Book Three: The Riddle of the Gods</u>

<u>available on Amazon</u>

<u>Book Four: The River of Time</u>

<u>available on Amazon</u>

Glossary

Adin / ə - din'/ : The first Shiva Bodanya. He was supposedly murdered by his brother, Siri.

Ahluhana / ä - lü - hä' - nä/ : The ancient name for the Sirini universe Goddess. It is also the original name for the planet.

Amun-Lan / ä' - mün - län /: The high priest who taught Meddhi-Lan.

Amya / äm' - yə / : The Queen of Deius and mother of Ayn. She died from plasma illness when he was very young.

Anko bird / änk' - ō / : A large bird that stands upright on two feet and has large feathers that are usually black and white. It is indigenous to Sirin, but was brought over to Deius in the time of The Great Adin.

Api / ä' - pee / : The beginning month of harvest season on Deius.

Atlar / at'- lär / : King of Kri and father to Ona.

Atlaris / at - lär'- is /: The sun God of Krian mythology.

Axis / ak' - sis / : Ayn's "pet," though he is much more. He is a cross between a cat and a bird in appearance.

Ayn / īn / : The boy-king and "Bodanya" of Deius. He is the supposed reincarnation of Adin.

Baran / ber' - ən / : Second general to King Atlar. He is the leader of The Lirhan, Kri's specialized army.

Bodanya / bō - dan' - yə /: "The chosen one" or the prophesied spiritual leader of Deius.

Darvis / där' - vis / : A young Krian who is an apprentice councilman to Octian.

Day of Seed: A Deiusian holiday that celebrates the harvest season.

Delma / del' - mə /: Krian Goddess of Mercy and love.

Deius / dā' - üs / : The planet where Ayn was born. It is part of the five remaining planets that inhabit the Un-Ahm galaxy.

Dini / dē' - nē /: A dog-like animal that is usually domesticated. It has furry, short wings.

Duna / dü' - nə / : Ayn's childhood pet. It is a Dini and is something like a dog, but with furry, short wings.

Dru-Ahm /drü äm / : A complex galaxy with intelligent life. It neighbors the Un-Ahm galaxy.

Elenon / el' - le - nän / : An eight stringed musical instrument originally created on the planet Ohr.

Frey / frā / : Ona's personal handmaid, best friend, and younger sister to Mair.

The Great Paradox: The Deiusian term for the slow decay of the atmospheres of the known planets near Deius. Also the term for the depletion of plasma within the Un-Ahm galaxy.

Holy Order of The Dei / dā / : The council of priests in the Dei Kingdom. They have guided the Royal line of Shiva for many years.

Jin / jin / : The youngest student of The Holy Dei.

King Rummund / rəm' - mənd / : Atlar's father and previous king of Kri.

Konaka / kō - nä - kä / : A dark brew made from Konaka beans and usually swerved hot.

Kri / krē / : The planet that is nearest to Deius as well as being their closest ally.

Lan / län / : The formal Deiusian name for a teacher.

Leif / lēf / : The only son of Octian who died in the Xen and Krian War.

The Lirhan / lēr' - ən / : The elite unit of soldiers under Atlar's command. Their fighting style is of ancient origin and known as one of the most dangerous within the galaxy.

Lod Enra / läd en' - rə / : The King of Ohr. He is father to Zin Ra and has had many disagreements with the priests of Deius for many years.

Loda La / lō' - də lä / : Queen of Ohr and wife to Lod Enra. She is the mother of Zin Ra.

Luceon / lü' - sē - ən / : Owner of the lounge that Zin plays at. His sister, Velna, calls him "Luc."

Magna Screen: Similar to a flat computer screen, but powered with plasma-energy.

MahMah stew / mä' - mä / : A traditional, Deiusian stew, mildly spiced and usually made with root vegetables such as potatoes and carrots.

Mair / mer / : Royal handmaid, adopted mother of Reese, and older sister to Frey.

Meddhi-Lan / me' - dē län / : The high priest who teaches Ayn as a child.

Octian / äk' - ti - ən / : Eldest councilman of Kri. He is the eldest brother of Atlar.

Ohr / ôr / : A planet in the Un-Ahm galaxy whose natives are of amphibian origin.

Ona / ō' - nə / : The Princess of Kri. She is the daughter of King Atlar and the late Queen Pira.

The Ona Flower: The sacred white flower of Deius. It represents purity and love.

Ney / nā / : The formal Deiusian name for a student.

Neya / nā' - ə / : New, beginner, also sometimes a slang for calling someone naïve or foolish – or in some areas of the galaxy, it is used as a negative slang word for a religious follower of Deiusian beliefs.

Paya-na fruit / pī - an' - ə / : A pink-colored Deiusian fruit that is sweet, but also slightly sour.

Pei / pā / : The priest who teaches Ayn as a child and is like a brother to him when he is growing up.

Pira / pēr' - ə / : Younger sister to Queen Amya. She married King

Atlar and became queen of Kri. She is Ona's mother, but died from plasma poisoning when Ona was only a small child.

Plasma: The liquefied version of the electromagnetic energy that surrounds the Un-Ahm Galaxy. It powers most modern civilizations of the known planets.

Polarity Syndrome: The scientific term for what Deiusians call "The Great Paradox." It is a term used to describe the depletion of plasma in the Un-Ahm galaxy.

Raifar / rā' - far / : Baran's father and First General to King Atlar.

Reese: Atlar's lover, as well as lead spy for the Lirhan. She and Baran have a past, but she considers herself a loner who fights for the love of her country.

Shiva / shē' - və / : The ancient name of the kings on Deius. It began with the reign of Adin.

Siri / sēr' - ē / : Adin's younger half-brother who was named after the sacred Deiusian sun. He was the ruler of Sirin during Adin's time, but was eventually written into history as the murderer of Adin.

Sirin / sēr' - in / : The mostly abandoned and desolate planet, which was named after Adin's brother, Siri, and is the original home of the exiled, dispersed Sirini people.

Siri-star/ sēr' - ē / : The holy star of Deius, also interchangeable with Adin's title: "Adin is the Siri-star of The Un!"

The Sirini / sēr' - in' - ē /: The cat-like people who are dispersed throughout the galaxy. They are most widespread on the outpost planet of X-314.

Sirin-fish / sēr' - in / : A fish with orange and purple stripes. It originally hails from the now extinct planet of Sirin.

Siya Dragon / sī' - ə / : A giant, red dragon of Deiusian legend.

Sri Unda / srē ün' - də / : A female scientist who discovered how to apply the many uses of electromagnetic energy. She coined the term "plasma" and began a movement to stop using the previous methods of attaining energy, such as oils and chemicals. She wrote a book called The Magnetic Connection that became popular during the olden days of Deius.

The Star of the Sun: A large, circular statue in the Holy Room of the Dei Kingdom. It represents the Sun being the most holy of symbols to the old Dei priests of long ago.

The Tah / tä / : The extremist rebels of Deius who value science more than religion.

Un-Ahm / ün äm / : The galaxy also known as "The Un." It consists of five planets: Deius, Sirin, Ohr, Kri, and Xen.

Undaniasis / ün' - də - nī' - ə - sis / : The scientific term for Plasma Sickness.

Varvin / var' - vin / : Zin's music teacher when Zin was a child.

Velna / vel' - nə / : The woman who owns a music shop on Xen.

Verlo / ver' - lō / : Mythical Krian Goddess of love and beauty.

Viha / vē' - hä / : The ancient swords used by the advanced soldiers of the Lirhan army.

Virtu-Pod: An Ohrian device that plays all forms of three dimensional media, including virtual clips of visuals and audio.

War-Ruse / -rüs / : An old, mysterious, and often poisonous elixir. The Lirhan use it when on undercover missions. It is taken orally and is used to disguise a person's physical characteristics, though it has extremely dangerous side effects once it has left the body.

X-314 (Xen) / zen / : An outpost planet originally colonized by the ancient kings of Deius. It is now unofficially run by the Ohrian mafia.

Xen City / zen / : The main city on the planet X-314.

Yol Notama / yōl nō - täm' - ə / : The new leader of the resurrected "Tah" rebellion.

Zin Ra / zin' – rä / : The Ohrian prince who befriends Ayn. He would rather study the arts than science and wants nothing more than to be free.

More Books by Lyra Shanti

The Veil of Truth

Book 2 of The Shiva XIV Series

The Riddle of the Gods

Book 3 of The Shiva XIV Series

The River of Time

Book 4 of The Shiva XIV Series

The Rainbow Serpent

A spiritual fairy tale

All books available on paperback and Kindle at

Amazon.com

About the Author

Lyra Shanti is a poet, playwright, novelist, and songwriter who currently resides in South Florida with life-partner, Timothy, and their two crazy cats. For more information about Lyra Shanti, go to: www.LyraShanti.com